14-09-2022

S
h
c
U
u
C

D0581113

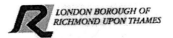

Richmond upon Thames Libraries

Renew online at www.richmond.gov.uk/libraries

STEPHANIE DECAROLIS is a lawyer living in New York with her husband, their two beautiful daughters, and their very spoiled cat. She is a graduate of Binghamton University and St. John's University School of Law. When she's not writing, Stephanie can usually be found baking, crafting, or taking photographs. The *worthy Museums* is her debut novel.

The Guilty Husband

STEPHANIE DECAROLIS

ONE PLACE. MANY STORIES

HQ
An imprint of HarperCollins*Publishers* Ltd
1 London Bridge Street
London SE1 9GF

www.harpercollins.co.uk

HarperCollins*Publishers*
1st Floor, Watermarque Building, Ringsend Road
Dublin 4, Ireland

This paperback edition 2021

3

First published in Great Britain by
HQ, an imprint of HarperCollins*Publishers* Ltd 2021

Copyright © Stephanie DeCarolis 2021

Stephanie DeCarolis asserts the moral right to be
identified as the author of this work.
A catalogue record for this book is
available from the British Library.

ISBN: 9780008462093

MIX
Paper from
responsible sources
FSC
www.fsc.org
FSC™ C007454

This book is produced from independently certified FSC™ paper
to ensure responsible forest management.

For more information visit: www.harpercollins.co.uk/green

Printed and Bound in the UK using 100% Renewable Electricity at
CPI Group (UK) Ltd

For my husband, who believes I can do anything,
and for my daughters whom I hope to inspire
to believe the same of themselves.

Chapter 1

Vince

DAY 1

It started, as so many things do, with a choice. Though it wasn't one consciously planned – a decision made, a line drawn in the sand. No, this felt more like something that happened while I wasn't looking. The gentle pull of the tide that sweeps you out to sea while you're preoccupied with the feeling of sunshine on your face. It all happened so slowly, and yet all at once. It started so small, a glance exchanged, a word whispered, but somehow, it's grown into something so large that it now looms over my life, casting a shadow on everything I once thought I'd die to protect.

I don't even know who I am anymore. I've become someone I barely recognize, making decisions I never thought I would make. What started with one mistake, one bad choice, has become many. One following the next until I could no longer keep up, I couldn't set it right. But in truth, I didn't really try. Not until it was too late anyway. I didn't know, in those glittering early days, what malevolent thing would curl around me like smoke,

1

so thick and so dark, that soon I wouldn't be able to see my way through it any longer.

I need to snap out of it. I need to focus. I stare at the spreadsheet on my computer screen, the cursor blinking at me impatiently. I know I should be working. I'll need these quarterly numbers before the board meeting this afternoon, but I'm distracted today.

I glance down at my cell phone that's resting, face down, next to my keyboard. I try to resist the urge to flip it over, again. To check for new messages. But the pull is too strong. Disgusted with my own disappointing lack of will power, I check my home screen. No new notifications. This is what I wanted, right? *Don't contact me again.* Then why does this silence feel like the quieting of birds before an impending storm?

'Vince?'

The voice rattles me and I drop my phone like a child caught sneaking sweets before dinner.

'Sorry,' my assistant Eric says, 'didn't mean to startle you.'

'No, no, I was just lost in thought for a moment. What's up?'

'There's someone here to see you,' he replies.

'Really? I don't see a meeting on my schedule. I'm supposed to sit down with the board in about an hour and I thought I had cleared my morning to finish up the quarterly reports.' We're about to launch a new branch of the company, expanding from software development into producing video games. It's a huge step for KitzTech and I have a lot riding on it.

'It's not a meeting … It's a detective,' Eric says.

'A detective? Do you know what it's about?'

'She said it's about one of our interns. Layla Bosch. She's … she was killed last night.'

I feel the blood rush from my face, the periphery of my vision start to blur. My stomach drops and I have the strange sensation that I'm suddenly in free fall.

'Do you … want me to send her in?' Eric asks.

'Of course, yes, send her in right away.' I straighten up in my seat, willing myself to regain my composure.

Eric leaves my office, closing the door softly behind him.

I rake my hands through my thick, wavy hair. I've started to notice that it's thinning lately, but Nicole says she can't see any difference. *Nicole*. What am I going to tell her? Do I have to tell her anything? I guess I'm about to find out.

I hear a quick rap on the door; a courtesy before Eric swings it open. We have an open door policy around here, and even though I'm the CEO, I constantly have consultants, associates, and my production teams coming in and out of my office throughout the day. I try to keep a relaxed and open feeling in our company; I think it's essential to keep the employees happy and the creativity flowing. But today Eric escorts the detective into my office and shuts the door behind him.

'Mr Taylor, I'm Detective Allison Barnes,' the detective says, extending her hand to me. I'm taken aback for a moment when I first see Detective Barnes. I suppose I've always imagined detectives the way I've seen them portrayed on television – middle aged, paunchy, rough around the edges. Detective Barnes is nothing of the sort with her thin frame, glossy brown hair pulled back into a smooth bun, and her rich olive skin. In another version of my life, I might have found her attractive, but today all I can focus on are her sharp hazel eyes, which are already looking me up and down, seeking out my cracks and flaws.

I walk around my desk to shake her hand, and offer her a warm smile. 'Come on in, take a seat.'

I gesture for her to sit in one of the low-slung leather chairs situated across from my desk. I walk back to my own chair and sit behind my large glass desk, assuming a position of power, confidence. It's all part of the show.

'Thank you,' Detective Barnes says, sitting primly on the edge of her seat as she takes in my spacious, modern office. My office is of a minimalist design, and, like the rest of our corporate

3

headquarters, it's painted a bright white. I notice the detective's gaze lingering curiously on the only splashes of color in here, the assortment of beanbag chairs and yoga balls that also serve as seating options in my office. 'I'm sorry to interrupt your morning, but unfortunately it seems that one of your interns, Layla Bosch, was killed last night.'

'Yes, my assistant, Eric, just told me,' I reply. 'That's truly awful. May I ask what happened to her?'

Barnes nods curtly. 'We found her body in Central Park this morning. I'm afraid that's all I'm able to tell you at this time.'

I feel my pulse quicken, my heart beating rapidly like a bird futilely thrashing its wings against a metal cage.

'My partner, Detective Lanner, and I are here to interview anyone who may have known Ms Bosch. We're trying to sort out if there was anything going on in her life, if there was anyone who may have wanted to harm her. Detective Lanner is meeting with your assistant at the moment.'

'Of course,' I say. 'Unfortunately, I personally didn't work too closely with Ms Bosch, so I'm afraid I won't be of much assistance to you, but I can have Eric pull up the names of her direct supervisors for you.'

'I figured as much. I didn't expect that the CEO of a big company like this would have much day-to-day contact with the interns, but I would certainly appreciate that list of her supervisors.'

I nod, and jot down a note to have Eric pull the names of everyone that Layla Bosch was assigned to work with.

'So,' Barnes continues, 'did you know Ms Bosch?'

'We like to call ourselves a family here at KitzTech, and that includes the interns. I make it a point to try to get to know everyone that works for me, but from what I recall Ms Bosch hasn't been with us for very long. She would have come in with the new class of interns only about five months ago, so I didn't have the chance to get to know her as well as I may have liked.'

'What can you tell me about her?'

4

'Well, like I said, I didn't have much opportunity to work with her personally, but I've heard great things through her supervisors. I hear she was a very ambitious and intelligent young lady that likely would have been offered a full-time position after the completion of her internship. But I'm afraid that's all the information I can offer you, Detective. I wish I could be of more assistance.'

'Thank you, Mr Taylor,' Barnes says.

'Just call me Vince. Everyone around here does.'

'We would like access to Ms Bosch's personnel file if you'd be so willing.'

'Of course. Anything you need. I'll have Eric pull that for you as well. And if there is anything else we at KitzTech can do to assist in your investigation, please don't hesitate to ask.' I slowly rise from my chair. 'I don't mean to rush you out, but I'm scheduled to meet with my board in just a moment unless there is anything else you need?'

'No, thank you, Mr Taylor. Vince. That'll be fine for now. I appreciate your time this morning, and I'm sure we'll be in touch.' Detective Barnes pulls herself up from the chair and dusts off her perfectly pressed pants.

I smile and extend my hand across the desk, hoping that she hasn't noticed the sweat beading along my collar. It's only a matter of time before she finds out that I'm lying.

Chapter 2

Allison

DAY 1

He's lying. Or, at the very least, there is something that Vince Taylor is not telling me, something hiding beneath his flawless smile. Vince was not at all what I was expecting when I asked to speak to the CEO of KitzTech. For one thing, I didn't expect him to be so startlingly attractive. My hand automatically goes to check my hair just thinking about him, and I can sense the color rising into my cheeks as I recall the tiny gasp I was unable to suppress when I first saw him walking towards me in his expensive jeans and crisply pressed shirt. He smelled of citrus and sandalwood, of exotic currents from faraway places.

Vince is casually handsome, as if he's become accustomed to how good-looking he is, but yet I suspect he's still very much aware of the charming effect his tall stature, broad shoulders, and honey-brown eyes have on everyone else around him. He's younger than I imagined he would be too. I'd guess he's around forty, with gentle laugh lines around his eyes and an easy, languid confidence that comes from living on top of his world.

Vince sat behind his fancy desk, in his absurdly large office, looking appropriately concerned about the death of his young intern, but something about him struck me as odd. I can't quite put my finger on it, but I have a gut feeling that there is more to him than the relaxed jeans, finger-combed hair, and movie star smile. I make a note to myself to look into Vince Taylor.

I walk down the large, glass spiral staircase at the center of the KitzTech corporate headquarters and into the brightly lit white lobby to meet my partner, Jake Lanner.

'Can you believe this place?' Lanner asks, gesturing at the grand, minimalist lobby. It's all polished glass and pristine surfaces. 'Did you notice they don't even have light switches?'

I quickly scan the walls. He's right. Not a single light switch, outlet, or wire in sight. I try to think back to the inside of Vince Taylor's office. Much like the lobby, his office was white and sparsely furnished, with the exception of a few brightly colored beanbags and yoga balls that seemed a bit ridiculous for a CEO's office. It was obvious that he tries to be the 'fun' boss that lets his employees call him by his first name and 'hang out' in his office that is easily larger than my apartment. But Lanner is right. I didn't see the familiar tangle of wires coming from the back of his desktop computer.

'I'm telling you, Barnes. The entire place is wireless. Everything is controlled by these little panels that blend into the walls. Watch,' Lanner says as he walks towards a glass doorway reading 'Café'. He places his hand on the outside of the door frame and a control panel illuminates asking for an employee ID.

'Can I help you?' a chipper young woman asks. Thick, trendy black glasses are perched on the bridge of her nose and she's wearing a form fitting, yet professional, black dress.

I turn and introduce myself and Lanner.

'Yes, you're the detectives here about Layla, right? Such a shame. I'm Rachael. I work at the front desk. Sorry to have missed you earlier but I was giving a tour of the facilities to some new applicants. Is there anything I can help you with?'

'No,' Lanner responds. 'We were just admiring all the tech around here.' He's in his element. Lanner loves anything techie.

'It's very cool, isn't it?' Rachael says, nodding. 'There's a panel like this outside just about every door. You just have to touch the panel to light it up. To get in and out of any of the community spaces around here you need to scan your employee ID, and to get into any of the restricted spaces you need to scan your fingerprints. We get a lot of people who stop in just to see the facility and we found that this was the best way to keep them out of the areas we don't want them wandering into. Would you like something from the café? I can scan you in.'

'No, thank you,' I respond. 'We were just leaving.'

'Okay, good luck with the investigation. I hope you find whoever did this,' Rachael says solemnly as she scans her ID, prompting the glass doors of the café to slide open before her.

Lanner and I begin walking toward the exit. 'So what's the deal with this place?' I ask him.

'What do you mean?'

'KitzTech. I know it's a technology development company, but this office doesn't exactly give me the "nerdy computer programmer" vibes I was expecting.'

'Nerdy? Come on, they created Friend Connect!' Lanner exclaims, evidently surprised at my lack of familiarity.

'That stupid social media site?'

'I swear, Barnes. I think you're the last person on Earth who still doesn't use social media. Even my grandmother has a Friend Connect page! But, yes. Friend Connect is a social meeting space where you can post pictures, connect with video calls, send messages, that kind of thing. It's crazy popular. KitzTech also put out Date Space. Do you know that one?'

'No, what the hell is that?' I ask.

Lanner rolls his eyes. 'It's another app where you can connect with singles in your area and it gives you a private, virtual space to connect before you meet in person. Slightly less sleazy than other dating apps. Trust me. I've tried out a few. But if sleazy is your thing, KitzTech also created Secret Message. It's an app that you can download on your phone to send discreet messages with anyone else using the program. The messages automatically disappear after they're read. You can imagine what that one is used for …' Lanner explains with a goofy smile.

'So, basically what I'm hearing is that Vince Taylor is probably pretty wealthy?'

'Try extremely wealthy,' Lanner replies. 'You gotta see his house.'

Lanner pulls out his phone and quickly taps away at it before turning it around and showing me a photo of what could easily pass for a luxury resort. The house, or I should say mansion, is incredible. An expansive villa set against a wooded backdrop. The aerial view Lanner found highlights the private pool, tennis courts, and long winding drive. The large property is extremely secluded and bordered by a stately stone wall – the only thing separating the grandeur of the home from the tangled woodland surrounding it.

'Just a touch larger than my apartment,' I scoff with a roll of my eyes, as I envision my tiny one-bedroom rental with the rattling air-conditioner that can't seem to keep up with the suffocating heat wave we've been experiencing.

'I'll say,' Lanner agrees. 'But if it makes you feel any better, his commute into the city from Loch Harbor probably sucks.'

That earns him another eye roll. 'You know, somehow that doesn't make me feel any better at all.'

'Anyway,' Lanner continues, 'did you get anything good from your interview with him?'

'Not really. He didn't seem to know the victim too well. She was just an intern and she's only been here a few months, but there was something about him that didn't sit right with me. I'm gonna scope him out later. You get anything good?'

'Not much. The vic worked with the development team. They were working on some new app or something. All very top secret,'

Lanner says. 'Pretty much everyone on the team had the same things to say about her though: she was a quiet girl, kept to herself, but very bright and very ambitious. Apparently she showed a lot of promise.'

'Any luck getting in touch with her next of kin?'

'No,' Lanner explains, 'but I had Kinnon drop by her address this morning and he got in touch with her neighbor. She's on her way down to the morgue now to ID the body.'

'Let's meet her there,' I say.

*

I hate the morgue. I can't count how many times I've been here during my years on the job, but it never gets any easier. The cold metal slabs, the blue-gray lifeless bodies, and the smell of formaldehyde make me shudder every time. But I have to keep it together. I've only recently been promoted to detective and this is the first major homicide investigation that I've been put in charge of, and so I don't want to show any signs of weakness.

Lanner and I have worked together for a long time. Although he made detective almost a year before I did, we more or less came up the ranks together, so he already knows my feelings on hanging out with dead bodies. But still, as lead detective on this case, I feel like I have something to prove. Lanner is a good guy, but he's still exactly that ... a guy. In a male-dominated police force, I can't afford to look like I can't handle the gore that comes along with the job.

'You ready?' Lanner asks.

'Of course.'

I pull back my shoulders, shake off the eerie chill that this place gives me, and walk into the lobby to meet Layla Bosch's neighbor.

We find her sitting on one of the small wooden chairs in the waiting room under a mop of frizzy black curls. She seems almost folded in on herself, making herself appear as small as possible, while she nervously picks at the skin on the side of her thumb.

'Hi, I'm Detective Allison Barnes,' I say gently as I approach. 'And this is my partner, Detective Jake Lanner.'

'I'm Mindy,' the woman says in a small voice, as she brushes a rogue curl away from her face. 'I can't believe this is happening. Are you sure it's Layla?'

'We think so,' Lanner says. 'We found her work ID badge on her when we arrived at the scene this morning. But we need you to identify the body, if you can, so that we can be sure the woman we found is Layla Bosch.'

'Yes, I can do that,' Mindy says, pulling herself to a stand. It looks as though she's doing her best to brace herself for what's to come.

'Follow me,' I tell her as I lead the way to the viewing room.

'Do I have to … go in the room?' Mindy asks, her eyes widening. 'You know … with the body?'

'No,' I assure her. 'The coroner will go into the autopsy room and he'll pull back the sheet, just away from her face. You'll see her here,' I explain, indicating a television monitor in the center of the room.

'And all you'll have to do is tell us if you recognize the body. If it's Layla,' Lanner adds.

'Okay. I can do that,' Mindy says, but she can't seem to stop her hands from shaking.

The television flickers to life and the familiar face of the coroner, Dr Allen Gress, appears on the screen. 'Are you ready?' he asks.

Lanner presses a button on the intercom next to the screen. 'We are,' he says. 'Go ahead.'

Dr Gress gently lifts a white sheet away from the victim's face. He's cleaned her up a bit since we've last seen her. Her face is no longer splattered with dirt, and her hair, which was matted with blood this morning, has been carefully brushed away from her face. The red dress, mottled with dark red blood, that she was wearing when we found her, has been cut away and replaced with a clean white sheet tucked neatly under her sides.

I hear Mindy take a sharp breath, and then she covers her mouth with her hands. 'That's her,' she says. 'That's my neighbor. Layla Bosch,' she manages before she begins to sob. Her hands tremble in front of her face and I can see red splotches blooming on her cheeks underneath.

'Thanks, Dr Gress,' Lanner says through the intercom. The coroner nods and pulls the sheet back over Layla's face as I switch off the screen.

I lead a tearful Mindy to a seat while Lanner goes to talk to Dr Gress about his findings thus far.

'Do you mind answering a few more questions for me?' I ask Mindy gently.

'Of course. Anything I can do to help.' Mindy's eyes fill with tears again and I hand her a tissue from a box on the small end table situated next to us.

'We've been trying to track down Layla's family,' I explain. 'We haven't been able to find any next of kin for her.'

'She doesn't have any family, I don't think. She told me that her parents and her only brother were killed in a car accident when she was very young. She was raised by her grandmother who recently passed, which is how she ended up moving to Brooklyn in the apartment next to mine. After her grandmother died she wanted a fresh start. Oh my God, I can't believe she's really gone.' The tears in Mindy's eyes begin to fall.

'Were you two close?'

'We were becoming pretty good friends, I guess,' she replies. 'Layla only just moved to town but I made an effort to get to know her. I live alone too, and I figured two single girls should look out for each other. She was kind of shy at first, kept to herself, but lately we've been spending more time together. Having a glass of wine after work, that sort of thing.'

'Did you ever meet any of her other friends? Boyfriends?'

'I don't think she had anyone else,' Mindy explains. 'She was new to town and really only ever talked about people she worked with. It didn't seem like she socialized with them much outside of the office though. I don't think she was seeing anyone either. If she was, she never mentioned it. I told her about my love life, or lack thereof, all the time. I think she would have told me if she was dating.'

'Thanks, Mindy. You've been really helpful,' I reassure her, handing her my card. 'If you think of anything else, you can call me any time.'

*

Lanner folds himself into the passenger seat of my car, his long lanky legs pressed up against the glove compartment. He slams the door behind him, making me wince. He always slams the damn door. It's infuriating. He immediately rips open a bag of chips, shoving a handful in his mouth. I watch the greasy crumbs fall onto the passenger seat of my car. Also infuriating. I don't know how Lanner manages to stay so thin with all the junk he eats.

'What did Dr Gress have to say?' I ask.

'He hasn't finished his autopsy yet,' Lanner replies while munching away, 'but his initial impression is that the cause of death was blunt force trauma to the back of the head. He's putting her time of death at approximately 9.30 last night. Give or take about a half-hour.'

'That's consistent with CSI's initial findings. When they looked at the site this morning they said that the blood spatter along the jogging trail looked like it came from a blow to the head. They're still canvassing the area, but no sign of the murder weapon yet.'

'What's the plan?' Lanner asks.

'I've asked Kinnon to put together a team to check CCTV

footage. There are no cameras in that area of the park, but maybe we can pick her up somewhere heading into the park. See if anyone was following her.'

'Good idea,' Lanner agrees. 'Where to now?'

'Let's go see what we can find at her apartment.'

Chapter 3

Vince

DAY 1

I park my Tesla in my driveway and take a deep breath, my hands still curved around the leather-wrapped steering wheel. I plaster on a fake smile and check my reflection in the rearview mirror. I'm surprised to see that despite the fear roiling inside me, I look like my usual self, or at least the image of myself that I've carefully cultivated over the years. The CEO. The tech mogul. The rock climber. The philanthropist. It frightens me how easily I'm able to turn it on. To tramp down my true feelings and play the part. But right now it's what I have to do. I have to pretend that the world is not crumbling beneath my feet.

I walk up the front path to my house, reminding myself that today is just any other day. It has to be, as far as Nicole is concerned anyway. I stand in front of the house for a moment, under the clear blue sky, steeling myself for the conversation I know I need to have. Our house, a Mediterranean villa styled after a home we once rented on the Amalfi Coast, stares back at me unforgivingly. Its stone archways, sweeping balconies, and soaring pillars already seem to be aware of the lies I'm about to tell within its walls.

I push open the double entry door and step onto the shining travertine floors of the foyer. Nicole loved these floors when we were first designing the house. I remember watching her poring over sample materials with our team of designers, choosing a palette of warm cream tones and cool grays for the home we were to build. She used color names like 'River Rock Gray', 'Dove White', and 'Vanilla Cream'. All natural hues, an earthy palette that would make the house feel both bright and tranquil, at one with the natural landscape surrounding it.

I drop my keys on the entryway table and call up the grand staircase which leads to the second floor bedrooms, but Nicole doesn't answer. I'm about to walk up the stairs when I catch a whiff of roasted garlic in the air, and decide to check the kitchen instead.

Our kitchen combines traditional Mediterranean design with ultra-modern amenities. The warm, sun-dappled room features natural stone surfaces with top-of-the-line stainless steel appliances fit for a chef. It's one of Nicole's favorite rooms in the house as it seamlessly flows out onto our pergola-covered patio where we often sit to eat outdoors. This space always feels warm and inviting, and today it's also filled with the unmistakable scent of Nicole's homemade lasagna. It's her specialty, her recipe perfected over the years. But Nicole isn't here.

I crack open the oven, something I know my wife would hate, but I can't resist the temptation to peer in at the bubbling cheese.

'You aren't opening the oven are you?' Nicole calls in.

'How do you always know?' I yell back.

'I know everything,' Nicole teases as she appears in the doorway of the kitchen. *No, you don't.*

'Lasagna looks delicious, babe.' I slide my arm around her slender waist. 'Were you in your studio?' I take in the sight of

16

her yoga pants, Lycra tank top, and her long blonde hair pulled back into a thick plait that hangs down her back.

'Yes, I wanted to get in a little yoga session before we indulge in all that pasta and cheese,' she says, patting her flat, toned stomach.

Nicole swipes an oven mitt off of the counter and lifts the steaming tray of lasagna from the oven. 'It needs to set for a few minutes.' She says this as if I'm not very well aware of her lasagna schedule by now. 'I'm going to take a quick shower and then we'll eat.'

'Sure. I'll set the table.'

Nicole rises up onto her tiptoes, and I lean over so that she can give me a quick kiss before she makes her way out of the kitchen. I can't help but steal another glance as she's walking away. With her trim, petite figure and the delicate way she pads out of the room, she reminds me of a little bird. But my wife is anything but fragile. She's been through so much and she's always remained so strong. I just hope she can do it again.

I remember the first time I ever saw Nicole. It was about ten years ago, when KitzTech was just a start-up. I was looking for office space to rent, and had found an ad online for a postage-stamp-sized room available for lease. I called the listing agent, and to my surprise, it was within my minuscule budget. I set up an appointment to see it that afternoon, and jotted down the address on a scrap of paper. A few hours later, I found myself staring up at the old brick building wondering if I had the right address. I opened the battered-looking door on the first floor of the building and walked into a small, but beautiful, art gallery. Nicole stepped out from behind a desk, wearing a delicate, flowing dress in a soft pink. Her long, white-blonde hair fell loose around her face giving her an almost ethereal look.

'Can I help you?' she asked.

I was so mesmerized by the frosty turquoise blue of her eyes that I couldn't bring myself to answer right away. 'Oh, uh, yeah, I think I may be lost,' I eventually stammered.

'Can I see this?' She gently took the scrap of paper with the office address from my hand. 'Oh, that's the unit upstairs,' she explained. 'The entrance is around the other side of the building.'

'Um, thanks.' I tried to tear my eyes away from her, but found it nearly impossible. She was the loveliest creature I had ever seen. I went to see the dank, musty office space upstairs and rented it on the spot. I didn't care that it wasn't at all what I was looking for. Because I needed to see that girl again. It felt like a *fait accompli*. I was meant to meet Nicole.

I don't know how I've strayed so far from the starry-eyed young man who accidentally stumbled into the art gallery that day. I don't know when exactly I lost that version of myself and became this person, the one with so many secrets to protect, but I am not proud of the transformation.

Just as I finish setting the table and putting together a quick chopped salad, Nicole walks back into the room pulling me from my reverie. She's barefoot with her long, damp hair thrown back over her shoulders.

'You even made a salad,' Nicole says. She's smiling as she takes a seat at the table and tucks her legs up under her.

'See? I told you I could cook.'

Nicole laughs. I never cook and we both know it. Burnt toast is the most I can manage most of the time.

'How was your day?' I ask before she has the chance to ask me about mine.

'It was good, I taught a few classes this morning, and then I had a client come in for a private session in my studio.'

We built a yoga studio for Nicole on a cleared section of our wooded property last year. It's built in a converted and air-conditioned greenhouse that lets Nicole's affluent and captious clients feel at one with nature without having to actually deal with any of the inconveniences of the outdoors.

'I'm glad the studio is working out so well.'

18

'The clients love it and I do too,' Nicole replies, nodding. 'It's so peaceful out there.'

There's a brief moment of silence while we both dig into the rich lasagna, letting the flavors melt on our tongues.

'Anyway,' Nicole says, 'how was your day?'

Here we go. 'Well … not so good, actually. A few detectives came by the office this morning. It turns out one of our interns was killed last night.' My voice waivers as I choke out the words and I clear my throat to steady myself.

'Oh how awful!' Nicole exclaims. She drops her fork and looks up at me, her eyes wide.

I feel my cheeks grow warm under her expectant gaze. I know she's waiting to hear more, waiting for an explanation.

'Yeah, it was an unexpected visit, to say the least,' I reply, trying to sound as casual as I can under the circumstances.

'I'm sure.' Nicole resumes twirling cheese around her fork.

She doesn't yet know that there's nothing casual about this. Not for me. Not for us. Nicole is the most caring and kind-hearted person I've ever met, but she doesn't understand yet. She couldn't. She's hearing this story at a remove; like one who learns of a death on the evening news and thinks to themselves, '*Such a shame*' while taking for granted the luxury of being able to simply flick the channel and let the tragedy gently drift from their minds. Aren't we all guilty of this though? Of failing to internalize the plight of others? We may feel compassion, perhaps even sympathy, but a stranger's pain doesn't keep us up at night when it doesn't reach out its cold, spindly fingers and touch our own lives. When the suffering isn't ours to carry, we wash it off hastily and unceremoniously and, if we're being honest, quietly think to ourselves that we're glad to be rid of it and the mild discomfort we fleetingly felt as a result of its proximity to our lives.

'Who was it?' Nicole asks, yanking me back from the darkness of my own thoughts.

'Huh?'

'The intern. Who was it?'

'Her name was Layla. She was new. I don't think you ever met her.'

'Such a shame.' Nicole shakes her head sadly. 'Do the police know what happened to her?'

I shake my head. 'All I know is that she was found in Central Park early this morning. They came by the office looking for anyone who knew her.'

'Did you know her? Layla?'

Now is the time to tell her the truth. 'No, not really,' I lie. 'I'm sure we crossed paths a few times, but like I said, she was relatively new at the company, so I didn't really have the chance to get to know her too well.'

'Well, I think it's terrible what the city is coming to. Can't even take a walk through the park without having to worry these days.'

I nod in agreement.

We eat the rest of our meal in relative silence, making small talk about the weather, her class schedule, the new video game branch we're planning to launch at KitzTech, but the darkness of Layla's death has already settled between us and Nicole doesn't know that it's only going to get worse from here.

*

I help Nicole clear the table, loading the dishes into the dishwasher and packing the leftovers into the refrigerator.

'I have to make a few calls,' I tell her. 'And then maybe we can have a drink by the pool?'

'Sure, sounds great.'

I head to my home office and wait until I hear Nicole open the sliding doors to the yard and close them behind her. I sit down in the plush leather chair behind my polished mahogany desk. Unlike my office at KitzTech, my home office is far more traditional. Large built-in bookshelves wrap the walls in warm wood tones, and a bar cart stands at the ready with a crystal decanter of amber whiskey which beckons to me now. I resist the temptation to pour myself a glass, even though I know that the phone call I'm about to make will not be an easy one.

I fish my phone out of my pocket and call my best friend, Jeff. Who also happens to be an attorney.

'Hey! Vince! Been a while, buddy!' Jeff exclaims.

'Sure has,' I reply, unable to match his enthusiasm.

'Uh oh, sounds like this isn't a social call then?'

'No, unfortunately it's not.' I take a deep breath. I don't know if I'm making the right choice, letting the truth out into the open, but I need advice and I know I can trust Jeff. 'One of the interns from my company was killed last night.'

'Oh, man! That's awful.'

'But here's the thing. I was sleeping with her.' *There. I said it.*

Jeff is silent for a moment. I look down at my phone to see if the call is still connected. 'Are you kidding me, Vince?' he says. He can't keep the judgment out of his voice. Or maybe he isn't trying to. Jeff and I have been friends since we were kids. He's never been one to mince words with me. 'You're married to *Nicole*. That woman is a goddess. What the hell were you doing getting some on the side?'

'I'm an idiot, okay?' I concede. 'But that's not the point. I was sleeping with her, and now she's dead.'

'Are you telling me you had something to do with it?' Jeff begins, 'Because if you are—'

'No! Jesus, Jeff! How long have we known each other? Do you really think I'd … kill someone?'

'No, you're right. Of course not. I'm sorry,' Jeff says, backing down. 'I just didn't see this coming. I always thought you and Nicole were the perfect couple.'

'We are. Were. It's complicated. I'll explain all of that another time. But right now I need your help.'

I fill Jeff in on my meeting with Detective Barnes this morning.

21

'So you didn't tell them about your involvement with Layla then?' he asks as I conclude my story.

'No. I didn't know what to do. No one knows about the affair and I thought if I mentioned it, I'd only make myself look guilty.'

'That's true, but if the police find out on their own, it's only going to look worse for you.'

'What the hell am I supposed to do?' I groan.

'Well, let me ask you this: how careful were you and Layla about covering your tracks?'

'We were very careful. She knew that this couldn't get out. She knew I was never going to leave Nicole, and that it would be some serious bad press for KitzTech. It was supposed to be a no-strings-attached thing. We only communicated through an app that sends messages over the Internet and they are automatically erased after they're read.'

'And you're sure that there's no record of those messages anywhere?' Jeff inquires skeptically.

'Positive. I developed that app myself.' *That much I feel confident about.*

'Well that's on your side, but these things have a way of getting out. You said this girl was only twenty-three. She was probably gossiping to all her girlfriends about banging her boss. As your lawyer, let me sleep on this, figure out if we should bring the affair to the police's attention or not. But as your friend, I'd advise you to tell Nicole. If this gets out, and she has to hear about it from anyone but you, I'm sure it won't go over well.'

'God, I'm such a fucking idiot,' I reply, dropping my head into my hands.

'Yes, you are,' Jeff agrees. 'Call me immediately if anything else happens.'

'Thanks, I will.'

I end the call and stare down at my phone for a moment. I know it's time. It's time to tell Nicole the truth. *Well, most of it anyway.*

Chapter 4

Vince

DAY 1

I walk out into the yard, running my hands through my hair. I have to stop doing that. Maybe that's why my hair is thinning. I can't lose Nicole. I just can't. What happened with Layla was stupid, reckless. It was just sex. A fleeting, visceral entanglement. But what I have with Nicole is real, and it was supposed to last forever. We may have hit a rough patch in our marriage, but I don't want this to be the end of the line for us. Jeff is right though. I have to tell her. I owe her the truth, and if she hears it from anyone but me, I know I'll lose her for good.

It's growing dark outside, the sky an inky midnight blue, but our yard looks like an oasis in the darkness. Underwater lights illuminate the pool in a celestial blue, and the lush garden surrounding it is dotted with soft fairy lights strung along the trees. Between two lounge chairs on the deck Nicole has placed a silver ice bucket with a bottle of white wine sticking out of the top, the cork already pulled. Condensation from the chilled wine is beading on the neck of the bottle and slowly sliding down into the ice below. Two crystal glasses stand on either side of the bucket waiting to be filled. I pour each of us a generous portion of the wine and take a small sip from the brim of my glass. I feel the of bite of the Chardonnay on my tongue.

'Wine?' I ask Nicole gently. She's sitting on the edge of the pool in a pink silk robe, her feet dangling into the water, swishing back and forth methodically.

Nicole shakes her head sadly but takes the glass from my hand. She doesn't have to tell me what this means. She's not pregnant. The latest round of IVF has failed.

'I'm so sorry, honey. But we'll keep trying. There's always next time,' I say reassuringly.

'Is there though? What will make the next round any different than the last one? Or the one before that, or the one before that?' Her words sound defensive but her voice sounds broken, defeated. 'I'll be turning thirty-two next month. I don't know how many more shots at this I'm going to get.'

'As many as it takes,' I tell her with certainty. 'You still have plenty of time. And I know how badly you want this. I do too. You're going to be an amazing mother some day. I know it.'

'Well, today is not that day, so we might as well make the most of it.' She takes a large gulp of her wine and places the glass on the edge of the pool. Nicole hasn't had more than a sip of alcohol in years to increase her chances of getting pregnant. But it seems like she needs this tonight. She slips off the silk robe and I see her naked silhouette set against the glow of the pool in front of her. She dives into the water hovering below the surface for a moment. When she resurfaces, her pale breasts just beneath the water's edge, she looks up at me with her impossibly blue eyes and says, 'Are you going to join me?'

I strip down slowly with Nicole watching me from the water, and slide into the pool beside her. Nicole wraps her legs around my waist and kisses my lips, slowly and passionately. Her kiss has the same bite as the wine.

There is no way I can tell her now.

24

Chapter 5

Vince

BEFORE

I hear a light rap on my open door which causes me to look up from my desk. I find myself staring at an unfamiliar, and strikingly beautiful, face surrounded by luxuriant, chocolate-brown hair that falls in soft waves down her back.

'Sorry to interrupt, Mr Taylor. I can come back another time if you're busy,' the woman says in a smooth, yet delicate, voice. She is standing in my doorway wearing a form-fitting black dress that accentuates her hourglass figure and the perfect roundness of her breasts which curve over the top of its V-shaped neckline.

'No, please come in,' I say, gesturing for her to take a seat in my office. 'What can I help you with?'

The woman strides into my office, the scent of her sugar-sweet perfume trailing behind her, and sits herself in a chair across from my desk. She crosses one long, tanned leg over her thigh and I can't help but notice her black leather heels and pink polished toes.

'My name is Layla Bosch, I'm one of the new interns. I just started last week,' she says extending a perfectly manicured hand to me. 'I just wanted to introduce myself, Mr Taylor.'

'Please, call me Vince.' I give her my hand and silently chide myself for taking note of the gentle curves of her body. 'I'm glad you stopped by. It shows initiative. How are you finding KitzTech so far?'

'Oh, it's great. Everyone has been wonderful. I really think I'm going to love it here.'

'I'm so glad to hear that. What department are you in?'

'I'm working with the development team. Jason was assigned as my supervisor, and he's just brilliant. I feel like I've already learned so much.'

Her deep brown eyes sparkle and they seem to dance as she speaks.

'That's great,' I reply. 'Jason is fantastic. We have a lot of new projects coming up and I'm sure he'll be keeping you guys busy.'

'Good, I'm looking forward to it. Anyway, as I said, I just stopped by to introduce myself. I won't take up any more of your time. But I hope to see you again soon.' Layla gracefully rises from her chair.

'Thanks again for dropping in,' I tell her. 'And I'm sure we will be seeing more of each other.' *At least I certainly hope so.*

I try to shake off thoughts of Layla as I turn back to my work. She's stunning, and my attraction to this woman, who is so much Nicole's opposite, takes me by surprise. I look over at the framed photo of Nicole that I keep on my desk, her icy blue eyes staring back into mine. Perhaps it's because Layla represents something foreign, the allure of the unknown calling to the part of me that sometimes yearns to break free from the routine that has become my life. *Yes, that's all it is.* This isn't attraction, it's wanderlust, the same pull that drives us to escape to the tropics when snow blankets our known landscapes. But, sooner or later, we all find ourselves longing for the comforts of home. I glance over at the photo of Nicole one last time. At her white-blonde hair, and her familiar smile. She is my home. I can't forget that.

Chapter 6

Allison

DAY 1

If the door to Layla Bosch's apartment is any indication of what we're going to find inside, I'm not sure I want to go in. The rusted, dented metal door has the number '12' carved into the chipping, vomit-green paint.

'This place is a dive,' Lanner says, matching my thoughts.

'Let's get this over with,' I tell him, unlocking the door with the key provided by Layla's surly landlord. You would think we'd asked her for the key to Fort Knox the way she reacted when I requested entry into Layla's apartment. I push the door open and step inside.

The inside of Layla's studio apartment is sparse. It hardly looks like anyone lived here, never mind a 23-year-old woman. The furniture consists of a small beige couch, a rickety wooden coffee table, a dated television on a cheap stand, a single bed topped with a plain, white quilt, and a tiny end table set next to the bed. There are no photos on the walls, no shelves cluttered with trinkets, no artwork, nothing to personalize the space at all.

I know that Layla only lived here for a few months, but it seems that when she arrived here to start her new life, she took very little of her past with her.

'Not much to it, is there?' Lanner says.

'Not at all,' I agree, as I poke through Layla's closet which contains a few cheap, work-appropriate outfits, a handful of dresses, and a pile of plain T-shirts and jeans. There are only three pairs of shoes neatly lined on the floor of the sparse closet and a few battered handbags with designer labels. 'Doesn't seem like she had much.'

'Guess KitzTech doesn't pay its interns too well,' Lanner jokes as he inspects a battered-looking laptop that sits on top of the coffee table. I watch him open the top of the computer, but it appears to be password protected.

'Bag that. We'll have the IT guys go through it,' I tell him.

Lanner nods as he slides the laptop into an evidence bag. 'That thing looks so old I'm surprised it even runs.'

We continue to look through Layla's few belongings for any clues about who this woman was and who may have wanted to harm her. I pick though a makeup bag and some hair products, and in her nightstand I find one photo of Layla and an older woman. That must be the grandmother that raised her. She's rail thin and appears to be in poor health, making it difficult to guess her age. I look down at the photo. The Layla staring back at me looks much different to the filthy, bloody version of her that I saw in the early hours of the morning. Her thick brown hair has a shampoo commercial shine, her skin has a glowing tan, and her smile looks genuine. She was stunningly beautiful. I carefully place the photo back in the drawer feeling saddened that her life was cut so short.

'Uh, Barnes, you may want to come take a look at this.' I find Lanner standing beside Layla's plain, simple bed. He holds up a small, leather-bound notebook that is tied closed with a leather string. 'Looks like a journal,' he says, thumbing through the pages.

'Found it under the mattress.' Lanner's eyes widen. 'Yeah, you're definitely going to want to look at this,' he adds, handing me the notebook.

April 2, 2019
Dear Diary,
Do people really write that? I'm not sure of the etiquette. I've never kept a journal before! But I thought this would be a great day to start. Today was my first day at KitzTech. Everyone seems so friendly and welcoming. I already know that I'm going to learn so much here and I'm keeping my fingers crossed that I'll get an offer for full-time employment down the road. But I'm getting ahead of myself. This was just day one. I wish I had someone to talk about the day with though. It feels so weird to be living on my own. My apartment is OK, but I miss Gran so much. It's hard to believe she's really gone. It's been just the two of us for as long as I can remember. But I know she would be proud of me for starting this new adventure. This is going to be the beginning of a whole new life for me!

April 9, 2019
Dear Diary,
I met my boss today, the CEO. I was so nervous introducing myself, but he was really nice. I hope I made a good impression. I really want to get a real job here. He's SO hot, by the way – not bad for a guy that's like 40!

I flip forward a few pages.

June 5, 2019
Hello, again Diary. I think by now we can drop the 'Dear', don't you? Especially since I'm about to tell you my biggest secret. I slept with my boss, Vince Taylor. And OH MY GOD it was incredible.

My jaw drops as I quickly leaf through the rest of the journal. One word stands out to me on nearly every page: 'Vince'. But when I get to the back of the little book, I see that a number of pages were neatly torn out.

'This is strange,' I say, showing the book to Lanner. 'Why would Layla have ripped pages out of her own diary?'

'Maybe she wasn't the one who took them out.'

'Let's see if we can find them anywhere.'

Lanner nods in agreement. We comb over Layla's small living space once again, but there are no signs of the missing diary entries.

'I don't think they're here,' Lanner says, giving up the search.

'I don't think so either.' I slip the black book into an evidence bag. 'Let's get this back to the station. And then it looks like we are going to have to have another chat with Vince Taylor.'

*

The moment I walk into the station, Officer Matthew Kinnon comes to greet me.

'Did you get anything from Mindy? The neighbor I tracked down?' he asks.

Kinnon is a good kid, but he reminds me of an over-excited puppy. He's new to the Major Case Squad, and eager to climb the ranks towards detective. I suppose I should be pleased that he shows so much initiative, but frankly I find him rather annoying.

'Not really. Here,' I say, handing him the diary and the laptop. 'Can you take the book down to Evidence and see if they can lift any prints off of it? And let's get IT started on her laptop.'

'What's the story with the book?'

'It's the vic's diary. Found it hidden in her apartment. As soon as Evidence is through with it, I'm gonna need it back though. I want to have it on hand when I do some more interviews.'

'Sounds like you found something juicy in her diary, huh?' Kinnon gives me a sly smile.

'Look, I have to go give the chief an update on the investigation,' I tell him, brushing off his question. 'Please don't forget to let Evidence know this is a rush.'

'You got it, boss.' Kinnon gives me a mock salute before turning on his heels.

I roll my eyes and make my way towards Chief McFadden's office.

The station house, like most government buildings, is long overdue for some updates. Our utilitarian metal desks are clustered together in the center of the squad room and topped with bulky desktop computers and dusty landline phones. The cement walls are painted a pale green and the old latex paint is slowly peeling away. The Chief has his own wood-paneled office at the back of the squad room, tucked away behind a heavy wooden door.

'Chief? Got a minute?' I say as I knock on his office door.

'That depends. Have any new evidence on your investigation?'

McFadden can be an intimidating man, despite his short stature, round waistline, and thinning rust-colored hair. He's known for his short fuse, but in my experience his bark is usually worse than his bite. I think he has a soft spot for the few female detectives on the force. He's always been a solid ally but he's never treated me with kid gloves.

'I might,' I reply. 'Lanner and I found a diary in the vic's apartment. Looks like she was sleeping with her boss. But a bunch of the pages were ripped out of the book. I have Evidence pulling prints now and then I'll go through all of the entries and see who else we might need to talk to. I definitely want to talk to the boss again first thing tomorrow morning, once Evidence is through with the diary. He told us he barely knew her when we interviewed him earlier.'

'Good,' the Chief replies nodding his head in agreement. 'What else are we doing?'

'I have a few of the guys going through CCTV in the areas

32

surrounding the park, but so far we haven't found any footage of the vic. I took her laptop as well. I have IT going through it now.'

'Very well. Keep me in the loop on this one.'

'No problem, Sir.'

Chief McFadden went out on a limb giving me this case and so I know that he's going to be keeping a close eye on my progress. But I don't mind. This is my chance to show him that I'm capable of running a major investigation on my own. I won't disappoint him.

*

I'm bone-tired by the time I get home. I push open the door to my apartment and drop my bag on the tiny kitchen table.

'Late night?' Josh calls as he sits up on the couch. His hair is poking out at odd angles and the television is still glowing in front of him. He must have fallen asleep playing video games again. I can't complain though. Josh works so hard. He recently opened his own gym and he's been putting in long hours getting the business up and running.

'Yeah. It was a crazy day. But, on the plus side, I got my first major case today. You're looking at a lead detective.' I manage a smile despite my exhaustion.

'Wow! That's amazing! I'm so proud of you, Ali!'

He pulls himself off the couch and wraps me in a tight hug. Josh and I have been dating for about a year now, and I can't even begin to count the number of times I've mentioned how badly I wanted this chance. He knows how much it means to me, and it feels good to see him sharing in my excitement. Josh's gym took off faster than we ever imagined, so lately it's been his successes that we've celebrated. I'm happy for him, I really am, but I can't deny that I'm also happy to finally be bringing home some big news of my own.

'What kind of case is it?' Josh asks.

'Homicide investigation. A woman found in Central Park.'

'Woah! That's huge! Bet the husband did it.'

'Ha.' I roll my eyes. 'She's not married but I have my suspicions about her boss.'

I know I shouldn't be telling Josh too much about the investigation, but I'm wrapped up in the moment of sharing my first big break with him. Besides, I didn't give him any information that won't be public knowledge soon enough if my hunch about Vince Taylor is correct.

'How scandalous,' Josh says, pulling me in for a kiss. 'I really am proud of you, baby. What do you say we take this celebration into the bedroom?'

I blush and smile up at him. 'Yes, lets.'

Chapter 7

Vince

DAY 2

I wake up to the sound of my cell phone vibrating on my nightstand. I look over at Nicole and she's still sleeping soundly. She's probably still recovering from her unusual overindulgence with the wine last night. I swipe my phone off the nightstand and check the caller ID. Jeff.

I roll out of bed and quietly walk downstairs into my office, shutting the door behind me.

'What's up, Jeff?'

'I gave some more thought to your … predicament. I think you need to come clean to the cops about your relationship with Layla,' he advises.

'It wasn't a relationship. Like I told you, it was a meaningless fling.'

'Well, whatever you want to call it, I think you need to get out ahead of this thing. I don't trust that a 23-year-old girl kept to herself that she was sleeping with her attractive, millionaire boss.'

Normally I would taunt Jeff for admitting that I'm attractive, but today I'm in no mood. 'Ugh, you're probably right,' I groan.

'The way I see it, the police have a job to do, which is establishing probable cause to make an arrest. You having an affair with Layla in and of itself isn't enough to rise to the level of probable cause. However, you are a public figure and these things have a way of coming out. If the police find out you lied about your involvement with this girl, that's certainly going to look suspicious and bring them that much closer to establishing probable cause. And so it may make sense for you to set the record straight now. But let me be clear, we don't want to give them more than we have to. We need to be cautious here. You're under no obligation to help the police charge you with murder.'

'Charge me with murder?' I swallow hard.

'We're not anywhere near that bridge yet, so let's just cross it if we come to it. I'm just trying to prepare you for the worst case scenario. Speaking of the worst case scenario, did you tell Nicole about your involvement with Layla yet?'

'No, I didn't. I was going to tell her last night but something came up and I just couldn't do it.'

'I'm coming to get you right now. Let's go down to the station and talk to this Detective Barnes together. We'll go over exactly what you are going to say in the car. You'll have to deal with Nicole afterwards.'

'Okay. Thanks, Jeff. I'll see you soon.'

I walk back upstairs to change quickly before Jeff gets here. *What does one wear for the day that they blow up their own lives?* I eventually decide on a pair of stonewashed jeans and a black polo shirt. I quickly wet my hair and comb it neatly to one side and spray on some of my favorite cologne. I take the time to shave my face and floss my teeth. I need to look clean-cut, trustworthy. I may look the part, or at least I hope I do, but my palms are sweating, a sure sign of the tension that's building behind the facade. I wipe my hands on my jeans and step out of the master bathroom.

'Are you going into the office?' A groggy Nicole asks, still tucked under our fluffy white duvet.

'Yes, just for a little while. I shouldn't be long.'

Nicole nods and nestles back under the blankets.

I jog downstairs just in time to catch the security footage of Jeff pulling up to the wrought-iron gates at the end of my driveway. I buzz him in and wait on the front steps for him to make his way up the drive.

'Are you ready?' he asks.

'Ready as I'll ever be.'

I slide into the passenger seat of his black Lexus. We drive a few blocks before Jeff pulls onto a side road.

'Just have to get gas,' he tells me. 'You want anything?'

'Actually, would you grab me a bottle of water?' The anxiety of sitting here helplessly while on my way to throw some fuel on the fire of a murder investigation has left me parched.

'No problem,' Jeff says as he climbs out of the car.

He returns a few minutes later looking ashen. 'I think you need to see this.'

He hands me a copy of the *World View*, a well-known tabloid that has published a handful of photos of me in the past. I see that my face is once again on the front cover.

Media Mogul a Murderer?
By Kate Owens for *World View*

Vince Taylor, CEO of the well-known tech giant, KitzTech, creator of ultra-trendy apps such as Date Space, Friend Connect, and Secret Message, is at the center of a murder investigation relating to one of his young interns, Layla Bosch (age 23). Bosch's body was found by a pedestrian yesterday morning along a popular jogging/cycling path in Central Park. A source close to the action confirmed that Taylor (age 39), the married multi-millionaire, was having an affair with the voluptuous victim in the months leading up to her unfortunate death. Was the sexy CEO involved in his intern's death? We don't know, but we can't wait to find out.

Along with the article, *World View* has printed the photo of me from the KitzTech website next to a photo of Layla at the intern summer kick-off barbecue. She's wearing cut-off jeans and a low-cut white tank top and she's standing in front of KitzTech headquarters, smiling innocently into the camera. She looks impossibly young. I wasn't even at that barbecue. It's only attended by the newly hired interns as a way for them to get to know one another, to build camaraderie, before starting their internships.

I feel the blood drain from my face and my hand starts to shake. I throw the paper into the footwell of Jeff's car.

'FUCK!' I shout, slamming my fist again the dashboard. 'How the hell did *World View* find out about the affair?'

'Who else knows about it?'

'You're the only person I told!'

'Well, it certainly didn't come from me,' Jeff says. 'So it looks like Layla wasn't as careful with your secret as you trusted her to be. That … or the police already know about the affair and they have a leak on their end.'

'I'm fucked!' I yell. 'There goes my chance to get ahead of this thing! And what is this bullshit? Can this rag of a publication just call me a murderer like that? Can't we sue them for libel or something?'

'No,' Jeff explains calmly. 'They didn't actually say you killed her. They certainly suggested it, but they were very careful to phrase their allegations as questions. They're skirting the line for sure, but at this point you really don't have a case against them.'

'So what now?' I drop my head into my hands.

'Now we go to the police and you come clean. It's still better that they hear the whole story from you.'

I nod and Jeff starts the car again. We drive to the police station in silence, and I feel like I've already been found guilty in the court of public opinion.

Chapter 8

Allison

DAY 2

I feel almost optimistic as I walk through the parking lot on my way in today, despite the oppressive heat from the morning sun which is already rising off the asphalt in dizzying waves. My plan is to read over Layla's diary one more time and then go have another chat with Vince Taylor. We're only on day two of the investigation and I already have a strong lead. I'm feeling pretty positive about it until I see Lanner's face.

'Have you seen this, Ali?' He's calling me by my first name. It must be serious.

'Seen what?' I take the magazine from his hand. It's a copy of today's *World View*. I read the headline: '*Media Mogul a Murderer?*'

'What the hell?' I ask aloud, slamming the paper onto my desk. 'How the hell did they find out about Taylor already?' There goes our upper hand with him. I wanted to take him by surprise with today's interview. Confront him with the diary before he had a chance to make up any more lies.

'I don't know, Ali, but the Chief is already asking for you.'

Shit.

*

'You were looking for me Chief?' I ask, standing in his doorway.

'Sit down,' he instructs. 'And close the door.'

I do as I'm told, feeling as though I was just sent to the principal's office.

'Any idea how *World View*, of all publications, got a hold of sensitive information about our investigation?' he asks. I can see his jaw working as he struggles to check his temper.

'No, Sir, I don't.' I start making a mental list of everyone who knows what I found in Layla's diary: me, Lanner, Chief McFadden, and the team down in Evidence. I suppose Kinnon also could have read it before handing it over to be processed. And … there's Josh. I know I told him more than I should have, but I didn't give him any names. And he certainly wouldn't be calling into any tabloids.

'Do some more digging,' McFadden tells me sternly. 'Find out if anyone in the victim's life knew about this affair. I'd hate to find out that someone in this office was feeding sensitive information to the press. But either way, we can't have reporters knowing more about our investigation than my own detectives.'

Technically I already knew everything that was printed in the *World View* article but I get his point. It makes us look like idiots when the tabloids break news about an ongoing investigation before we do.

'Yes, Sir,' I say leaving his office with my tail between my legs.

I walk back out into the station room, pretending I don't notice the whispers swirling around me. Everyone wants to know how the press got a hold of this story and what Chief McFadden had to say about it behind closed doors.

'You okay?' Lanner asks.

I ignore the question. 'Is that diary back from Evidence?'

'Yeah, it's on your desk. No prints on it except the vic's. But it's leather so kind of hard to lift prints. Still no way to tell if she tore out those pages herself or not.'

'Thanks. Let's see if we can get Vince Taylor down here for an interview right away.'

'No need, he's already here. Showed up a few minutes ago with his lawyer. I put him in interview room two. Thought you might want to be the first one to talk to him.'

*

I watch Vince in the interrogation room through the two-way mirror before going in. He's bouncing his heel nervously in his creamy black leather driving shoes. *Could he look more pretentious?* His lawyer is furiously whispering something to him. Vince's head is bent forward and his shoulders sag. A sign of remorse? Or maybe defeat.

'Hello again, Mr Taylor,' I begin as I walk into the room, taking a seat across from him at the cold metal table.

'Detective Barnes,' Vince says as he clambers out of the chair, his long legs stumbling under the table as he extends a hand to me.

I shake his hand coolly. 'I'm told you wanted to speak with me?' It's not time to show my cards just yet. There's still a chance he hasn't seen the *World View* article this morning.

I see Vince swallow hard, the muscles in his throat working up and down. I post a pleasant smile on my face but in reality I'm studying Vince Taylor closely. Every movement, every twitch, giving away that underneath his smooth, charismatic facade, he's already breaking.

'Yes,' his attorney interjects. 'I'm Jeff Mankin. Mr Taylor's attorney. My client asked me to bring him down here today to make a statement pertaining to your investigation into Layla Bosch.'

'I appreciate that, Mr Taylor. What was it that you wanted to share with us?'

Vince looks at me and then back at his attorney before he begins. 'I, um, had a brief affair with Ms Bosch.'

'Are you saying you were in an intimate relationship with the victim?'

Vince looks uncomfortable, squirming in his seat, and I can see the tips of his ears turning red. It gives me a sense of satisfaction to see Mr Perfect so shaken. I know I'm on the right track.

'It wasn't a relationship exactly. It was just … a physical thing,' Vince corrects.

'Did anyone else know about your affair?'

'No. Definitely not. Not unless Layla told someone, but I don't think she would have …'

'How is any of this relevant?' Mankin interrupts.

I ignore him and continue my questioning. 'How long did this … affair … last?'

'It started about two months ago, maybe even a little before then. I don't know exactly. It wasn't like I intended for it to happen; we just kind of fell into it, and anyway I ended things a few days—'

'Vince,' Mankin growls. But the words are already tumbling out of Taylor's mouth. A nervous stream of consciousness that I've seen with so many witnesses before him. It seems as though he barely registers his attorney's warning.

'—A few days before … she died,' Vince concludes. His ears are burning red now and I notice him pulling at his collar.

I have him on the ropes, and I need to keep him talking. Let him walk into my trap. 'And this relationship you had with Ms Bosch, was it serious?'

'He just explained to you that it wasn't,' the attorney interrupts.

'And Layla knew that,' Vince confirms. His attorney shoots him a sharp look.

'Well, Mr Taylor,' I respond. 'It's interesting that you'd say that.'

43

I toss the evidence bag containing Layla Bosch's little black diary onto the table. 'Do you recognize this?'

'No, I don't,' Vince says. He keeps his composure but I see his eyes dart to his attorney giving him away. There's something he's not telling me. And it seems that he hasn't told his attorney either because I see Jeff Mankin look back at his client, a hint of anger in his eyes.

'This is Layla's diary. We found it in her apartment. And oh boy, has it been an interesting read. Seems she had quite a lot to say about you and your "affair" as you call it. Do you want me to read you one of my favorite passages?'

Vince doesn't respond. He's frozen, staring at me in wide-eyed horror as I begin to read:

'*Vince told me that he loves me today. And I can't believe it, but I think I love him too. He told me that we're going to be together someday. He's going to do whatever it takes. I just hope he does it soon. I can't stand the waiting anymore. I'm ready for the world to know about us.*'

'No, no, no, that's not true at all—' Vince exclaims, panic rising in his voice.

'Vince!' Jeff Mankin interjects, glaring at his client, a clear warning to shut his mouth.

'Right,' I continue, 'so either Layla lied to her own hidden diary or you're lying to me. Which seems more likely?' I cross my arms over my chest and lean back in my chair. This man is so used to everyone tiptoeing around him, worshiping at his feet. *Not this time, Vince Taylor.*

'Look, Detective,' Mankin says, 'my client came here voluntarily today. He's been forthcoming with you about his relationship with Ms Bosch—'

'Well, that's not entirely true. When we spoke yesterday he told me that he barely knew her.'

'You mean when you questioned him in his place of employment in front of his employees? He didn't feel comfortable raising the issue of his relationship with Ms Bosch then, but he came here voluntarily first thing this morning to tell you about it,' Mankin retorts.

'Sure, after the *World View* article already exposed his secret.'

'That's another thing,' Mankin says, his voice rising. 'It's interesting that some trashy tabloid informed my client that he was a person of interest in this investigation before you did. Seems to me like you need to regulate the information coming out of this office a little better. And, for your information, we were already on our way here when we saw that ridiculous article.'

'That tip-off certainly didn't come from this office if that's what you're implying. You might want to speak to your client about who else knew about his love affair with the victim!' I'm losing my temper. I need to rein it in. I can't let this attorney get under my skin. If I lose my cool I lose control of this interview.

'It wasn't a love affair!' Vince interjects, running his hands through his hair. 'I don't know why she would say that, but it wasn't. We both knew what it was. It was just a meaningless fling, a bit a fun. A mistake, really ...'

'That's enough, Vince,' Mankin says sternly, cutting his client off. 'Detective,' he continues, turning to me, 'my client came here to inform you of his involvement with Ms Bosch and he's done that. But it had absolutely nothing to do with her death. And so, unless you're charging him with anything, this interview is over.'

'I just have one more question, Mr Taylor,' I say as Vince and his lawyer begin preparing to leave. 'I'm going to need to know where you were the night of August twenty-fourth, the night Ms Bosch was murdered.'

Chapter 9

Vince

DAY 2

She wants to know where I was the night Layla was killed. I knew this question was coming of course, and Jeff and I rehearsed my answer about a hundred times on the drive over here after we saw that damn article, but now that Detective Barnes has actually asked it out loud, it all feels too real. Layla is dead and Barnes thinks I killed her. She seems so smug about it too, leaning back in her chair, arms folded over her chest, with that obnoxious grin on her face. She thinks she knows me. She thinks she has me all figured out. But she's wrong.

I know how Barnes sees me. The entitled rich guy, the cheating husband, the lecherous boss preying on young interns, but she doesn't know the first thing about me. She doesn't know that I grew up poor, my parents scraping by on food stamps, she doesn't know that everything I own was hard earned, and she doesn't know about the fertility treatments, the doctor's appointments, the injections, the scans, the invasive questions about my sperm count and our sex lives. Barnes doesn't know how our failure to produce children gradually took over my marriage. Every conversation revolving around Nicole's empty womb and the pain that it brought her. She couldn't know about how it tore at my heart to watch the woman I love struggling like that and how much I had to bite back my own pain about our inability to start a family, because Nicole's sadness was so all-consuming. There was simply no room for mine. She doesn't know how lonely I felt carrying that grief alone. Barnes couldn't possibly understand what drove me to Layla, but I am keenly aware of how dangerous her misconception of me can be.

I have to hold back my rising anger. I need to answer her question. 'I had to work late and then I spent the night at my apartment.'

'Your apartment?'

'Yes. We keep an apartment in the city. We live over in Loch Harbor, Connecticut, which is almost an hour's drive out of the city most days, so it's convenient for when I need to work late that I can stay in Manhattan.'

'Sure does sound convenient.' Barnes' voice is dripping with sarcasm. 'And you're sure you worked late that particular evening?'

'Yes. We're preparing to launch a new branch at KitzTech very soon, and I needed to get everything in order to present it to the board yesterday. It's a huge undertaking and I find that I often do my best work at night when the office is quiet.'

'Uh huh. I see,' Barnes says eying me suspiciously. 'I don't suppose anyone can verify this information?'

'No, but my security system can.' I feel like I've finally won a point in this match. 'I scanned my ID and my fingerprints to get in and out of the office. It will show you that I was there until about eleven o'clock at night.'

'You have a record of that?' It sounds like her confidence is beginning to waiver. *Good.*

'He does,' Jeff interjects. 'And he'd be happy to provide it to you … if you think you can keep it out of the tabloids that is,' he adds with a smirk. 'That'll be all for today, Detective.' Jeff taps me on the shoulder, letting me know that it's time to shut up and leave.

We stand up under Barnes' watchful gaze. She's had to accept my statement for now, but I know that she doesn't believe me. She's still convinced that I killed Layla.

*

Once we're safely back in Jeff's car I let out a sigh of relief. 'You think that went okay?' I ask him.

'You're kidding, right? No, that did not go okay!' Jeff slams his hand on the steering wheel. 'We were blindsided by that fucking diary. And don't even bother lying to me again, telling me you've never seen it before, because I saw your face when she pulled it out. I've known you your whole life, man. I can tell when you're lying. Or at least I thought I could.'

'What is that supposed to mean?' I'm suddenly feeling defensive. 'I haven't lied to you about a single thing.'

'Oh really? "It was just sex", "she knew it was just supposed to be a bit of fun". Sure doesn't sound that way to me, Vince.'

'I don't know why Layla wrote those things, Jeff, but I swear to you I never told that girl that I loved her and I was certainly never going to leave Nicole for her.'

'Well whether you said it or not, your girlfriend was clearly under a different impression.' Jeff stares out at the road ahead of him, his face screwed up in anger. I see a familiar deep 'V' forming in the creases between his brows and I think it might be best to let him cool down for the time being.

The drive back to my house is quiet. Jeff and I have known each other for almost thirty years, and yet we have nothing to say right now. We pull up to my house with only the sound of Jeff's tires crunching on gravel to break the silence. I swing open the passenger door and step out in front of my house.

'Good luck with Nicole,' Jeff says, extending the proverbial olive branch. 'I have a feeling you're going to need it.'

*

I take a moment alone in front of the house before I have to go in and face Nicole. Sometimes I still can't believe that I live here, in this house. The tiny house I grew up in could easily fit into the four-car garage alone. This is our dream house, mine and Nicole's. We had it built about five years ago, right after I took KitzTech public. It's far larger than what we really need for the two of us, but when we first stood on this vacant lot and designed the home we would build here, we thought we would be filling it with children of our own. What we created is a beautiful, sprawling villa nestled into the serenity of the wooded landscape. The house contains all the latest technological advances: smart spaces that automatically dim the lights and control the temperature based on the individual preferences of whoever is in the room; waterfall showers that recall your preferred water temperature and pressure; and a refrigerator that can text me to let me know when I need to pick up milk on my way home. But this house was also built for Nicole, with its bright and airy rooms, tranquil water features throughout the property, and, of course, her one-of-a-kind yoga studio. The house is the perfect combination of the two of us, a seamless blending of nature and technology. We built our own perfect world here, and I'm about to destroy it. There is no way around it. I have to tell her about my involvement with Layla now. But I know it's going to hurt her, and I never wanted to be the cause of any more pain in her life.

I push open the double doors to the front of the house and step into the spacious open foyer. I spot Nicole already walking down the stairs and she stops the moment she sees me. Her eyes are red-rimmed and she's clutching a tissue in one hand, a sheet of paper in the other.

'Nic,' I say walking towards her.

She steps towards me and hands me the paper. It's a print out of this morning's *World View* article.

'A client sent it to me.' Her voice is soft, as if it pains her to even form the words. I can tell she's fighting back tears, more tears. She looks up at me, her impossibly blue eyes swimming, waiting for me to tell her it's not true. But I can't.

'I'm so sorry, I didn't want you to find out this way, I was going to tell you—'

'So it's true then?' Her chin begins to wobble. 'You were really sleeping with your intern?'

'Nic, please let me explain—' I start, but she turns away from me, her face crumbling in disgust. My wife can barely stand to look at me. 'It's true. I was … involved with her. But it didn't mean anything, it was nothing—'

Nicole turns back to face me, her voice rising in anger. 'Nothing? You threw away our marriage for nothing then?'

'No, I …,' I stumble. 'I just … with all the fertility treatments, and IVF, it got to be too much, I started to feel—'

'Just one more thing my inability to give us children has caused.' Nicole begins to sob. I try to reach out to her, I want to hold her close to me, to promise her that everything is going to be okay, to take away the hurt I've caused her, but she pushes away from me.

'I need to be alone right now, Vince. I need some time to think.'

Nicole walks upstairs to our bedroom, leaving me alone with only the gentle sound of our bedroom door clicking closed behind her.

But maybe it's for the best that Nicole is distracted for the moment because there is something important I need to take care of right now. I walk into my home office, flip open my laptop, and log in to the KitzTech server. I tap into our security system, the one I designed myself, and with just a few lines of code it now looks like I used my employee ID to leave the building at 6.03 p.m., returning at 6.26 p.m., (picking up a quick dinner, should

Barnes ask), scanning my fingerprints to get into my personal office at 6.31 p.m., and I swiped out at 10.43 p.m.. I even throw in a trip to the men's room at 9.14 p.m., for good measure. I download the security records and transfer them onto a flash drive to give to Jeff.

I feel like a criminal altering the security code. And maybe I am. But work was the best alibi I could come up with. I can't have anyone knowing where I really was the night Layla died.

*

It's late in the evening by the time Nicole walks out into our yard to find me sitting on a lounge chair with my laptop open, trying to distract myself with work as usual. The sun and its heat have long dipped below the horizon and she's wearing an oversized sweater, the sleeves dangling loose over her hands. She looks so small as she sits down gently on the edge of my chair. I close my laptop and toss it onto the empty chair next to me, but before I can open my mouth to speak, Nicole begins.

'I need to ask you something, Vince. I'm only going to ask you once, and I need you to tell me the truth, okay?' Her fingers nervously toy with the hem of her sweater.

'Yes, anything.' I'm relieved that she's at least looking in my direction again.

'Where were you the night that girl died?' Her eyes are wide and imploring, her cheeks streaked with tears that look silver in the moonlight.

'I had to work late and then I spent the night at the apartment.' It frightens me how easily the lie comes. 'We're launching that new video game branch soon and I needed to get the quarterly projections together to present to the board the next morning—'

'I know that's where you told me you were that night, but is it the truth, Vince?' Her voice is quiet, unsure. *She thinks I'm capable of murder.*

'Yes. It is,' I lie to my wife.

'Okay,' she says, her eyes falling to her lap. 'I believe you. But it's going to take me some time to trust you again. I don't know how I'm going to get past this.' She shakes her head slowly, and I can feel her disappointment in me radiating off her in waves. I don't think I've ever felt as low as I do in this moment.

I look at my wife now, really look at her. *When was the last time I did that? When was the last time I truly saw her?* She seems to have grown smaller than she was only yesterday, she's folded in on herself, her head bowed, shielding her face behind a veil of long, blonde hair.

I reach for her hand. Words alone can't express how truly awful I feel, how much I hate myself, for having put her through this. But she recoils at my touch, deftly sliding her hand out from beneath mine.

I think back to the early days, to when we were so in love that we couldn't keep our hands off one another. My mind flashes with images of my lips on hers, her head on my chest, her fingers interlaced with mine. Those golden days of lazy Sunday mornings spent naked in bed and stolen kisses that never seemed to end. And now my wife, the love of my life, is repulsed by the feel of my skin on hers. And it's my own fault. *I've done this to her. To us.*

'I understand,' I say, my heart breaking as I do. 'And I'm so sorry. But I promise you that I'm going to earn your trust back. I love you more than you'll ever know.'

Nicole looks up at me then, her eyes round and baleful. They're rimmed with red and tears, more tears, gently slide down her cheeks. She nods slowly, silently, as she wraps her sweater tightly around her shoulders before making her way back into the house alone.

Chapter 10

Vince

DAY 3

I wake up in a guest room, alone, to the sound of the house phone ringing and the front gate intercom buzzing non-stop. It takes me a moment to place where I am. The spare rooms in our house, of which there are several, remind me of a hotel. They're tastefully decorated, designed to accommodate even the fussiest of houseguests with an array of toiletries, fresh flowers, and Egyptian cotton sheets, but utterly devoid of any of the sentiment which makes our house feel like our home.

I hoist myself out of bed and accidentally catch sight of myself in the full-length mirror that Nicole put in each of the guest rooms. My face is darkened with stubble and my hair is jutting out in all directions. I look, and feel, as though I've aged ten years overnight. I make my way to the master bedroom and push open the door to find Nicole sitting up in bed, holding her knees to her chest.

'This has been going on all morning,' she says sadly. 'The intercom has been buzzing for hours. I checked the front gate camera. It's a bunch of reporters. Please make them leave, Vince.' She looks up at me, her eyes pleading.

'I'll take care of it.'

I'm no stranger to the spotlight, but Nicole didn't sign up for this. She was with me before the money, before the fame … before the affair. She didn't ask for any of this and I feel like I need to protect her. I walk downstairs to the front door and look at the security camera pointed at the wrought iron gate at the end of our long, winding driveway. I press the intercom button and I'm immediately bombarded with at least five voices yelling into the intercom, shouting their questions at me as quickly as they can: *Were you questioned by the police? Were you in love with Layla Bosch? Were you leaving your wife for Layla? What happened to Layla, Vince?'* I assume other news outlets have picked up on the story printed in the *World View* yesterday and now each of these vultures wants to tear into my marriage, my private life.

'My wife and I have no comment at this time and we would appreciate it if you would respect our privacy and back away from our property immediately,' I reply over the intercom before shutting it off entirely. I also unplug the house phone line to end the calls which seem to be coming more and more frequently now.

I pull out my cell and call Jeff. 'There are a pack of reporters outside my gate, barking like rabid dogs. Is there anything we can do about it?'

'Good morning to you too,' Jeff grumbles. I must have woken him up. I can still hear the sleep in his voice. 'As long as they aren't actually on your property, unfortunately there's nothing we can do about it. Did you speak to them?'

'Only to tell them that I have no comment.'

'Good. Don't interact with them again. They'll get bored and move on to the next story soon enough.'

'Okay, thanks, Jeff,' I reply gratefully.

Jeff grumbles something about how calling him in the early hours of a Saturday morning should cost extra, and ends the call.

I trek back upstairs to find Nicole exactly as I left her. 'Are they gone?' she asks.

'No, unfortunately not, but I've unplugged the intercom. They won't be bothering us again. Let's just lie low for today and I'm sure they'll be on to the next story by tomorrow. And if they aren't, I'll hire someone to handle security.' I try to make my voice sound confident, reassuring, but in reality I'm not so sure that this story will blow over as quickly as I'm hoping it will. 'Do you have any clients coming for a session today?'

'I was supposed to teach a pre-natal yoga class this morning, but I've just emailed my clients to tell them that I'm feeling ill. I don't want to have to explain to them why they have to pass through a gang of reporters to get my to studio. Explaining why they have to pass through security guards wouldn't be much better. This is Loch Harbor, it's supposed to be a safe community. A security team marching around the front gates is going to scare all of my clients off for sure.'

'I'm so sorry, Nic.'

'So you've mentioned.' She sounds tired, defeated. I hear her release a sigh, followed by the sound of her stomach rumbling.

'Go relax by the pool. I'll bring you out some breakfast.'

'Okay,' she says tentatively. 'I guess.' Her eyes barely meet mine. I know she hasn't forgiven me, but at least she's letting me try to make things right.

Nicole changes into a cornflower-blue bikini and tops it with a white sheer cover-up, while I run some water through my hair and try to wrangle it into something presentable before I give up entirely. I quickly put on a pair of olive-green board-shorts and a plain white T-shirt, and by the time I've finished, Nicole has already gone downstairs.

I hurry down the stairs and into the kitchen where I can see Nicole curled up on a sun lounger, her nose in a book. I begin to prepare breakfast for her, something I know she'll love. I don't expect her to want to share a meal with me, but I want to do this for her. I open the refrigerator and pull out an assortment of fresh fruits, mangoes, strawberries, raspberries, peaches, and watermelon, and I begin to slice them and arrange them neatly on a large platter. I pop four slices of bread into the toaster, reminding myself to set the toaster to medium heat so as not to burn it, and pour two brimming glasses of orange juice.

The meal reminds me of our honeymoon in Hawaii, where Nicole and I would wake early in the morning to sit on our secluded balcony with a plate of fresh fruit between us and watch the dolphins swim past our little bungalow. That trip cost us what felt like a fortune at the time, nearly all of our meager savings after our wedding, but it was worth it for ten days of sun, making love on the beach, and feeling like the luckiest man on earth to be sharing it with Nicole.

I balance the platter of fruit on one arm and hold a glass of juice in each hand. I manage to push open the sliding door to the yard with one foot, and I'm feeling quite pleased with myself. I see Nicole laying on the lounge chair in her bikini, soaking in the early morning sun with her book in her hand and her cover-up thrown over the back of the chair. After all these years the sight of my wife is still enough to take my breath away. I don't know what I was thinking getting involved with Layla. It's a mistake I will regret for the rest of my life. But right now, I need to focus on Nicole. On getting us back to where we used to be.

'Breakfast is served, Mrs Taylor. I brought you the Hawaiian honeymoon special,' I say, giving her a little bow.

Nicole offers a tight smile at the sight of me holding the platter of fruit. It isn't much, but it's something. And now I'm really feeling very pleased with myself. Nicole stands up, letting her long locks fall around her shoulders, and at that very moment a camera flashes, the sound of a shutter click reverberating around our yard.

I instinctively drop the platter, the clattering sound making Nicole jump, and look around for signs of the intruder. I catch a glimpse of a man in a baseball cap jumping off of the stone wall that surrounds our yard, but he's gone as quick as his camera flash.

I look back at Nicole, but she's already running towards the house, holding her cover-up to her chest. I'm left standing alone by the pool, the forgotten fruit and shards of glass glistening in the sun at my feet.

I clean up the mess and walk back inside. *What is that smell?* The toast. Burnt, of course. It seems like ever since I met Layla, I can't seem to do anything right.

Chapter 11

Vince

BEFORE

'Eric?' I call out of my office. His desk is just down the hall. 'Were you able to get those copies I needed for my three o'clock?' No answer. I walk past his desk but he's not there. He's probably wrapped up with the launch advertisements. It's been a hectic week. Oh well, before I was a CEO, I was a programmer; I'm sure I can figure out a copy machine. And besides, I'm not above making my own copies. I swipe the folder of revenue projection I left for Eric earlier off of his desk and make my way down to the copy room.

'Good afternoon, Vince,' one of the secretaries says with a little wave as I walk by. *What's her name again? Tiffany? Brittney? Something like that.*

'Good afternoon to you too.' I give her a wink and a crooked smile. She looks like she just might faint. I will never get used to that. Before I was *the* Vince Taylor, King of KitzTech, women weren't exactly falling at my feet. I had to ask Nicole out six times before she finally agreed to go for coffee with Vincent, the nerdy computer programmer that worked in the office upstairs. I suspect that the expensive clothes, over-priced haircuts, and flashy car have something to do with the change. I have to admit, it does feel good though, and I don't mind playing along. Even though I've never been the 'playboy' type, it's part of the Vince Taylor persona.

I make my way into the copy room and shut the door behind me. This copier is far more complicated than the one I bought second-hand when I was in my tiny rented office space. I'm studying all the buttons and settings intently when I hear the door open. I turn around to see a young woman with tears in her eyes, a wadded up tissue in her hand.

'Oh, Mr Taylor! I'm so sorry! I didn't realize you were in here!' she says, her embarrassment apparent.

'It's okay, please, don't worry about it. You're Layla, right?'

'Yes, oh my god, this is so humiliating, crying in front of my boss!' A blush begins creeping up into her cheeks. 'I'll go, I can come back to make my copies later.'

'No, I'll be done in just a second. As soon as I can sort out this damn machine. Why don't you take a seat while I finish and then it's all yours.'

Layla walks into the cramped copy room and takes a seat on a stack of bankers' boxes piled up next to the copier.

'Is everything, okay?' I ask her.

'I'm fine, really,' she says. 'This is going to sound ridiculous, and probably way more information than I need to share with my boss, but today would have been my grandmother's birthday. She raised me, and she recently passed, so it's been a rough day.'

'I'm so sorry to hear that. You know what, why don't you make your copies and then we'll take a walk down to the café. They make an amazing red velvet cake. We can have a slice in your grandmother's honor. I was planning to get something to eat before my next meeting anyway.'

'That's just about the sweetest thing I've ever heard,' Layla responds as she rises up to stand next to me at the copier. 'I'd love that.'

Ours eyes meet and I know I'm in trouble.

Chapter 12

Allison

DAY 3

High Tech Hottie Under Heat
By Kate Owens for *World View*

Once again Vince Taylor, CEO of the famous technology development company, KitzTech, finds himself in the spotlight. But this time it's not for dropping the latest app we all have to have.

As previously reported by World View, *Vince Taylor is a person of interest in the investigation into the murder of the lovely Layla Bosch (age 23), an intern at KitzTech, and it seems that things are certainly heating up. A source close to the investigation has informed* World View *that Taylor, everyone's favorite high tech hottie, was having a steamy affair with the late Layla Bosch. Vince Taylor and his wife, Nicole Taylor, have declined to comment on the alleged affair, but we're now told that the NYPD is in possession of Layla's personal diary that describes, in sordid detail, her hot and heavy relationship with her boss. We've been informed that Vince was brought in for questioning by the police yesterday morning.*

What exactly was going on between Layla and her boss? Was it just lust? According to Layla's diary, it seems it may have been love. My my, Mr Taylor. What will they find next?

I cannot believe what I'm seeing. How the hell did *World View* know about the diary? I read the online article again and again hoping that somehow I had it wrong. But no, there's no denying it now, someone is feeding information to the press. This article was published along with the same photos of Layla and Vince that were featured in the previous article, as well as a new photo of Vince's wife, Nicole, which appears to have been taken in their backyard. She's undeniably beautiful, with long, icy-blonde hair and a flawless figure which is on full display in her little blue bikini, but the poor thing looks like a startled doe in this photo, all wide-eyed and open mouthed.

I have to feel bad for the woman. She just found out her husband was having an affair with an intern (so cliché) and now she has reporters poking at the wound. I've been in her shoes. I get it. Well, sort of. Before Josh, I dated this guy, Mark, for three years. It was serious. We moved in together, adopted a puppy, and when he got down on one knee I immediately said 'yes.' I just knew he was the one. But then I found out about Beth. Mark had been seeing her for months and I, blinded by love, hadn't seen any of the signs. *Some detective I am.* I only found out about the affair by pure, dumb luck. Beth texted Mark's phone, and I mistakenly picked it up while he was in the shower, thinking it was mine. As soon as I saw her message on the home screen, '*I can't stop thinking about you, xoxo,*' I knew things would never be the same. I gave Mark his ring back, he took the dog, and he left. But Mark did teach me one very valuable lesson: never take anyone at face value. More often than not, the ones that seem too good to be true, are the ones hiding the biggest secrets.

I know one thing for sure though, McFadden is not going to

be happy about the newest *World View* headline. I pick up my phone and call Lanner.

'Before you even ask, yes, I saw the *World View* article, and no, I don't want to talk about it. But we need to find out who their source is. Now.'

'Yes, ma'am,' Lanner says. 'I'll pick you up.'

Lanner is outside my building within fifteen minutes. I waited outside on the sidewalk for him. I was too pent up in my apartment, feeling like a caged animal pacing back and forth; an angry bear that hadn't been fed. I need to get to the bottom of the *World View* problem. The way I see it, there are two possible scenarios here: either someone from our department is leaking information to the media, or there's someone else out there who knew about Layla's involvement with Vince Taylor and has chosen not to come forward about it. Someone who knew Layla well enough to know the contents of the private diary she kept.

I slide into Lanner's passenger seat and aim the air conditioning vent at my face. I was only outside for a few minutes but I can already feel the sweat pooling at my lower back and seeping through my white dress shirt. 'This weather is disgusting.'

'You know what they say, bad things happen in heat like this,' Lanner replies.

'No one says that. You just made that up.'

'No, really! I read a study about it. Crime rates increase when the heat index rises.'

'Well if that's true then I expect we're about to get saddled with a ton of new cases because this is ridiculous,' I conclude, fanning myself.

'What's the plan for *World View*?' Lanner asks, getting back to the task at hand. 'You know they aren't going to give us their source, right?'

'Can't hurt to ask. Maybe showing up in person will be a little more persuasive. I looked at the last two articles. They were both covered by the same reporter: Kate Owens. She's the one we need to speak to.'

'Kate Owens ...' Lanner repeats to himself. 'Why does that name sound so familiar?'

I can see the wheels turning in his head as he works it out. 'Oh! I remember her!' I see his face light up with recognition. 'She was that reporter that used to write for *The Minute*! Big scandal. She was fired suddenly and then did a whole talk show circuit about how her boss had made inappropriate advances towards her, but there was no proof so she couldn't prove that she was fired for rejecting his old wrinkly ass.'

'And she ended up working at *World View*? Quite a fall from *The Minute*.'

'Yeah, I doubt any other paper wanted to touch her after she cried harassment.'

'Men are dogs,' I grumble.

'Present company excluded, I assume?' Lanner asks with a smirk.

'That's up for debate. Anyway, I doubt it's a coincidence that Kate Owens is the one receiving these tip-offs given her history. She seems like the perfect fit to run a story about Vince Taylor and his dead intern.'

'That much we can agree on.'

Lanner pulls out a bagel and offers half to me. I take it, and although I don't say it, I appreciate that he remembers that bagels are my favorite.

*

'We're here to speak with Kate Owens,' I say to the frizzy-haired older woman behind the front desk at the *World View* offices. I flash my gold detective's badge for emphasis.

'Let me see if she's available.' The woman sighs as though we've asked her to do us a favor and not the very job she presumably gets paid to do.

'Kate,' she says into the phone, 'couple of detectives here to see you.' The woman gives us a distrustful glance as she listens to Kate's reply on the other end of the line. 'Come on,' she finally tells us. 'She'll meet with you in the conference room.'

The surly woman lifts herself from her chair with what appears to be great effort and slowly leads us down the hall to a dated and drab room at the back of the office. 'She'll be right with you,' the woman says, as she leaves Lanner and I alone in the room, shutting the door behind her.

'She was pleasant, huh?' Lanner comments as he looks around the room, at the peeling wallpaper, faded green carpet, and array of mismatched office chairs clustered around the table in the center of the room.

'Shocking. Given that she works for such a classy publication.'

Just then Kate breezes into the room. Evidently no one informed her that she no longer works for *The Minute*. She's dressed in a professional, but stylish, navy blue sheath dress, accented with a crisp white blazer and patent leather peep toe heels. Her golden blonde hair is cut in a short, angled bob that only a woman with Kate's desirably narrow face and defined chin could pull off.

'What can I help you with today, Detectives?' she says as she sits down in a leather desk chair crossing her long, tan legs in front of her.

'We're here to talk to you about the pieces you've put out about Layla Bosch and Vince Taylor,' I tell her.

'I figured as much.' Kate gives me a small but warm smile. 'But if you're here to ask who my source is, you know I can't give you that information. And even if I wanted to,' she adds, 'these tips came to me over an anonymous e-mail.'

'So you ran these stories without knowing if they were true?' I follow up.

'All I can tell you, Detective, is that the e-mails sent to me gave me enough detailed information that I felt I could confidently print these articles. And the fact that you two are sitting here today leads me to believe that what I wrote was, in fact, accurate.' Her voice is calm yet confident. It seems that Kate Owens has not been rattled in the least by the presence of two NYPD detectives.

I catch a glance of Lanner looking down at his phone under the table. 'Barnes, we have to go,' he tells me.

'Just a moment, Detectives,' Kate interjects as we're standing to leave, 'there is one more thing I want to tell you before you go. But this stays between us. My boss wouldn't be happy if he knew I told you.'

I nod in agreement, encouraging her to continue.

'That photo we ran with the article this morning? The one of Vince Taylor's wife in her backyard? Our guys didn't take that photo. Someone anonymously dropped it in our mailbox early this morning, just before the article went live online. I didn't want to include it. I don't agree with that kind of thing. This is about Vince Taylor, not his wife. She doesn't need some sleazy photographer trespassing on her property to get photos of her in her bikini. It's trashy and I don't think we should be encouraging people to behave that way, but the Powers That Be wanted to include it. This is *World View* after all, so ...' she concludes with a shrug.

'Thanks, Ms Owens,' I tell her, shaking her hand firmly. 'If you come across any information that could assist in this investigation, we would appreciate it if we were your first call.'

Kate nods affirmatively.

Lanner and I briskly walk out to his car. 'What was that about?' I ask. 'Why did you rush us out of there?'

'Chief wants us back at the station. There's a witness waiting to talk to us. Says he has info about Vince and Layla.'

'Let's go.'

Chapter 13

Vince

DAY 3

'Hey, Jeff, I know it's a Sunday, but would you mind coming by the house today? I don't know if you saw the latest *World View* article yet, but this is getting out of hand. They used a picture of Nicole on their website. I won't have her dragged through the mud. I think it's time we got ahead of this thing,' I say.

'Yeah. I'll be there. Give me about a half-hour.'

'He's coming,' I tell Nicole. 'We're going to take care of this. There will be no more reporters hounding you.'

'Of course there will be, Vince,' she replies with an exasperated sigh. 'You invited this into our lives. You're a public figure, everyone wants to know our business, and you handed them plenty to run with.'

'I know you don't want to hear it anymore, but I'm sorry, Nic. I really am.'

'I know you are, Vince. But that's not enough to make this stop.'

I've let her down. I can hear it in her voice, I can see it in her sullen eyes that seem to have lost their sparkle. Nicole has never looked at me like this before, like I'm a failure. Even when we didn't know if KitzTech was going to make it, even when I invested all of my life's savings getting the company off the ground and we thought we were going to lose it all, she never saw my failures, only my ambition. She stood by me, she believed in me when I didn't. I know I owe her so much more than I've given her, but what hurts the most is knowing that she's lost her faith in me.

'I'm going to put something together for lunch,' she tells me plainly.

'You don't need to go to the trouble.'

'I need to do something, anything, that feels normal right now. Besides, the least we can do for Jeff is feed him after dragging him out here on his day off.'

I leave Nicole to it while I go upstairs to take a shower.

I step into the shower in the master bathroom. With its slate walls, river rock floor, and waterfall stream, showering here feels like you're standing under an actual waterfall in a secluded corner of the rainforest. I increase the water pressure and let the water beat on my back, easing some of the tension from my shoulders. I breathe in the steam, mixed with the scent of the eucalyptus leaves Nicole likes to hang in here. I'm starting to understand the appeal. Nicole says that the scent helps to clear the airways and create breath awareness during her yoga practice. Maybe she's right. I can feel the crisp, clean aroma filling my lungs and calming me from within.

I almost feel like a new person by the time I finish showering and shaving. I put on a pair of light blue shorts and pair them with a white linen shirt and make my way downstairs. I can hear Nicole moving about in the kitchen.

'Do you need any help?' I ask as I walk in.

'No, I'm just about finished.' I watch as she chops some plump, red cherry tomatoes and adds them to a large bowl of salad. She's also prepared a cheese platter, finger sandwiches, and a pitcher of lemonade. She is incredible, even under the worst of circumstances. *How could I ever have taken her, our marriage, for granted?*

'Lunch looks great, thank you for putting this together.' I bend down to kiss her lightly on the cheek. She bristles slightly as my lips brush her face, the knife in her hand suspended momentarily above the cutting board.

'I'm just not ready for this yet, Vince,' she says as she steps away from me. 'I can't pretend everything is normal between us right now.'

'I'm sorry, you're right. I'll give you the space you need.'

'Honestly, the only reason I haven't left already is because I don't want to face that pack of reporters on my own. If we just stay here, together, in the house, there's no further story for them.'

She's right about one thing, it would only hype up the tabloid drama if Nicole was spotted walking out on me, but it still stings to hear her say that that's the only thing keeping her by my side right now.

We're interrupted by a knock on the door.

'Vince, it's me,' Jeff calls through the closed front door.

'I'll go set us up outside,' Nicole says, grabbing the large salad bowl off the kitchen island and making her way towards the sliding doors leading to our back patio.

I walk to the front door and open it just wide enough for Jeff to walk through without giving any lurking reporters with a zoom lens a peek into our home. Jeff is dripping with sweat.

'Your intercom wasn't working. I couldn't get in through the gate. I had to park on the street and hike up here,' he complains.

'Oh, sorry, man. I shut it off because the reporters press it constantly. It was driving us insane. And anyway, it's just a driveway. You didn't have to scale Mount Everest to get up here.'

'Well it feels like it in this heat.' Jeff wipes his brow dramatically.

'Come on, Nicole made lemonade.'

I lead Jeff into the backyard where Nicole has set up her lunch spread on the large outdoor table situated under the shady pergola. She's already poured each of us a glass of fresh lemonade. Jeff swipes his off the table immediately, the ice rattling in his glass as he takes a large gulp.

'As always, Nicole, you are amazing,' he says, as he finally puts down his nearly empty glass. 'A guy could get used to this.'

Jeff is a perpetual bachelor. He's never shown even the slightest interest in settling down. Although he's had girlfriends here and there over the years, none of them ever seemed to stick. And Jeff appears to be just fine with that, choosing instead to spend his free time as he pleases: traveling, going to bars, and meeting the occasional woman off of my dating app, Date Space. While Jeff is a good five inches shorter than me, with noticeably thinning hair and a soft midsection, he seems to be doing alright for himself. He always has a new Date Space story to tell me every time we get together. It makes me feel like all the effort I put into maintaining my abs over the years has been a colossal waste of time.

'Okay,' I say, directing us to the task at hand. 'We have to do something about the press.'

'There weren't too many outside your gate just now. Just a few stragglers left. See? I told you they'd be onto the next scandal soon enough. Vultures,' Jeff manages between bites of an egg salad sandwich.

'Do you think I should issue a statement or something? To get them off my back?'

'I really wouldn't advise it just yet.' I watch Jeff pile a precarious amount of cheese onto a cracker. 'As soon as the cops stop wasting their time sniffing around you and figure out who actually killed this girl, you'll be old news.'

'I just don't like the road this narrative seems to be going down. The press are making it seem like I was responsible for her death,' I say, exasperated. Nicole looks over at me, briefly catching my eye. *Does she doubt what I told her? That I was working late the night Layla was killed?* 'How did they even know about the diary?'

'Who knows,' Jeff replies. 'Maybe a friend of Layla's or maybe a cop. We have no idea who else knew it existed. But regardless, I'm sending those security records over to the detectives today,' Jeff assures me. 'That should get them off of your back, and once they lose interest in you, the press will too. I'm telling you.'

'It's just been a lot,' Nicole adds quietly.

Jeff softens instantly upon hearing her voice. I can see him switch from 'hardened defense attorney mode' back to just being our friend. 'I can't even imagine what you're going through, Nic. Both of you,' he corrects. 'The things *World View* has been reporting are hurtful and salacious, but, as I explained to Vince, technically not bordering into libel. Unfortunately there's nothing we can do to stop them at this point. I am going to strongly urge both of you to just lie low for now and not interact with the media at all. And if you can manage it, presenting a united front will go a long way in ending the public drama. A happily married couple isn't exactly front page news, if you know what I mean.'

'I don't know about *happily*,' Nicole replies, eying me coldly. 'But I understand your point, Jeff.'

'Alright, guys,' Jeff says, pushing his chair back from the table. 'I hate to eat and run, but I want to get those security records over to the cops and see what I can do about putting an end to this madness. Can you get me a copy, Vince?'

'Sure, I already put them on a flash drive for you last night. I'll go grab it from my office.'

I jog back inside to grab the flash drive while Nicole begins gathering the lunch plates on the table. I find the flash drive laying on my desk and I quickly swipe it into my hand. I pause for a moment, thinking over what I'm about to do: hand over falsified records to the police on a homicide investigation. My palms are starting to sweat and I swallow hard. *No, it has to be done.*

I walk out of my office and through the kitchen towards the yard. As I near the center island, I see something that stops me in my tracks. Nicole is standing beside the outdoor table, the pitcher

71

of lemonade in her hand. Jeff is standing next to her, too close for my taste, and he lightly brushes her upper arm with the back of his hand. Nicole turns away from him, wiping a tear from her eye. Jeff has been a friend of mine, of both of ours really, for years. Of course he would comfort my wife through a difficult time, but I don't know, something about the scene feels so intimate, so tender, that I can't help but stand back and watch it play out before me. Nicole is still facing away from Jeff, staring out over the pool, and Jeff again tries to put his arm around her shoulder but she shrugs him off. I stride towards the door, breaking up whatever is going on.

'Everything okay?' I ask as I step outside.

'Yea, Nic was just feeling a little overwhelmed,' Jeff replies. Nicole doesn't respond. She's still staring out into the yard, her back to both Jeff and I.

'You find that flash drive?' Jeff asks.

'Right here.' I press it firmly into Jeff's palm.

'Great. Call me if you need anything.'

Jeff makes his way out of the yard, and once I hear the back gate click behind him, I approach Nicole.

'You alright?'

'No, Vince. I'm not. All of this … It's too much. I'd say I'm very far from *okay*.' Her words are a cocktail of anger and pain. Her arms wrap over her chest, a barrier protecting her from the rest of the world … from me.

'I know it is. But you heard Jeff, it will all be behind us soon,' I reassure her.

Nicole nods, still not making eye contact with me.

'Speaking of Jeff …' I venture, 'was he acting strangely just now?'

'What do you mean?' Nicole finally looks up at me. Her eyes are hard and cold.

'Was he being a little forward with you?'

'You have to be kidding me, Vince. After … what you did …

you really have the nerve to suggest something is going on with Jeff, of all people?'

'No, I wasn't suggesting you did anything wrong, I was just asking if you thought he was … I don't know … coming on to you.'

'No, Vince. He wasn't,' Nicole says pointedly. 'He was just being kind, checking in on me. And honestly, it's nice to know that at least *someone* is thinking of me in all of this.'

'Nicole, *I'm* thinking of you, I—'

'Really, Vince? Were you thinking of me when you decided to have an affair with your intern?' She lets her arms fall to her sides, her hands clenching into fists in righteous indignation.

She has every reason to hate me, I remind myself. *I deserve this.*

'No, I—' I start to protest.

'No, Vince you weren't. Maybe if you stopped to think of me, even *one time*, this wouldn't be happening to us right now.'

'Nicole, please just listen—'

'No. I think I've done quite enough listening for today.' She throws her hands up in frustration. 'I can't have this conversation with you right now. I'm going inside.'

Nicole walks away leaving me with the remains of our lunch to put away. I don't want to feel distrustful of my best friend, but I know what I saw. And it's making me question everything. How long has he been in love with my wife? Could he be the one leaking information to *World View* to try to drive a wedge between us? I know Nicole thinks I have it all wrong, but I also know what it looks like when a man is in over his head.

Chapter 14

Vince

BEFORE

'It didn't work. Again,' Nicole sighs into the phone. 'I really thought it was going to take this time. I don't know why I get my hopes up.'

'I'm so sorry, honey. I can come home right now. I didn't plan on staying this late anyway.'

'No, that's alright. I'm going over to Kathy's. To take my mind off of things for a while.'

'Okay. That's a good idea. Have a nice time.'

Nicole hangs up the phone and now I'm alone with my disappointment. I didn't want to tell her this, but I had my hopes up that this round of IVF was going to be the one that worked too. I don't know why, I just felt so positive about it. For the first time, I really let myself imagine what our lives would look like nine months from now, me holding a tiny baby in my arms, wrapped in a pink and blue hospital blanket, soft whiffs of fine hair poking out the top. Ice-blonde, like Nicole's. It felt so real, I could smell that new baby smell, picture her tiny fingers curled around mine. I know rationally that this baby never existed, she was never mine, but yet the loss feels just as real.

I grab my jacket off of the hook on the back of my door and head towards the parking lot. There's no way I'm going to be able to work any more tonight. All I can think about is the baby that wasn't meant to be.

As I walk out towards my car, a velvety darkness creeping into the evening sky, I click the automatic start button on my keyring and the headlights of the Tesla flicker in response. In the glow of the headlights, I realize, for the first time, that I'm not alone. I see a figure jump with surprise at the sound of my car starting, whipping around to face me.

'Layla?' I ask. 'What are you doing here so late?'

'Oh, the interns are having a competition to see who can pitch the best new app idea tomorrow and well ... my idea kind of sucked. I stayed late reworking my entry.'

'I'm sure it's not as bad as you think.'

'I hope not! I'm told the winner gets to pitch their idea to the boss.'

I know about the intern contest; I started it. I like to see which of the prospective hires has what it takes to think outside the box and come up with unique and marketable ideas.

I should go home. I should leave right now. But I can't stomach the idea of going back to my big, empty house. The one that may never be filled with the children we built it for. 'Do you want to show me your idea now?' I ask Layla instead. 'I won't tell anyone that I got a sneak preview.'

'Really?' she responds excitedly. 'That would be so amazing! Should we go back inside?'

'Actually, I think I have a better idea.'

*

Layla slides into the booth across from me, sipping a rum and coke through a red swizzle straw. I can't help but notice that the straw is the same exact shade as the red lipstick on her full, glossy lips. *No, Vince. Don't go down that road.*

The waitress arrives, delivering a basket of french fries to our table, sliding them between Layla and I. The fries shine with grease in the dim overhead lighting, and they're spilling over the side of the red plastic basket they were served in. I pop a fry into my mouth to distract myself from staring at Layla's.

'I have to say, Vince, this isn't the type of place where I would expect to find a CEO hanging out.'

'Hey, I like sports bars as much as the next guy. Even if I don't care much for watching sports. There's something about cheap beer from the tap and greasy fries that I just can't resist. Besides, I used to come here all the time, when KitzTech was just a start-up and I was the only employee.'

'I really think it's amazing how you created this whole company from nothing.'

Layla leans in to take a sip of her drink and a lock of chocolate-brown hair falls over one eye. She gently tucks it behind her ear and looks up at me with kohl-rimmed eyes. I notice for the first time that her brown eyes are flecked with gold, like an intricate mosaic.

'Thanks,' I reply, waving off the compliment. But the truth is that I am very proud of KitzTech and how far it's come. It's grown larger than even I ever imagined. 'So, what's this new pitch you're working on?' I need to steer the conversation away from me and back to the safety of work-related topics.

Layla proceeds to fill me in on her idea for a new video editing app where users can combine multiple videos into a sort of a collage, set to music and ready for social media. 'Just imagine newlyweds creating professional-grade videos of their favorite moments from their wedding, new parents sharing the milestones from their baby's first year, coaches sharing the highlight reel of

76

their teams' seasons, all formatted for social media, all stamped with the KitzTech logo. It could be huge.'

I can hear the excitement in her voice. She's right. It could be huge. The idea is brilliant. 'I'm very impressed, Ms Bosch. This is one of the best intern pitches I've heard in a long time.'

She flashes me a smile, all white teeth behind cherry-red lips. 'Really? You like it?' she asks animatedly.

'I love it. In fact, if you don't win this contest, I think I'm still going to develop it … And fire whoever didn't give you first place,' I answer with a laugh.

'Oh my gosh, this is so exciting! I'll get us another round to celebrate.' She slides out of the booth in the direction of the bar before I have a chance to protest. Not that I want to. I find that I'm enjoying her company, the relaxed atmosphere, and talking over drinks about something other than ovulation cycles, progesterone levels, and basal temperatures.

'So,' Layla says, after returning to the table with two more drinks in her manicured hands, 'tell me about the real Vince Taylor.' She props her elbow on the table and rests her chin on one hand, looking at me intently as if she's genuinely interested in getting to know me, the real me. It's been a very long time since someone has been interested in knowing who I am behind the public persona.

'Well, I hate to disappoint you, but I'm not really all that interesting. I am a computer programmer, after all,' I start with a laugh. 'But let's see, I love rock climbing. Mostly because it gives me a chance to be on my own out in nature, just me and the challenges I choose to take on. I love finding a new climb, figuring out the best way to tackle it. It's like a puzzle. And it's such a rewarding feeling when you finish a successful climb.'

'Wow, that sounds amazing. Does your … wife climb with you?'

I can't tell whether she's actually interested in the answer or whether she's really just asking if I'm married. I assumed she knew, the wedding ring being a dead giveaway. 'Not really,' I reply.

'She'll join me for a hike sometimes, but climbing is something I like to do on my own. It's my thing, my escape, ya know?'

'I do.'

I take another sip of my beer. 'How about you? What's your story?'

'Me? I just moved to New York from Pennsylvania. I lived there most of my life with my grandmother, and when she passed I decided to make a new start of things. I applied for this internship, and when I managed to get accepted, it felt like it was meant to be and I moved to New York City immediately.'

'Do you like it here? In New York I mean?'

'It's been a little bit of a culture shock after growing up around more cows than people, but I wanted something new and I've certainly found it.'

I try to picture the woman sitting in front of me on a farm. Trading in her stilettos for cowgirl boots, the skirt that clings to her hips for overalls. The image makes me laugh.

'What's so funny?' Layla asks, a sly smile working its way onto her face.

'Just trying to picture you on a farm, is all,' I reply, which garners a laugh from Layla too.

'I was never cut out for small town life,' she says. 'Most of the other girls I grew up with got married and had kids right out of high school. I guess I just always wanted something more. Like you. I wanted to make a name for myself before I started a family.'

I look down into my beer. Little does she know how much I'd give for a family. Layla must notice the dark cloud growing over me because she asks, 'Did I say something wrong?'

'No, not at all. It's just been a rough day.'

'Do you want to talk about it? I know you don't know me very well, but I'm a really good listener.'

And I find that I do. I do want to talk to her. I don't know if it's the alcohol, the easy way she has about her, or the years of pent-up sadness I've been carrying around for the children I never had, but I find the words spilling out of my mouth before I can stop them.

'My wife, my wife and I, we're having trouble getting pregnant. We've been trying for three years now, IVF, fertility drugs, you name it. But nothing seems to be working. And today we found out that her latest round of IVF has failed again. I feel so disappointed, but I can't tell her that because she's already carrying so much on her shoulders. I don't think she even realizes how hard this is for me too. And it can feel really lonely working through it alone. Not that it's Nicole's fault really. I have just never been able to bring myself to burden her with the weight of my disappointment too. And she's been so wrapped up in her own pain, that she can't see mine. But it's more than just the disappointment for me, I also feel so much guilt. I've never told anyone that, but it's true. I made Nicole wait until KitzTech took off before I would try for kids, and now that we're trying and it's not working, I can't help but think that maybe if we would have started sooner, maybe if I had made our family a priority instead of work …'

'I'm so sorry, Vince,' Layla says softly, gently reaching across the table to place her hand over mine. 'I'm sure this is so hard on both of you.' *Both of us.* Layla is the first person to acknowledge that our trouble conceiving is not just Nicole's burden to bear, it's mine too. Talking to her about all of these things I've kept to myself for so long, sharing the weight of it, has already made me feel less alone.

I look into Layla's eyes and I feel like she sees me, understands me, in a way no one else has for a very long time.

Chapter 15

Allison

DAY 3

'Oh good, you guys are back,' Kinnon says the instant Lanner and I walk into the station. 'There's a guy here who says he has some information about Layla Bosch that you might want to know. I put him in interview room one.'

'Thanks, Kinnon,' Lanner replies, giving him a rough pat on the shoulder before we make our way to the interview room.

When I walk into the room, I see the witness, a young man who can't be much older than Layla was, bouncing one knee nervously while his fingers tap rhythmically on the cold metal table.

'Sorry to keep you waiting,' I say, extending my hand to the young man. 'I'm Detective Allison Barnes, and this is my partner Detective Jake Lanner.'

'We've met,' Lanner informs me. 'You're an intern at KitzTech, right?' he says to the witness.

'Yes,' the young man replies. 'My name is Brian Geller; I worked with Layla before she … died. There's some stuff I didn't tell you when we first met a few days ago. I just … I didn't think it was relevant. But now that I've been reading all that stuff about Layla and Vince in the papers, I don't know, I thought maybe I should tell you. It could totally be nothing, but just in case it's not, I don't wanna be the guy that didn't say anything, ya know?' I can hear the nerves jangling in his voice.

'Of course. We appreciate you coming to talk with us,' I reassure him. 'You never know what's going to be important in an investigation. Why don't you tell us what you know.'

'Okay, so, I was working late one night, and when I went to leave, I walked out into the parking lot and I saw Vince and Layla talking. I couldn't make out what they were saying but it seemed like Vince was real pissed about something. I thought it was probably about the new app, and so I tried to listen in.'

'Why would Vince be angry with Layla about a new app?' I ask.

'Well, see, here's the thing. There's this new video editing app we're working on, and Layla claimed it was her idea but it wasn't. It was mine. She must have pitched it to Vince as if she came up with it, because he gave her all the credit. Layla wasn't exactly the genius everyone thought she was. Not to speak ill of the dead or anything, but I don't even know how she got this internship. It seemed to me like she didn't know the first thing about software development. Must have lied on her résumé or something. Anyway, I volunteered to work with her to develop an idea for a new app, thinking I was doing a good thing showing her the ropes, and she seemed like a nice enough girl … But then I ended up doing all the work, and Layla got all the praise for my idea. So when I saw Vince reading her the riot act that night, I thought she'd been found out, that he realized she wasn't really qualified for her job. Gotta admit, it felt kind of validating after she'd stolen my work. So I stuck around to see where it would go. But then I started to think that maybe something else was going on … maybe it wasn't about work at all.'

'Why is that?'

'Because I saw Vince grab her arm. Looked pretty rough. And

Layla pushed him off of her. Vince got into his car after that and slammed the door behind him. I felt a little bad for Layla, wanted to see if she was okay, so I went over to talk to her after Vince drove off. I think she was surprised to see me there, and she asked me how much I'd seen. I told her I just saw her and Vince having a disagreement, and she immediately started to cry. She told me he'd threatened to fire her over a mistake she'd made at work, and begged me not to tell anyone what I'd seen. She said it was too embarrassing. I promised her I wouldn't, but I didn't really believe her story. I don't know, I've just never seen Vince lose his cool like that before, and it seemed way too personal to be about work.'

'When did this happen?' I inquired.

'About a week before Layla … died.' Brian starts bouncing his heel nervously again. 'Like I said, it could have been nothing. Layla came in to work the next day as if nothing happened, and she never mentioned it again. Didn't get fired either. So I don't really know. Just with all of this stuff in the news about Vince and Layla having … an affair or whatever … I thought maybe I should tell you.'

'You did the right thing, Brian,' I assure him. 'If you think of anything else, anything at all, please let us know.'

'Okay, yeah.' He sounds relieved. 'I'll do that.'

He shakes my hand and Lanner leads him out of the interview room.

Once Brian is out of sight, I turn to Lanner. 'What do you make of all that?'

'Sounds like there was a lot more going on between Vince and Layla than Vince let on.'

'I agree. And we need to figure out exactly what that was.'

Lanner calls Kinnon to join us in the interrogation room.

'How'd it go with the witness?' Kinnon asks.

'Alright,' Lanner replies. 'He didn't know much, but seems there was trouble in paradise between the vic and her boss. Can you do us a favor and do a little digging into Vince Taylor? I want to know everything there is to know about this guy.'

'You got it,' Kinnon replies eagerly before scuttling out of the room to get started.

'He's so annoying,' I tell Lanner as soon as the door closes behind Kinnon.

'Aw, come on Barnes. Give the kid a break. He just wants to help.'

I can't resist rolling my eyes. Lanner always wants to see the best in everyone.

*

'Got something for ya,' Kinnon says as he approaches my desk a few hours later. He drops a manila folder on my desk with a dramatic flair.

'Give me the highlights.'

Kinnon seems happy to oblige, a triumphant smile spreading across his face. 'I started looking into Vince Taylor, just like you asked. And this guy seemed squeaky clean. Like too clean to be true, ya know? Donates a fortune to kids with cancer, shows up at every benefit, gala, red carpet event you can imagine, his wife always on his arm. Every time he's in the news it's for a new donation he's made, or a new bit of tech he's developed. Good looking guy too, seems like he's the total package—'

'Okay, so are you just here to tell me that you have a man crush on the guy or did you actually find something useful?'

'Right, yeah, I'm getting to that,' Kinnon responds, undeterred. 'It turns out that Vince Taylor, formerly known as Vincent Taylor, has one very big skeleton in his closest. Looks like Layla Bosch wasn't the first inappropriate relationship he's been in.' Kinnon crosses his arms across his chest, looking very pleased with himself.

'How so?'

'Well, back before Vince was Vince, back when he was still known as Vincent, a girl he went to school with accused him of rape.'

'What? How did we not know about this sooner?'

'Looks like he was never charged. The girl recanted her allegations. A few days after her initial complaint she filed another report saying she made it all up. Gotta wonder why …'

'Can you track her down? Get us her current contact information. I want to talk to this woman.'

Chapter 16

Vince

DAY 4

I wake up on Monday morning with a pounding migraine. I barely slept last night, my head swirling with thoughts of Layla, of Nicole and Jeff. I had misjudged Layla so badly. I didn't see her true colors until it was way too late. Was it possible I had done the same with Jeff? I can't imagine he'd betray me so badly that he'd splash my personal life all over the tabloids, but then again I didn't think he was in love with my wife either. Nicole has barely spoken a word to me since yesterday afternoon. We passed by each other all day, moving about our house like strangers. Two lone wolves circling their own territories, neither of us willing to be the one to cross over the divide.

After hunkering down in the house all weekend hiding from the press, I'm looking forward to going into the office today. Doing what I do best and maybe feeling like everything is normal, even if just for a few hours.

I shower quickly and get dressed for the day in jeans and a fitted black T-shirt, my signature office attire. I comb my hair neatly and tussle it a bit with my fingers, just the way my stylist instructed me to so that my hair looks neat, but yet somehow as though I just walked out of the ocean. The fact that I even have a stylist to defer to is still laughable to me. It was Nicole's idea. She thought I needed a better public image than 'dorky computer whiz with glasses'. What followed was a complicated hair routine, corrective eye surgery to ditch my thick glasses, a personal trainer, and a closet full of designer jeans and black T-shirts that stretch across my newly toned biceps.

Just as I'm stepping out of the bathroom, I hear my phone buzzing on my nightstand.

'Hey, Vince. It's Eric. Are you coming in today?'

'Of course.'

'Okay, I just wasn't sure whether you would be what with everything … anyway, the board is scheduling an emergency meeting right now. I don't know if I was supposed to tell you but … I thought you should know.'

'I'll be there as soon as possible. Thanks, Eric. You did the right thing.'

I grab my wallet and keys and shove them into my pocket. I sprint out of the room, taking a moment to glance back quickly towards the master bedroom, but the door is still closed. No sign that Nicole is awake yet. I sigh and bound down the stairs to the front door.

I start the Tesla and tear down my driveway and open the front gates with the remote clipped to my visor. I'm surprised to see there are no reporters waiting for me. Maybe it's too early in the day for them to have pulled themselves out of bed yet, or maybe Jeff was right and they're moving on to the next scandal. Good. It's about time.

I race down the expressway towards my office in midtown Manhattan, my palms sweating on the steering wheel. The drive usually takes just under an hour without traffic. I don't generally mind the commute; it gives me time to unwind on my way home from work. And it's worth it to be able to live in a town as beautiful as Loch Harbor where we could build our dream home on a lush, sprawling property. I've never had any desire to live in the city; apartments stacked up on top of one another, the people, the taxis, the noise. Everything about New York City is loud, rushed, crowded. We wanted to live in a place where we could hear birds chirping in the yard, watch a fire crackle in our own fireplace, and find the type of peaceful tranquility that simply doesn't exist in the city. But today, for the first time, I wish I lived closer to my office. An emergency board meeting, one I wasn't summoned to attend, can't possibly be a good thing.

After the drive, which felt like an eternity, I pull into my designated parking spot under the building and rush into the main lobby. I run up the central spiral staircase, taking the stairs two at a time, and head for the main conference room. I burst through the door hoping that I don't look as frantic as I feel.

'Vince, we weren't expecting you today,' Darren, the CFO, says by way of greeting.

'Well, I'm here, and I heard you were meeting without me, so I thought I should join you.'

'Actually, there are some things you should know. Since you're here,' Darren tells me as he resumes his seat, my seat, at the head of the long conference table. All heads turn towards me. The conference room is full of executives, ones hired to oversee KitzTech once I agreed to take the corporation public, and all eyes are trained on me as if I'm the enemy. This is *my* company. I created it from nothing. Perhaps they've all forgotten.

'Go on then,' I say authoritatively. 'What is it that you need to tell me about my own company?'

'The investors are backing out. They're pulling funding for the new branch,' Darren replies.

'What?! Why?'

'Because of you, Vince. And everything that's been floating

around in the media. No one wants to be associated with KitzTech right now.'

'There has to be something we can do!' I can feel the panic rising in my voice. I've invested a lot of my own money into this new venture. I can't afford for it to fail. It would break me.

'That's what we're here discussing today. We still have a few investors left. We may be able to stay the course. But if this gets worse, the only solution we see is for you to step down as CEO.'

'I will not step down! This is MY company. I created this place. KitzTech wouldn't exist without me!'

'At this rate, KitzTech won't exist *with* you. We all hope it doesn't come to that, Vince. But if we lose any further funding, the board does have the right to vote on whether or not to force your resignation. I'm sorry. I truly am. But we need to do what's best for KitzTech and its stockholders.'

'Unbelievable,' I mutter to myself as I storm out of the conference room.

Darren is excellent at his job, and he's kept a tight rein on the company's finances, but I've always felt that he resented my role as CEO and the public face of KitzTech. I have to wonder whether he's using my personal troubles to his advantage. Is he really just protecting KitzTech or is he trying to free up my seat at the head of the table?

I go back to my office, sealing the door behind me. No open door policy today. But no sooner do I sit down at my desk than I hear a knock on the door.

'WHAT?' I bellow. Eric cracks the door open and pops his head in. 'Sorry, Eric. Shitty morning. What's up?'

'Um, I'm sorry to make your day worse, but you might want to check out the *World View* website. Security said there are a bunch of reporters already crowding the front entrance.'

I can't even bring myself to respond. My body immediately feels numb, although my fingers are already furiously tapping the keys of my keyboard by rote. Eric wisely leaves me to it and again closes my door.

As soon as the *World View* website loads, I gasp. My face is splashed on the front page. The photo must have been taken through my front gate with a zoom lens when I went to take the garbage out or something over the weekend. I didn't realize how terrible I looked. I'm wearing baggy, flannel pajama pants and a shapeless grey T-shirt. Salt and pepper stubble shades my chin, my hair is in disarray, and I appear to be scowling angrily into the distance. I'm almost so shocked by the photo that I forget to read the headline:

Creator of Friend Connect Gets Too Friendly With Intern
By Kate Owens for *World View*

As first reported by World View, *Vince Taylor (age 39), CEO of the popular technology development company, KitzTech, was allegedly involved in an illicit affair with his young intern, Layla Bosch (age 23), in the months leading up to her unfortunate death last week. Taylor is now the prime suspect in the investigation into Layla's murder and has been questioned by the police on multiple occasions. An arrest has not yet been made.*

World View *has now been provided with a copy of what we believe to be a page from Layla's personal diary, and we think the heat is about to turn way up on this investigation. On August 18, 2019, just one week before her death, Layla wrote:*

'*I think I need to end things with Vince. It's all just becoming too much. I know he loves me, but I'm just not sure I feel the same anymore. He said that he saw me out to dinner with a friend last week. I tried to tell him that Adam is just a friend, nothing more, but he didn't believe me. He told me that he could never bear to see me with anyone else. I know this is what I wanted, a future for the two of us, but his love is starting to feel too intense. How did he even know I was out with Adam? Is he following me? I tried to tell him that I needed space, but he wasn't having it. He just kept telling me that he couldn't be without me. I don't know what to do.'*

The document obtained by World View *is being turned over to the NYPD to verify its authenticity and to assist in the police investigation into Layla's murder.*

I can't believe what I'm reading. This reporter … she has to be lying. Surely this has to be considered libel at this point, because what she wrote, it never happened. And yet … there is enough truth in the details that I know she didn't grasp the story out of thin air.

I suddenly notice that my cell phone is buzzing in my pocket. I pull it out just in time to catch Jeff's call.

'What the fuck is this, Vince?' he asks angrily. 'I thought you told me everything there was to know. Did you forget to mention the part where *she* wanted to leave *you*? Because if you're not going to tell me everything, I can't possibly defend you—'

'I did tell you everything! This article is complete and utter bullshit. As a matter of fact, I want you to press charges for libel this time.'

'None of it is true?' Jeff asks skeptically. 'Because before you go suing anyone, I need to know what you're up against.'

'Well, most of it is a lie.'

'You're going to need to tell me exactly what the hell is going on here, Vince.'

I take a deep breath. I don't know how to make him understand this. 'Okay. I happened to see Layla out one night. I was having dinner with an investor and Layla was sitting at the bar with a man. I pretended not to see her at first, but she cornered me when my client went to the men's room. She assured me that the man she was with was just a friend. I will admit that I was a little bit jealous, we were already sleeping together at that point, but I told her it was none of my business who she chose to spend her time with.'

'And?'

'And nothing. That was it. That whole thing about not being able to live with her seeing someone else, and her wanting to end things, none of that happened! I swear to you, Jeff.'

'Alright.' The exasperation is evident in his voice. 'I'll make a call to a friend from law school and see what we can do about a libel suit, but I have to warn you, it won't unring the bell. Even if you sue *World View* into bankruptcy, the damage is already done. Public opinion has been formed.'

Jeff is right. I know he is. I can spend all of my time and money tying *World View* up in lawsuits, but what they printed was already let loose into the world. The rumors are already swirling around me. And around KitzTech. 'What the hell am I supposed to do then?' I ask. 'Just sit here and take it?'

'For now, the best thing you can do is lie low and not give the media anything else to talk about. We don't even know if the page they purport to be from Layla's diary is real. But I'm sure you will be the first one to hear from the police if it is.'

How could I have been so wrong about Layla?

Chapter 17

Vince

BEFORE

'Thanks for letting me tag along today, Vince. It was such a great learning experience for me,' Layla says as we leave a working lunch with our developers.

'You're welcome, but you weren't tagging along. This new app was your idea, and you've worked really hard on it these last few weeks. I know I've asked you and the team to put in a lot of extra hours with me lately; I thought you should have the chance to see this through to the end.'

'So what now?' she asks as we step out onto the sunny sidewalk. It's the early days of summer, before the heat becomes oppressive, where the feeling of sunshine on your face still warms you from within. 'Should we catch a cab back to the office?'

'You know what, it's such a beautiful day, why don't we walk. It's not too far. That is, if you're okay walking in those shoes.' I glance down at the black heels at the end of her long legs.

'Sure, let's walk. I don't mind at all.'

We begin to walk back to the office, passing the busy storefronts along Fifth Avenue, the carefully curated window displays show-casing luxury items: supple leather handbags, glittering diamond jewelry, elegant gowns draped over waifish mannequins. I've become so accustomed to the casual opulence around me that I'd forgotten what it probably looks like to someone like Layla who is new to this city. I catch sight of her reflection in the polished glass as we pass by yet another designer storefront. Her face turned up, her wide eyes taking in the dizzying sight of the towering skyscrapers surrounding us.

'I forgot for a moment that you're new to New York,' I tell her. 'The city is really something special isn't it?'

'It sure is. Do you ever get used to it?'

'Sadly, you do. I'd almost forgotten how spectacular it can be.'

We walk on in silence for a moment before I have an idea. 'You know what? Change of plans. I'm taking you somewhere special. Consider it your official initiation into being a real New Yorker.'

Layla smiles brightly. 'I can't wait.'

I raise my arm and hail us a cab.

*

The taxi pulls up to Pier 83 on the edge of the Hudson River. The pier is bustling with tourists, cameras slung around their necks, wide-brimmed visors perched on their heads. This is one sight I've never gotten used to, and today is a perfect day. The water is a sapphire blue, the sun glinting off of it like scattered diamonds. Seagulls circle overhead, and large ships gently bob in their ports.

'This place is amazing!' Layla exclaims.

I'm so pleased to have been the first to introduce her to one of my favorite parts of New York City.

'This was a great surprise,' she adds.

'Oh, this isn't the surprise. Come on.'

I lead Layla over to the green and white building with the

large, circular edifice atop it reading 'Circle Line', and pay for two tickets for the Liberty Cruise.

'What is this?' Layla asks.

'You've never heard of the Circle Line? You really *are* new in town. It's a cruise along the Hudson River. It will give you a whole new perspective on the city. Just wait until you see the Statue of Liberty up close.'

'Oh my Gosh! I'm so excited!' Layla squeals with delight.

*

Layla and I stand at the front of the cruise ship, our elbows folded on the railing in front of us, as the Statue of Liberty grows larger before us. I look over at Layla. Her eyes are closed, her chin angled up, basking in the sunshine and the salty sea air. I notice a light spray of freckles over the bridge of her nose and the way that she doesn't seem to mind the feeling of the wind in her hair.

'Are you cold?' I ask, suddenly realizing that she's wearing a sleeveless dress and the air is crisp as it whips off the water.

'I'm fine,' she responds kindly, though I can't help but notice that she pulls her arms closer to her body, protecting herself from the wind.

'Here.' I take off my suit jacket and drape it over her shoulders. She's swimming in it, but she smiles up at me appreciatively.

'Thank you. So this is what all the real New Yorkers do in the middle of their workdays?'

I laugh. 'No, not quite. It's kind of touristy, to be honest. But it's still my favorite way to see the city.'

'Thank you for taking me. This is wonderful.' Layla turns towards me, pulling my jacket tight around her slim shoulders. Suddenly we're only inches apart, and she's looking up at me, her eyes sparkling. Before I have time to think about it, my lips are on hers. I can taste the salt from the sea on her mouth, and her warm body feels like it fits perfectly against mine; like a part of

94

me that I didn't realize I was missing until this very moment. Just the way I used to feel when I held Nicole – before a child-sized wedge had grown between us.

Nicole.

'Layla, I'm so sorry. I don't know what came over me. I should not have done that.'

'Don't apologize, Vince. I wanted it too.'

'I'm married though. This can't happen again.'

'Of course not. I completely understand. It never happened, okay?' She squeezes my hand reassuringly. Her voice sounds kind, understanding, but I don't how she could possibly understand the emotions racing through my head right now: desire, longing, regret, shame, guilt – a dizzying combination.

'Thank you,' I say.

Layla turns back to face the water, the Statue of Liberty now looming large in front of us, casting a shadow over our little boat. I keep my eyes trained on Lady Liberty, but I can't stop thinking about the feeling of Layla's lips on mine.

Chapter 18

Allison

DAY 4

'Kate, you promised me you would contact us if you found anything pertinent to our case,' I bark into the phone.

'And I am.'

'Only after I read about it in *World View*!'

'Look, I have a job to keep too. And it's not like the diary page I printed had a murder confession in it. I printed an excerpt from the page and now I'm turning the original over to you just as I said I would. Do you want it or not?'

'Of course I want it!'

'Good. A messenger is already on his way.' She ends the call.

I was so sure that Vince had taken those pages out himself. I had convinced myself that they held some incriminating information about him that he didn't want anyone else to see. Seems I was partially right: the pages are incriminating, but whoever has these pages now clearly doesn't like Vince Taylor very much. What reason would anyone have for sending this entry to the press other than to point the finger at Vince? I don't know who might want to take down Vince, or why, but at least I have a place to start.

I walk back over to my desk and dig out the phone number Kinnon found for the woman who filed a police report about Vince, or should I say Vincent, nearly twenty years ago. I don't know how Kinnon managed to find her current phone number, but I'm not totally surprised. He's very tech savvy. It's probably why Lanner has taken such a liking to him.

The phone rings over and over again. I'm beginning to doubt that Kinnon found a working number, when I hear someone pick up.

'Hello?'

'Shannon Combs?'

'Combs was my maiden name, it's Shannon Hartley now. Who is calling please?'

'My name is Allison Barnes. I'm a detective with the NYPD. I wanted to ask you some questions about a police report you filed.'

'I haven't filed any police reports.' I can hear the confusion in her voice.

'This was an old report. Made nearly twenty years ago.'

Shannon goes silent. For a moment I think she may have hung up, but then she speaks again in a soft voice.

'Are you calling about Vincent Taylor?'

'Yes, I am.'

'I have nothing to say.'

'Ms Hartley, if you could just—'

'I'm sorry, Detective, I can't help you. Please don't call me again.'

I hear the receiver click loudly in my ear.

Well, that *didn't go as I'd expected.*

Just as I hang up the phone, a messenger arrives with a white envelope addressed to me. I open it carefully and pull out a handwritten note from Kate Owens.

Detective Barnes,
As promised, here's the document I received which is report-
edly a page from Layla's diary.
Before you ask: no, I don't know where it came from. Good luck.
  – Kate.

I carefully extract the page from the diary wearing a pair of Latex gloves. I hold it up to the torn edges of the diary that has been sitting on my desk, willing me to find Layla's killer. It's a perfect fit. I slip the new page into an evidence bag and walk it down to the Evidence Room hoping they will be able to tell me more about who had it last.

Chapter 19

Vince

DAY 4

My phone has been eerily silent. Surely Nicole has seen the latest *World View* article, but she hasn't tried to reach me. That can't be a good sign. My e-mail inbox, on the other hand, has been pinging non-stop. Reporters from all over the country have taken an interest in this story and are now badgering me for a comment. 'What happened to Layla, Vince?', 'Were you involved in her death?', 'Were you stalking her, Vince?' They ask these questions so simply, as if I may decide to hit reply and e-mail them a confession to murder. I delete every single one without responding, but I know that it's only a matter of time before this story grows out of control, like a cancer spreading its poison as far as it can reach.

I know Jeff advised me not to engage, but how can I be expected to just sit here while my life is picked apart, my freedom and my marriage hanging in the balance?

I pack up my things and leave my corner office at KitzTech. Although Darren isn't my favorite person at the moment, and his motivations are questionable, he did raise a good point. This

99

negative attention is only going to harm the brand I worked so hard to create. For the good of the company, I need to step away for the time being. I shoot an e-mail to Darren to let him know that although I won't be stepping down as CEO, I'm going to take some personal time. I don't need to bring the drama to KitzTech's front door.

I take the stairs to the underground parking lot and slide into my car. It roars to life in the cavernous underground parking structure. I begin to nose the car out onto the city street, but the exit ramp is blocked by a herd of reporters and photographers. They snap photos of me, the flash blinding me, as I slowly try to drive past them and maneuver my way around the crowd. They're probably hoping I accidentally run someone over so they'll have more headlines to run.

'MOVE!' I shout as I lean on my horn.

The group slowly disperses, finally giving me enough room to pull onto the street and out of the scope of their lenses.

By the time I get home, the stress of being surrounded by reporters hasn't subsided. It's only when I pull into my driveway that I realize that I've been clenching my teeth.

'Nicole?' I call out as I walk through the front door. No response. I call again up the stairs towards the bedrooms, but she doesn't answer.

Maybe she's with a client. I walk out the back door, past the pool, and into the wooded grounds that surround it. The sky has grown gray, the sun ducking behind a thick cloud, threatening the rain that we so desperately need to break this heatwave. I follow the cobblestone path to Nicole's studio. I can see her inside the glass structure, kneeling on an aqua-blue yoga mat. Her legs are folded neatly under her. She's wearing lavender-colored yoga pants and a matching sports bra. Her hair is braided neatly, a rope of blonde trailing down her back. She is facing away from me, and I watch the smooth muscles in her back working beneath her skin as she stretches and lengthens her body during her practice.

I see her shoulders rise and fall as she breathes deeply into her stretches. She looks so peaceful in this moment, and I decide not to disturb her.

Just as I am turning to leave, I think I hear a rustling in the underbrush. I snap my head around just in time to catch sight of movement in the tree line, a dark shadow that recedes before I can fully make out its form. I freeze, holding my breath, and wait to see what it may have been. We do have wildlife in the woods, squirrels, chipmunks, small, quiet creatures that would hardly catch my attention. The stone wall surrounding our property prevents the local deer from wandering into the yard.

The woods seem still now. Just the sounds of birds chirping overhead. Maybe I was imagining things. I have been on edge in the past few days. But no, there it is again. It's coming from behind Nicole's studio. It's probably one of those damn reporters. Just like the bottom feeder who scaled the property wall to photograph Nicole in her bikini yesterday.

And that's it for me. I will not stand for my wife to be gawked at like a zoo animal in her own home, especially in this space that might be the only place she can find peace right now. I feel something inside of me come undone. All the anger I've had to bite back for the last few days is set free, and without a second thought I find myself sprinting through the woods. My legs are pumping furiously, the ground soft and spongy beneath the soles of my leather shoes. I feel my footing slip, my ankle twisting painfully as it rolls on the soft earth, but I do not care. Not now. I am a man possessed and I am going to find out who was lurking around my wife.

I see the outer wall now, visible between the trees. I draw near just in time to see the form of a man, a dark hooded sweatshirt pulled over his head, hoisting himself atop of the stones. He appears to be shorter than I am, and having some trouble maneuvering his way over the wall. I know I can catch him. He's nearly within my reach. There is something so familiar about his form, about the slope of his shoulders, the roundness of his back as he clambers to safety. Could it be Jeff?

'Stop!' I yell.

But the man ignores me as he continues to scramble to find his footing. There are only a few yards separating us now. I rush towards the wall, but my injured ankle finally gives out and I fall to the ground. The man doesn't turn around. He takes this opportunity to propel himself over the wall and drop down onto the other side. I pull myself up from the ground, my clothes caked with the damp soil, petrichor permeating the fibers. I want to follow him, this man who breached the seclusion, the safety of our home, but I know that I won't be able to catch up to him now, not with my ankle in this state. It's throbbing now and I can feel the swelling growing beneath my skin, pulling it taught.

I've let Nicole down again. I couldn't even protect us in our own home. I hobble back towards the cobblestone path heading towards the house. I'm pathetic. But I won't be anymore. I can't let this go on. I need to protect myself and my wife. I know Jeff told me to lie low, but I just can't do it anymore. Not while my life is under siege. Besides, the more I think about it, the more certain I am that it was Jeff, my best friend, who I just caught leering at my wife when she thought she was safe and alone. I can't be certain, but I do know that I don't trust him right now. I'm going to need to handle this Layla situation my own way. After all, I'm the one that let it get out of hand in the first place.

Chapter 20

Vince

BEFORE

'We can't keep doing this,' I say breathlessly as Layla's lips pull away from mine. I can feel the velvety traces of her lipstick on my lips.

I gently disentangle her arms from around my waist. It's late, and I'm fairly certain that we're the last ones in the office, but I'm still worried that someone might walk in and see us together.

'I know,' she replies. She sounds disheartened but she doesn't argue the obvious.

'I'm married.'

'I know that too. I didn't mean for this ... us ... to happen.'

'I didn't either.' I run my fingers through my hair as I fall back into my office chair. My head thrown back in frustration and longing.

These encounters with Layla have been happening more and more frequently over the last few weeks, since our first kiss on the Circle Line cruise. It may be in my head, but lately it feels like every time I turn around she's there. Maybe I'm just noticing her more now, after what happened between us, but I can't help but feel that her skirts have gotten shorter, her shirts clinging more closely to her curves. It seems that Layla is everywhere now. Biting her glossy lower lip and watching me with that seductive look of hers. It's no wonder I can't stop thinking about her. While I'm working, while I'm driving home to my wife, and while I'm alone in the shower. It hasn't been easy to keep things from going further, from falling off the cliff that I'm standing perilously close to. But I know that I can't.

Layla climbs onto my lap. Her skirt hiking up above her knees as her legs straddle mine. She kisses me long and deep.

'Layla, don't …' I begin, but my protest doesn't sound convincing even to me.

'Listen, Vince. I know you're married. I know you love your wife. I'm not expecting you to run off with me or anything. But I don't think either of us can deny that there's something here – a pull between us.'

She's right. I feel a burning connection with her, a magnetic attraction that's pulled me towards Layla since the first moment I saw her. We came together so easily, so naturally, that it was almost as if neither of us had a choice in the matter.

'Besides,' she adds with a coy smile. 'No one ever has to know.'

Before I can continue with my half-hearted efforts to stop her, she reaches a hand between my legs and I feel my body surrender long before my mind has.

I know that I'm about to cross a line that I can never come back from, but in this moment all I can focus on is the feel of Layla's wanting hands, the weight of her body on top of mine. I am overcome with need, a need for her, and I lift her off of my lap and sit her on my desk, her legs still wrapped around my waist. Her skirt is uselessly bunched around her hips and I run my fingers over her black, lace panties, the fabric smooth beneath my fingers. I've never touched her before. Not in this way. And it feels as if my private, forbidden thoughts of her over the last few weeks have materialized before my eyes. Layla writhes beneath my touch. She wants this as much as I do. I glance up at her and she gives me a mischievous smile as she grabs a fist full of my shirt and pulls me on top of her. All of the anticipation leading to this moment, the lingering glances, the stolen kisses, is boiling over now and I no longer have the power to stop what's coming.

Chapter 21

Allison

My desk phone rings and I snatch it off of the receiver.

'Hello?'

'Hey, Barnes. It's Keith down in evidence. I finished pulling the prints from that diary page you sent me. The only prints I could find belonged to the vic. But, I should warn you that pulling prints from paper isn't always an exact science. Sometimes they're hard to lift because of the texture of the paper. I can't say for certainty that no one else ever touched this page. All I can tell you is that only the victim's prints are identifiable on it right now.'

'Thanks, Keith. I appreciate it,' I say as I end the call. *Damn.* That missing page was helpful in showing that Vince's relationship with Layla was more involved than he wanted us to believe, but it didn't bring us any closer to proving that he was responsible for her death. I know Vince Taylor lied to me about where he was the night Layla died. I just know it. I don't care that his security records show that he was at his office. I'm not buying it.

I walk over to Lanner's desk and find him halfway through a fried chicken sandwich.

'What's up?' he asks, his cheek stuffed with food.

'Only Layla's prints were on that new diary page.'

'Damn. I was hoping we'd find Taylor's, to be honest. It would make this case a whole lot easier to wrap up.'

'Sure would. I know he was involved somehow.'

'Barnes, I know you've got good instincts, but do you think we've been too focused on Taylor?'

'I don't think so. My gut is telling me we're on the right track with him. But I think you have a point. We need to consider all angles. Let's go over what we have so far.'

Lanner nods. 'Kinnon went through the vic's phone when it was first found on her body. That's how he got in contact with the neighbor, Mindy. But there wasn't much on it. She has the Friend Connect app, but her login info wasn't saved so he couldn't access the account. Doesn't look like she was too active on it anyway. I checked out her public info. From what I can tell, she only joined up once she started at KitzTech and she's only connected with the other KitzTech interns.'

'Guess I'm not the only one that doesn't care about Friend Connect then. Anything else on the phone?'

'There were a couple of texts back and forth with Mindy, making plans to get drinks and stuff like that. There were a few with co-workers about work-related stuff too. Nothing useful. I did find it a little odd though. Most people her age communicate solely through texts. I expected to find a lot more.'

'She was new to the city. Maybe she hadn't made many friends yet.'

'Right, but she didn't keep in touch with a single person from back home? Looks like she bought this phone once she moved to New York and there's not a single text, call, or e-mail from anyone she didn't meet here.'

'Mindy did say Layla wanted a clean slate,' I respond with a shrug. 'What else have we got?'

'Nothing useful came from the CCTV footage we pulled from the areas around Central Park. IT just finished with her laptop this morning. I haven't gotten the report yet though.'

'Let's call down and see what they've got.'

I punch the extension for the IT department. Stu picks up on the first ring.

'Stu Fringe here. How can I help ya?'

Stu is incredible at his job. He's helped us out on countless cases. If there is anything hiding on Layla's laptop, I have no doubt he will have found it. Although Stu couldn't be less 'cool' with his unwieldy red hair, wire-rimmed glasses, and slight lisp, I secretly suspect that Lanner is jealous of his tech skills. Personally I think it sounds like Stu is speaking a foreign language every time he discusses his findings with me, my eyes glazing over within seconds, but I do appreciate that he's always polite enough to break the information down into layman's terms for me without judgment.

'Hey, Stu. It's Barnes and Lanner. Calling to see what you found on that laptop we sent over on the Bosch case.'

'Oh, hi, guys! Truthfully I didn't find much. I suspect she bought this laptop second-hand. First of all, it's like, not the best. The processor is still running on … right. You don't care about all that. Anyway, it looks like the hard drive was wiped clean about six months ago. Probably when she bought it. There wasn't anything personal on it. No photos, contacts, that sort of thing. Looks like she mostly just used it for work and job applications. She did, like, a lot of research on KitzTech and Vince Taylor. Her browsing history is all KitzTech related. One weird thing though – seems like she watched a ton of videos about software programming.'

'Why is that weird?' I ask. 'Wasn't that her job?'

'Well, yeah, but do you have any idea how competitive those internships at KitzTech are? They only take on the best programmers from the best colleges. Not someone that has to look up basic coding on YouTube, if you know what I mean.'

'Interesting. Thanks, Stu. Very helpful as usual.'

'Happy to help. Let me know if there's anything else I can do for you guys!'

I end the call and turn towards Lanner who is looking at me expectantly.

'What do you make of that?' he asks. 'Seems like Layla lied on her job application to KitzTech.'

'Or … she and Vince were already involved before she ever started at KitzTech and he gave her the job to keep her close by. Either way, one of them is lying, and we need to figure out who it is.'

*

By the time I get home I'm bone tired. I push through the door to my apartment and I'm greeted with a gust of warm air. How does it feel even hotter in here than it does outside? The air is so thick with humidity that I feel like I'm walking through fog. I can hear the window air conditioning unit chugging away, but it's clearly losing this battle. Josh and I have named it 'The Dinosaur' both because of its age and the way it sounds like it's roaring whenever it's on. The damn thing is so loud that we often have to choose between watching TV or living in tolerable conditions.

I toss my keys onto the counter of the small efficiency kitchen that is just beside the door. I notice rogue grains of rice stuck to the stovetop. I guess Josh did some cooking today.

'Rough day?' Josh asks. He's leaning back into the couch, legs spread, shirt off. I can see the sweat beading at his temples. He must have only just turned on The Dinosaur.

'Very.' I pull off my shoes and chuck them aside. I begin stripping out of my work clothes before I even make it into our minuscule bedroom. The apartment was once a studio, but in a ploy to charge more rent, the landlords erected a flimsy wall to cordon off a corner of the room and called it a one-bedroom. It's so small that Josh keeps his clothes in the coat closet. There's not enough room for two dressers in the bedroom.

To be fair, when I rented this place, I thought I'd be living here alone, and it seemed like more than enough for just me. Meeting Josh was an unexpected development. After Mark, the last asshole I dated, I swore off men for the foreseeable future. I wanted to focus on my career, on myself. But then I happened to meet Josh purely by chance.

It was one of the rare occasions that I let Lanner talk me into going out for a Friday happy hour with some of the guys from the station. I usually hate those things. They all get so drunk and rowdy. Meanwhile, when I drink, I tend to grow quiet. I withdraw into myself and I end up just feeling displaced, as if I'm watching the party pass me by. I see everyone smiling, letting loose, but I've never been able to let myself go in that way. I hate feeling out of control. But on that particular night it was someone's birthday, not that I can recall whose, and I had agreed to tag along to some crappy dive bar near the station. I only planned on staying for a drink or two, but two drinks soon turned into three, then maybe four, and by then I'd had enough. I stumbled out onto the sidewalk, annoyed at myself for getting drunk when I hadn't intended to. It was bitterly cold, and I wrapped my coat tightly around myself, bracing myself against the wind that was whipping around me. In the distance I could hear the familiar bells of the Salvation Army Santas collecting donations. The streetlights were wrapped in spiraling red and white lights making them look like over-sized candy canes. I stuck my hand into the frigid wind to hail a passing cab, but the driver either didn't see me or chose to ignore the drunk woman needing a ride home.

'Need a hand?' said a broad-shouldered man with a wide grin and deep brown eyes.

'No, I think I know how to hail a cab.'

'Could have fooled me,' he replied, his crooked smile growing even wider.

'Very funny.' I raised my hand again, but yet another cab sped by. 'You've gotta be kidding me.'

The man laughed. 'I'm Josh.'

'Allison.'

Josh stuck two fingers in his mouth and whistled loudly, an ear-splitting sound that seemed to reverberate off of the brick buildings lining the street around us. He raised his other hand into the air, and within a matter of seconds, a yellow cab pulled over to the curb, its tires crunching on the graying snow mounded along the edge of the road.

'You got lucky,' I said.

'Whatever you say …' Josh teased, shrugging his shoulders.

'Well, go on then, get in,' I told him.

'No, this one was for you. Unless … where are you headed? Maybe we can split the fare?'

'Brooklyn.'

'Me too.'

We slid into the back of the cab that smelled distinctly of cigarette smoke and body odor, but the interior was warm and it was a welcome reprieve from the icy air outside.

Josh sat next to me on the leather bench seat, his legs spread confidently. I noticed that his thigh grazed mine, but I couldn't be sure if it was intentional or not. Josh hummed to himself as the cab crawled through the tight roads of Manhattan. *What an annoying habit*, I thought, but as I cast a sideways glance in his direction he looked genuinely happy, humming along with the radio and tapping his knee in time to the beat. Unlike me, Josh seemed confident and unapologetic about who he was and where he fit into the world. The cab picked up speed as we made our way out of the city and into Brooklyn.

'So,' Josh finally said. 'What's your story?'

'What story?'

'Like, what do you do, for starters?'

'I'm a cop.'

'No kidding?' His voice sounded both surprised and impressed.

'Nope. Definitely not kidding.'

'Well, that's pretty badass.'

'Thanks.' I paused for a moment. I never know how men are going to react to the news that I'm a cop. Some find it intimidating I think, while others make tasteless jokes about whether I get to take my handcuffs home. Not that I date much, but when I have, I've found that as soon as the topic of my career comes up, the tone of the evening changes immediately, one way or another. But this time was different. Josh seemed so casual about it, as though the idea of a reasonably attractive female cop wasn't beyond the pale of his limited male imagination.

'What about you?' I asked.

'I'm a personal trainer. But not for long. I'm opening my own gym. Ever heard of CrossFit?'

'Yeah, of course.'

'It's going to be something like that. More of a workout club than a gym where the trainers will create daily workout challenges and our members will feel a sense of community. I think it keeps the momentum going, ya know? We'll play cool music, hype it up on social media. My gym is going to be the place everyone wants to be. I'm calling it Lift.'

'Sounds really cool,' I replied, even though I hate the gym, and that one sounded particularly off-putting to me. I keep myself in shape, but I prefer to work out at home or run on my own with only my headphones to keep me company. But the way Josh's face lit up when he spoke of his plans, the bare ambition in his voice, was undeniably attractive. *Maybe there's more to this guy than the cute smile*, I thought. And it *was* pretty cute.

'Thanks,' Josh said. He was beaming.

As the cab pulled up in front of my building, Josh suddenly seemed shy. 'So … do you think I could get your number?'

'Really?' I asked. I was surprised to hear him ask. He just seemed like one of those friendly people who talk to everyone they meet. I hadn't realized he was interested in me that way.

'Yes, really.'

'Oh, okay then.'

I gave him my number and he promised to call soon. He in fact called the very next morning.

That was over a year ago. And Josh is still just as positive and happy as he was the day I met him. I think he's good for me. He reminds me to get out of my own head sometimes.

I walk out of our bedroom in a pair of cotton shorts and one of Josh's Lift shirts that hangs loose on me.

'That shirt looks good on you,' Josh says with a coy smile.

'Thanks.' I flop down on the couch next to him.

'Hang on,' Josh tells me as he jumps up off the couch. He walks into the kitchen and pulls open the refrigerator. I hear the glass jars of jelly, salad dressing, and mayonnaise lined up on the door rattling as he does so. I poke my head over the back of the couch to see what he's up to, and I watch him pull out a bottle of white wine and twist off the foil top. He pours us each a portion into plastic cups.

'Picked this up on my way home earlier,' he says, clearly proud of himself.

I know the cheap wine is inevitably going to give me a headache, but I appreciate the gesture and I take the cold glass gratefully.

'Thank you.' The wine feels blissfully cool on my tongue. 'This really was thoughtful.'

'Well I saw the *World View* article this morning. Kind of figured you weren't having the best day. Do you want to talk about it?'

'No. I definitely do not. I want to talk about anything *except* that case right now. I think I need some time to clear my head, maybe looking at it with fresh eyes tomorrow will help.'

'You got it, babe. In that case, I'll tell you about my day instead.'

Josh begins to tell me about the competition he's hosting at Lift and how many new members have been signing up to be a part of it. Admittedly I'm only half listening as the wine is already going to my head, but I love listening to the animated cadence of his voice when he talks about something he's passionate about. Before long we fall into a quiet rhythm, me tucked up against Josh's side as we switch on the TV to some stupid reality show and pretend we can hear what the contestants are saying over the sound of The Dinosaur humming away.

*

I wake up in the middle of the night, the sheets tangled around my legs. I look over at Josh and he's lying on his back snoring gently with one arm draped over his eyes. I don't know how he sleeps like that. Something is pulling at my mind. I can't quite place what it is, but there's something about this case that has been bothering me. Maybe it's because it all seems to revolve around a world I don't understand. Vince's world. A world where people connect through wires and cables and Wi-Fi. Where genuine connection, looking into someone's eyes while you share the details of your life, is reduced to an awkward inconvenience. Social media has let us design how we want the world to see us, while conveniently cropping out all of the unsightly messes that make up a real life.

I pad out of the bedroom and fire up my old laptop. I really should replace it soon. Stu would probably have a heart attack if he saw this thing. I tentatively type in the address for Friend Connect. Ugh, I've resisted joining for so long. I just don't understand the appeal. Why would I want to know what some girl I went to high school with is eating for lunch? But if I'm being honest with myself, that's not the only reason I haven't joined. I know I have a lot to be proud of with my career, but the rest of my life isn't exactly where I thought it would be by the time I turned 35. I thought I'd be married now, house with a white picket fence, and a kid or two. It stings to see everyone I used to know living the life I used to think I'd have. I type in my information.

Name: Allison Barnes.

No, I shouldn't give my real name. The last thing I need is for suspects to be looking me up on Friend Connect. *Delete, delete, delete.* I decide to go with Ali Marie – my middle name.

Birth date: October 21, 1985

Occupation: … I think it's best to leave that one blank.

'Upload profile photo?' it prompts. *Fine. I suppose I'll have to.* I flick through the handful of photos I have stored on my laptop, looking for one that I wouldn't mind showing everyone I know. There's one of Josh and I from a friend's engagement party last summer that was hosted at a rooftop bar. It's a candid photo that was taken by the photographer the couple of the hour had hired. I'm wearing a sundress and sandals, my hair is down for once and it's brushed into soft waves. Josh is looking off into the crowed laughing and smiling as he always is, but it's the look on my face that causes me to pause for a moment. I'm looking up at Josh, while I lightly hold his arm. I look like a love-struck teenager. I do love Josh, I really do, but I'm always so careful to keep my guard up. I can't help it. The tough exterior is just part of who I am. It seems that this photographer snapped a photo of me in one of the rare moments when I let the armor slip. I click the photo and upload it as my Friend Connect profile photo. Maybe it's not the most accurate representation of who I am, but isn't that what this stupid site is for? To convince everyone that you're this shiny perfect version of yourself that you could never possibly maintain?

Upload complete. I guess it's official. I'm on Friend Connect now. The first thing I do with my account is search for Layla Bosch. I can see her name, but there's no photo attached to her profile. And then it dawns on me. The missing piece of the puzzle that has been needling me.

I pick up my phone and call Lanner.

'Guess what?' I say the instant he picks up the phone.

'Do you realize that it's three in the morning? There's only one reason I like women calling me at three a.m., and I have a feeling this isn't that.'

'Can you stop being a pain in the ass for two seconds? I thought of something about our case.'

'What is this important revelation that couldn't wait until a decent hour?'

'I can see that Layla was on Friend Connect, but—'

'Wait, are you on Friend Connect now?' Lanner laughs.

'Maybe. But that's not the point. What about Date Space? How can we find out whether she was using that app too? Maybe that's how she really met Vince! Maybe that's how she ended up landing a cushy job she didn't know the first thing about!'

'She did have the app on her phone, but she also had all of the other KitzTech apps. I'm sure all the employees do.'

'Don't you use that sleazy thing? Can't you look her up?'

'I could try, but most people don't use their real names on there. Hang on.'

I hear Lanner shuffling in bed. A few seconds later he's back on the line.

'Nope. Couldn't find her. But like I said, that doesn't mean she didn't have an account under a different name. Let's see what Stu can find in the morning. You know, when normal people are awake.'

'Fine. Go back to bed, Sleeping Beauty.'

I end the call and climb back into bed next to Josh who hasn't moved a muscle since I left. Right before I drift off to sleep, I see my phone light up with an e-mail notification: '*You have a new Friend Connect request from Jake Lanner.*' I roll my eyes and give in to sleep.

Chapter 22

Vince

DAY 4

I stretch my arms over my head, my spine cracking. I lift my hand to my neck, massaging it gently at the side as I stretch the sore muscles. I spent the majority of the afternoon locked away in my office, tying up some loose ends before I take some time away from KitzTech. I feel like a parent leaving their child unattended for the first time. At least I think I do. What would I know about parenting? But ever since I started KitzTech, I've kept a tight hold on the reins. Even on the rare occasions that I'd take vacation time, my phone was always glued to my hand, ready to put out any fires that could spark in my absence. I know my staff are well-trained, they can handle things in my absence, and yet letting go of the helm for the time being feels like being swept out to sea.

But the truth is, work hasn't been the only thing on my mind. I've been consumed with thoughts of Layla. Of what I can do to stop her death from tearing through my life, my marriage, like a runaway freight train. The last four days have been a whirlwind of emotions: anger, fear, panic, and also sadness. In this quiet moment, it washes over me anew. Things between Layla and I may not have ended well, but I never wanted this for her. Her young life cut short, reduced to nothing more than a headline, another poor girl lost to the dark undercurrent of New York City.

I hear Nicole's soft footsteps overhead. She's probably getting ready for bed. I look over at the Chinese takeout containers pushed to the corner of my desk, grease congealing in a film over the remaining noodles, giving them a nauseating gray sheen. I heard Nicole in the kitchen earlier, making herself something to eat. I crept into the kitchen like a dog with its tail between its legs, but Nicole fixed me with a cold glare and I instantly stopped in my tracks.

'Don't,' she said. 'I can't do this tonight.' She swiped her plate off of the counter and took it upstairs with her.

I skulked back to my office, limping on my injured ankle, with my tail tucked even further between my legs, and ordered my pathetic dinner for one.

I have to do something now. About Layla. About this investigation. I can't wait for another headline to take us by surprise, to pull Nicole even further away from me. The chasm between us is already growing so wide that I don't know how I'll ever be able to reach her again.

But what could I possibly do? If things were different, I would ask Jeff. But I already know he'd tell me to stay out of it, to just sit here and wait to be arrested. *Maybe that's exactly what he's hoping for.* No. Not Jeff. He wouldn't do that to me. We've been friends since we were ten years old, playing baseball together in a kid's league. Not that I was any good. I couldn't have hit the side of a barn, but Jeff was a superstar. All the dads on the sidelines were already talking about seeing him in the Majors some day. When Jeff approached me after practice one day and asked if I wanted to walk to the arcade, I couldn't believe my luck that the coolest kid in school wanted to be my friend. I didn't realize he even knew my name.

My friendship with Jeff carried me all through high school. I knew I wasn't the coolest kid. I had thick, dark-rimmed glasses, far before they were fashionable, and my interest in computers hardly helped me make friends. But with Jeff on my side, the popular crowd tolerated my presence. I wasn't part of their inner circle, but I was allowed to exist on the periphery of the good life. I tagged along with Jeff to all the right parties, and even though the popular guys never talked to me, and the girls didn't seem to notice I existed, I was there, sipping my beer in some forgotten corner. And I got to walk home with Jeff, laughing in the streets about who got too drunk, who hooked up with who, and all of the juicy high school drama that felt like the most important thing in the world at the time. Jeff was my life raft. But what did he get from that friendship? I'm still not entirely sure.

Later in life, when all my time in front of a computer finally paid off, and women like Nicole finally started to notice me, Jeff made all the right noises. He told me he was happy for me, that he knew I'd make it some day. But I couldn't help but feel like he was jealous. He was always supposed to be the superstar, and I was supposed to be the sidekick, just happy to exist in his shadow. Jeff claims he's happy with his lot in life. He has a successful legal career, a fast car, an expensive condo on the beach, and no one to answer to. But sometimes I think that he wishes he had more. He's reminded me so many times over the years how lucky I was to find someone like Nicole. But now, I'm starting to think that Jeff doesn't want 'someone *like* Nicole', he wants Nicole. She is the one thing I have that Jeff doesn't, something money can't buy – someone who loves me.

It's painful to feel like I no longer have Jeff in my corner, and I don't want to feel distrustful of my friend, but someone somewhere is going to a lot of trouble to make it look like I was responsible for Layla's death. I can't take any chances trusting the wrong people. I will have to do this without him. I run a search for a private detective agency. Maybe they'll know where to start.

I look at the list that Google generated for me. Apparently 'private investigator' is a popular career choice. I start browsing websites. Most of them promising to find evidence of cheating spouses, to catch employees stealing from their employers, to pull up sludge for cash payments up front. I feel dirty just looking at their websites. I'm about to give up, when I come across David Mullins, a retired detective who now takes on select cases. He advertises that he'll only work with you if he feels it's worth his while. Perhaps not the best business plan, but it makes me feel like I can trust him. I type out an e-mail to David Mullins, hoping that he finds my plight worth his while:

> Dear Mr Mullins,
> My name is Vince Taylor, and if you've read the World View lately, you may think you already know my story. I was having an affair with an intern at my company, and now she has been found dead in Central Park. The police seem to think I'm responsible for her death, but there is far more to this story than what's been printed under the salacious headlines. I hope you might be willing to assist me, as I'm not sure where else to turn.
>
> > Sincerely,
> > Vince Taylor

My fingers linger over the keyboard wondering if I'm making the right decision. If I should listen to Jeff or to my instincts. I click the send button, and hope for the best as I make my way back to the guest room where I seem to have taken up permanent residence.

Chapter 23

Vince

BEFORE

I breathe in deeply and exhale slowly, blowing a long plume of air between my lips, as if I'd just taken a pull from a cigarette. Layla's hand is resting on my bare chest, one leg splayed over mine. The white, Egyptian cotton sheets are bunched into ropes and tangled around us like creeping ivy as the early morning light seeps in through the bedroom window. I look down at Layla, her brown hair tussled, her cheeks flushed with sex. Her eyes are closing sleepily as she absently runs her fingers up and down my sternum, her touch as light as the wings of a bird.

This is the first time I've taken Layla to my apartment. I couldn't risk sleeping with her in the office again. It's happened a few times, and I know we were lucky not to have got caught yet. But renting a hotel room for a few hours felt too tawdry. Bringing her here was yet another boundary I've crossed. Nicole rarely stays in the apartment, only on the odd occasion that we attend an event in the city, but her spare toothbrush is in the bathroom, her dresses hang in the closet. This is Nicole's territory,

121

and I've invited another woman into it. Into our bed. Layla's scent is permeating Nicole's pillows and my stomach clenches at the thought of it. Will Nicole notice? The sheets will be laundered, the apartment restored to its pristine condition by Marta, our housekeeper, but will Nicole somehow know? Will she pick up on the traces of Layla's intrusion?

I look around the room, at the evidence of my poor decisions: Two wine glasses on the nightstand, one with a perfect imprint of Layla's lips on the rim, the dregs of blood-red wine clinging to the bottom of the glasses; Layla's clothes scattered on the floor, in a telling trail leading from the front door to the bedroom.

'I'm going to get a glass of water,' I say. 'Would you like some?'

Layla nods sleepily, her eyes fully closed now, a look of dreamy bliss on her face.

I walk out into the kitchen and pull open the heavy door of the stainless steel refrigerator. This apartment, which I purchased primarily for occasions when I had to work late and didn't want to make the drive back to Loch Harbor, is nothing like our home. It lacks all of Nicole's warm touches. Everything is cold and modern. The marble floors are cool beneath my feet and the kitchen, largely unused, looks more like a showroom than a home. Nicole thought the idea of purchasing an apartment in Manhattan was absurd when we live less than an hour away. Maybe she was right. Maybe this place was a mistake.

'Do we really need all this, Vince?' Nicole said when she first toured the expansive penthouse apartment, with all its polished surfaces and soaring ceilings. 'Don't you think it's a bit much?'

'We can afford it,' I reminded her with a shrug.

'Just because we can doesn't mean we have to.'

I don't know why I was so insistent. Perhaps it was because I grew up never knowing if we'd have enough money to keep the lights on, and I felt like I had to prove to myself how far I'd come since then. I didn't want to live in Manhattan, but I loved the idea of owning a piece of this highly coveted island. I didn't see it at the time, but this apartment, this penthouse, is nothing more than a status symbol. I wanted to own real estate in one of the old, distinguished buildings in Central Park West. I wanted to lay claim to what few others could have, to prove that I was no longer the boy who wore hand-me-down jackets that I'd fished out of the school's Lost and Found box, which was stuffed with the items the other kids casually discarded and never thought of again. No, if I could own a piece of this building, its old-money status evident by the baroque architecture, uniformed doorman flanked by red velvet ropes, and the private elevator exclusively servicing the penthouse apartments – the world would know that I mattered. *I* would know that I mattered; and I would no longer feel like an impostor amongst the ranks of the wealthy.

'Nicole, I know it's a lot but just look at the view.'

She walked over to the large Palladian window in the center of the living room and looked out over Central Park. A green oasis flourishing in a sea of concrete.

'It *is* impressive. But I don't know …'

'I do,' I told her, taking her in my arms, and kissing her neck. 'You'll see. We're going to love this place.'

I'd had such high hopes for this apartment then. I imagined glittering nights out in the city, Nicole on my arm. Attending galas, the opening at the Met, ballets in Lincoln Center, and then retiring back here, tipsy with champagne and desperate to find our way to the bedroom. But that fantasy didn't exactly become a reality. Soon after I bought the apartment, our love-making became organized with near military precision. The spontaneity of nights out fizzled away, and champagne was a thing of the past. And now Layla is here in Nicole's place, draining the final drops of color from the dreams I once had for my wife and I.

'Did you get lost?' Layla teases as she walks out of the bedroom with one of my white collared shirts wrapped around her. It hangs off her shoulders seductively and her bare thighs are on display. She's looking at me with her deep brown eyes, and smiling innocently, her hands hidden beneath the crisp cuffs of my shirt.

'Sorry, I was just lost in thought for a moment.' I hand her a glass of water.

'Thanks.' She walks over to the grand window in the living room and looks out over the park, just the way Nicole once did. 'This place is amazing, Vince. It's like a palace! I feel like a princess in a tower up here.'

I smile, but in my head I'm thinking, *this is not your castle, this is not your kingdom*. I suddenly feel a desperate need to get Layla out of the apartment. It was stupid to bring her here. I don't know what I was thinking. Actually, I do. I was thinking about her. About having her. I wasn't thinking about how it would feel to see her standing in Nicole's footprints.

'Have you been to Central Park yet?' I ask.

'No, I haven't had the chance since I moved to New York.'

'Perfect, let's get dressed. I'll show you the park.'

'Won't you be late getting into the office?'

'Who cares? I'm the boss. Besides, if anyone asks, I took you to another investors' meeting this morning. Came up last minute.'

Layla rises up onto her toes and kisses me deeply, her tongue probing my mouth. I feel a flutter in my gut, but I force it down.

'I said go get dressed, you,' I chide as I tap her bottom playfully.

'You're the boss.' Her voice is sensual and full. 'I'm just going to shower first, if that's okay?'

'Of course.'

Layla makes her way towards the bathroom in the master bedroom. I watch her walk away, the curve of her bottom poking out from underneath the hem of my shirt, her hips swaying rhythmically like a model on the catwalk. I wonder whether she's doing it intentionally, whether she knows what she's stirring inside of me, or whether it's derived from a more natural, subliminal control of her sexuality.

I hear the shower turn on as I follow her into the bathroom. I watch her drop my shirt to the floor, tantalizingly slowly, and step under the cascade of water. She lifts her face to the water, allowing it to drip down her throat and onto her breasts. I watch her pull her hands through her hair and I turn away. If I watch any longer, we'll never make it out of this apartment.

I pull on a pair of jeans and one of my signature black shirts. Just as I'm yanking on my socks, I hear a key in the lock. I freeze. My heart hammers against my chest like a rabbit caught in a trap. Did Nicole not believe me when I told her I was working late and staying in the city last night? Did my lies seep through the phone sounding flimsy and wavering, revealing me for what I am? My mouth goes dry and there is nothing I can do but walk out into the living room and watch the front door slowly creak open.

I know that when Nicole steps through that door, I will fall to my knees and confess. I will beg her for forgiveness. I will do anything she wants if she will just give me another chance. I feel my knees go weak, I'm ready to throw myself at her mercy as I see her foot begin to step inside.

The door swings fully open, and a startled Marta is staring back at me. Both of us wide-eyed in surprise.

'Oh, Mr Taylor. I'm so sorry. I did not know you were going to be here today. I always clean on Tuesdays and—'

'No, Marta, it's okay. I'm just leaving for work. This was my fault, I forgot to tell you I'd be in this morning.'

We both fall into an awkward silence before it dawns on me that Marta can hear the shower running in the master bath.

'Right, I was just about to get into the shower,' I say, running my fingers through my hair.

Marta's face glows red. 'Yes, Mr Taylor, of course. I'll come back later.'

She hurries out, dragging her cart of cleaning supplies behind her, and letting the door fall closed in her wake.

Jesus. That was too close. I can never bring Layla back here again.

*

Layla laces her fingers through mine as we walk across the park. I wince at the intimacy of the gesture and hope she doesn't notice. After the close encounter with Marta I feel like I need to distance myself from Layla. The hazy glow of our drunken, passionate sex last night has worn off and in the cold light of day it feels cheap and shameful. I was no longer in the mood for a stroll through the park with Layla, but I didn't know how to tell her I'd changed my mind, and besides, I needed to get her out of that apartment immediately.

Layla, on the other hand, seems to still be basking in the after-glow of our indiscretions. She clung to my arm in the elevator, looking up at me with her big doe-eyes. My stomach roiled.

I gulp down my growing anxiety that someone may see us together, and gently disentangle my fingers from Layla's under the guise of pointing out a cardinal soaring between the lacy elm trees above us.

Central Park has always held a special significance to me. My father used to take me here every year around the holidays. It is the one thing we'd always do together. Things weren't always easy, but the times we spent here felt magical, an escape from our real lives. For a few hours we could pretend we were the type of people who casually strolled Central Park all the time. In reality, things were quite different. My mother was diagnosed with cancer when I was young. She was dying for most of my life, until she finally succumbed to her illness when I was eleven. My father, who never finished high school, worked long hours in a tire factory to provide for me and to take care of my mother's medical expenses. He never once complained, though I know he always wished he could provide more for us. He couldn't afford to take us on family vacations, or pile presents under a Christmas tree, but he never missed a Christmas in New York.

Up until my father passed, following a heart attack about four years ago, Christmas Eve in Central Park was our tradition. Just the two of us. As a child, I remember how he'd take my hand as we waited on the cold, cement platform for a train to take us from New Jersey into Manhattan. I buzzed with excitement, bouncing giddily at his side. Once in the city, we would take a cab to Central Park, and I felt like a celebrity in a chauffeured car as we passed through the bustling city, whizzing past skyscrapers, billboards, and all the twinkling lights in the shop windows.

My visits to Central Park with my father are some of my fondest, and most vivid memories. I remember the horse-drawn carriages, adorned with Christmas ribbons, which carted elegantly dressed couples with thick woolen blankets laid across their laps. The cold December air escaped the horses' velvety muzzles in curling puffs as silver sleigh bells tinkled on their reigns. The smell of roasted chestnuts and soft pretzels warming over coals wafted through the air as I strolled through the park next to my father, who, when I was a child, seemed impossibly tall. On one glorious Christmas Eve, snow fell around us like confectioners' sugar, clinging to my coat and gloves, the world sparkling with frost.

I shake off the memories, precious, intimate treasures that I don't want to share.

'We should probably get to the office,' I tell Layla, making a show of looking at my watch.

The park holds no magic for me today.

Chapter 24

Allison

DAY 5

I drum my fingers on my desk. *Tap, tap, tap. Tap, tap, tap.*

'Do you think you could maybe stop that?' Stu says gently.

'Stop what?'

'The tapping. And maybe also that thing you're doing where you're hovering over my shoulder?'

'Oh. Sorry,' I say, forcing myself to sit down and wait patiently. I'm not a patient person. One of the many virtues I do not possess. I asked Stu to look over Layla's phone again, to see if there is any way we could see whether she had a Date Space account, maybe find out who she connected with there.

'Barnes?'

'Yeah?'

'The tapping.'

I look down and realize that I've been tapping my foot against the side of the desk. *Tap, tap, tap.*

'Sorry.' I grin sheepishly.

'Okay, here's what I can tell you.'

I lean in closer.

'Layla did have a Date Space account. Her username was BreakfastAtTiffanys. She didn't list her real name on the account, and there's a photo but you can hardly tell it's her. See?'

Stu turns the phone to face me. He shows me an image of who I assume to be Layla. It was taken from the waist up, highlighting her ample breasts which are piled into a black bikini that does not seem up for the task of containing them. She's wearing a floppy sun hat, which she's seductively pulled down over one eye with a delicate hand ending in pink manicured nails. The hat casts a shadow over her eyes, but her cherry-red lips glisten enticingly in the sunshine. It strikes me that this photo was probably carefully selected. It's suggestive enough to garner attention (plenty of attention is my bet), but keeps her real identity hidden, in case she wanted to avoid recognition by any local suitors outside of the designated Date Space chat.

'Can you see when Layla joined Date Space?' I ask.

'Looks like it was January of this year.'

'Four months before she moved to New York then,' I say, more to myself than to Stu. 'Any way to find out who she was talking to on there?'

'No, there isn't. Once a conversation space is closed, the app doesn't keep a record of who you spoke to.'

'Damn.'

'Secret Message is the same. She has the app, but she has no unread messages. Once a message is read, it's automatically erased. Can't be retrieved.'

'Double damn.'

'Sorry, Barnes. Wish I had more for ya,' Stu says as he shuts down Layla's phone once again.

Back to the drawing board. There has to be some way to find out more about Layla. And there's only one person I can think of who might be able to help us with that. I walk over to Lanner's desk.

'I think we should go talk to Mindy again, Layla's neighbor. Stu just told me that Layla had a Date Space account, but we don't know who she was talking to. Let's see if she ever mentioned it to Mindy.'

*

Lanner pulls up to Mindy's apartment building, Layla's former residence. It's a squat little brick building with small rectangular windows cut into the facade, each fitted with metal bars. For a girl who was sleeping with a multi-millionaire, she wasn't doing too well for herself. There's no parking on the street in front of the building. Lanner circles the block a few times before he finds a spot that can accommodate his department-issued Chevy Impala. We walk up the block in the suffocating heat. It radiates off the sidewalk and coils around me like a snake. The air is stagnant and laced with the smell of urine and simmering garbage. Lanner and I approach the building in silence. It's as if the heat evaporated all of the words off of our tongues.

By the time we walk up the four flights of stairs to Mindy's apartment, I'm drenched in sweat. Lanner knocks on the door while I peel my shirt off of my skin and fan myself with it.

Mindy comes to the door, opening it cautiously, the chain lock still in place. We called her before showing up, so she should be expecting us, but I suppose you can never be too careful. Especially after her friend turned up dead just a few days ago.

'Oh, hi Detectives. Just a moment,' Mindy says as she closes the door and disengages the chain. 'Come on in.' She sniffles. She mentioned earlier that she's working from home today, nursing a cold.

Mindy's hair looks like a lion's mane in the sticky humidity. Black curls leap from her scalp as if they're trying to escape her head. She must notice me looking because she pulls it back self-consciously.

'Sorry about the heat. The air conditioners in this building suck.'

'I know how you feel,' I tell her. 'Mine's just as bad.'

'Did you guys find out what happened to Layla?' Mindy motions for us to take a seat on her sofa, which is thankfully positioned right in front of the feeble air conditioner. It's blowing lukewarm air, but sitting in the breeze still feels like we've reached an oasis.

'Not yet,' I explain. 'We're following up on a few leads and had a couple of questions for you.'

'Sure. Anything I can do to help.' Mindy swipes at her nose with a wadded-up tissue.

As Lanner and I had discussed on the drive over, he's going to handle the social media questions as I'm still a 'newbie' as he phrased it.

'Did Layla ever mention Date Space to you?' Lanner asks.

'Yeah, sure. She knows that I've made a few unsuccessful attempts at Internet dating, and when I told her I was ready to call it quits, buy a few cats, and become a spinster at the ripe old age of twenty-six, she suggested I try Date Space. She told me that her employer, KitzTech, created it and that it's a fun and safe way to meet guys. I don't know if you've ever tried it, but it sets up these private chat spaces for you to talk to anyone you connect with so that you, like, don't have to exchange numbers until you're ready, and you can even video chat and stuff.' Mindy fidgets in her seat and she seems to be having trouble meeting Lanner's eye, her cheeks glowing pink. It's no wonder she prefers meeting men online first. She strikes me as painfully shy.

Lanner smiles, making Mindy squirm just a little bit more. Sometimes I forget that women find him attractive. We've been partners for so long that his shine has sort of worn off for me. I see him more like a brother; someone who drives me crazy, but I care about fiercely.

'Did Layla use Date Space herself?' Lanner asks.

'I don't know. She didn't mention it if she did. But did you, like, see her? There's no way a girl who looks like that needs to meet guys on the Internet ... Not that there's anything wrong with that of course,' Mindy rushes to add as she looks over at me. 'Plenty of good-looking people do Internet dating. How else do you meet people these days, ya know?' Evidently she thinks I'm exactly the type of person who spends my evenings scouring the Internet for dates.

'I'm just saying,' Mindy continues, 'Layla had no trouble meeting people. Every time we'd go out to a bar or whatever, all the guys in the place would stare at her.'

'Does anyone in particular stick out in your mind?' I ask. 'Anyone approach her?'

'No, not really,' Mindy says, looking up thoughtfully. 'Layla never even seemed to notice all the attention she was getting. I imagine she was used to it.'

'You still have my card?' I ask.

Mindy nods. 'Yes, I do.'

'Call me any time if you think of anyone who showed a particular amount of attention to Layla. Anyone you may have seen more than once.'

'Okay, yeah, sure,' Mindy agrees.

Lanner and I shake Mindy's hand and thank her again for her time, and we show ourselves out of her apartment.

When we step back out onto the sidewalk, the heat hits me like a punch to the face. I feel a wave of dizziness crash over me.

'Sit down, Barnes,' Lanner instructs as he lowers me to the curb. 'I'll go get you some cold water.'

Lanner jogs across the street to a bodega. 'Apples 99 cents per pound' advertised on a bright pink poster tacked to the front window. I watch him hurry through the door, but it's what is above the door that has really caught my attention. A CCTV camera aimed directly at me, sitting on the sidewalk in front of Layla's building, its lens glinting in the sun.

Lanner rushes back with a bottle of water. I gulp it down greedily, feeling the blissfully cold liquid trail down my throat.

'Thank you,' I say when I finally manage to pull the bottle away from my lips. 'But we need to go back in there for one more thing.'

'What's that?'

'Their CCTV footage,' I reply, pointing up at the camera. It stares back at me, an ever watchful eye.

Chapter 25

Vince

I refresh my e-mail over and over again. For the first time in …
I don't even know how many years, I'm not going into the office
today. The temptation to log into the KitzTech server and check
in on things is very strong. I know I should keep my hands off
the wheel, at least for now, but I find that I'm having difficulty
relinquishing control. And so instead, I'm sitting on my living
room couch, my laptop warming on my thighs, just waiting for
David Mullins, the private investigator, to respond to my inquiry.
I need to relax. It's still early and he probably hasn't even had his
morning coffee yet, never mind decided whether or not to jump
on the train wreck that is my life right now.

I hear Nicole coming down the stairs.

'Hey,' I offer.

'Hi.'

Okay, not the warmest greeting, but at least she's speaking to me.

'Can we talk?'

'I suppose we have to. Just let me make myself some tea first.'

Nicole makes her way into the kitchen. I hear her filling the kettle, the tea cups clinking. I can't see her from here, but I can picture her up on her tiptoes searching for her favorite tea cup. The white one with the gold rim. As Nicole waits for the kettle to whistle, I refresh my e-mail approximately fifteen times, before I toss the laptop aside in frustration.

Nicole walks back into the living room on catlike feet, carefully balancing the delicate china tea cup brimming with peppermint tea. Its bracing aroma fills the room, cool and clean. Nicole perches on the edge of the sofa and takes a tentative sip, steam rising from the cup in spiraling tendrils.

'You saw the *World View* article yesterday?' I begin sheepishly. Nicole nods.

'None of it is true. I swear to you, Nicole. I don't know why Layla—'

'Please don't say that name to me.' Her voice takes a hard edge.

'I'm sorry. It's just that, she's lying. She lied.'

'It seems like, for some reason or another, she was under the impression that you were very much in love with her. You "couldn't bear to see her with anyone else" were her exact words, I believe.' Nicole's voice is cold, unforgiving. She doesn't believe me. And why should she? I've broken her trust.

'I don't know why she'd think that, but it's not true. I never felt that way about her, and I certainly never said those words to her. You have to believe me. I know I haven't given you any reason to trust me, but I swear to you I'm telling you the truth.'

'I want to believe you, Vince, I really do. But I feel like I don't even know you anymore.' Her eyes mist over with tears, but they don't fall. Not yet. It's as if she's looking at me from behind protective glass.

'Of course you do, I'm the same person I always was.'

'No, Vince, you're not. The man I married wouldn't have done this to me. He just wouldn't have. You've changed, I don't know when exactly it happened, but you did, and this … this has changed us. I don't know if things can ever go back to the way that they were before.' Nicole takes another a small sip of her tea, the steam rising in front of her face once more. A misty barrier forming between us.

'I've made mistakes. I know that. You deserve so much better than I've given you, and I promise you, Nicole, I'm going to get back to the man I used to be. The man you loved. Please just give me that chance.' I can hear the desperation in my own voice, the measured confidence I usually exude a long forgotten memory. The guilt, the shame, the regret, the injustice of it all wash over me, one emotion lapping over another, swirling together until I can't parse them apart anymore. In this moment, all I know is that I'd do anything to make Nicole believe me. *I can't lose her. I can't.*

'I'm trying,' Nicole replies. 'I've *been* trying. I've given you the benefit of the doubt all along. I still believe you didn't kill that girl, and that's the only reason I've agreed to stand by your side through all of this, but I can't take any more surprises. Have you told me everything? Do you promise me?'

'Yes. I swear to you that I have.' I swallow down the lie. I haven't told her where I really was the night Layla died. But I can't. If I told her where I was, I'd have to tell her why I was there, and no one can ever know about that. I want to spare Nicole from having to live with that ugly truth, but I know my reason for the lie is also a selfish one. If the truth ever got out, that would be the end of all of it.

'Okay. But I promise you Vince, if I find out you've kept anything else from me, I'm leaving you.' Her words land with such finality that it drags the air from my lungs.

'I assume you're not going into work today?' she adds more as a statement than a question, one eyebrow raised.

I look down at the rumpled white shirt I'm wearing, the same one I slept in. The underarms are yellow with sweat, and a food stain, half-heartedly blotted, marks the front. How quickly I've descended into disorder.

I explain to Nicole what's happening at KitzTech, my

conversation with Darren and the looming threat of losing more investors for the new video game branch. Her eyes grow round.

'You, we, invested a lot into that new branch,' she says, sounding worried.

'I know, and that's why I'm taking some time out of the office, out of the spotlight there, until things calm down.'

We both fall silent, not knowing where to go from here. We're in uncharted waters. Our marriage, once thought to be a sturdy vessel, has been dashed on the rocks, and we're clinging to the wreckage now; two castaways praying for landfall.

Mercifully I feel my phone buzzing in my pocket. I fish it out and check the home screen. Jeff.

'Hey, Jeff. I hope you have good news.'

'Not exactly. I spoke to my buddy from law school. He handles libel and defamation cases. Sort of out of my wheelhouse. But anyway, he agreed with me. You don't have a libel case just yet. Because you're a public figure, it's not enough to just prove that *World View* printed false information that was damaging to your reputation. The standard is quite a bit more rigorous for you. You'd have to establish that *World View* acted with actual malice in printing false information.'

'What does that mean exactly, actual malice?'

'It means that you have to first prove that what *World View* said was, in fact, false.'

I feel annoyance bubbling up inside of me. I don't know how many times I can tell him that the things *World View* has been printing about me are not true. Well, most of it isn't at least …

'Anyway,' Jeff continues, 'then you would have to prove that they *knew* that what they were printing was false. And well, I don't think you can do that. They reprinted a primary source, Layla's diary. For one thing, they never claimed that what she wrote was true, they just claimed that those were Layla's words, which, presumably they were, and for another thing, they would have no way of knowing that what she wrote was a pack of lies.'

'Well, you were right,' I grumble. 'This wasn't good news.' I thought that maybe the threat of a lawsuit would be enough to warn off the tabloids, especially *World View* which seems to be leading the pack.

'Sorry, buddy. I wish there was more I could do for you.'

'Actually, there is one more thing.'

I glance over at Nicole who has picked up a paperback. Her eyes are scanning the page, but I suspect she's more interested in my call with Jeff.

'Did you stop by the house yesterday?' I ask.

Nicole peers up at me from over the top of her book, but quickly looks down again.

'No. Why do you ask?'

'No reason. Never mind. It's nothing.'

'Okay, then. I've got to get to court,' Jeff says. 'Call me if you need anything.'

'What was that about?' Nicole asks as I end the call.

'Oh, nothing really. I thought I saw Jeff's car in town yesterday. Just wondering if he'd tried to stop by while I was out.'

'Alright …' Nicole replies skeptically as she turns back to her book. 'You could have just asked me if he'd been by.'

I open my mouth to reply, ready to bury one lie with another, but just at that moment, my e-mail pings with an alert, pulling my attention. It's David Mullins.

Mr Taylor,
Thank you for your interest in my services. I'd like to meet with you in my office today at 11.00 a.m., if that suits you. Please advise.
      Best,
      David Mullins, P.I.

I reply immediately.

I'll be there.

*

I arrive at David Mullins' office building at precisely eleven o'clock. I hope the locale is not representative of his skills as an investigator. The building, which appears to be a converted warehouse, is dismal. The metal walls, painted a nauseating green, are chipped and peeling, and rust streaks under the windowpanes make it appear as if the building itself is crying. I walk inside and take the metal stairs up to the second floor, the sound of my footfall echoing around the stairwell. Mr Mullins' website said that his office is located in Suite 203. I think 'suite' is probably a misnomer for anything located in this building. I approach the door to his office, an old wooden door with a wired glass insert. It reminds me of the door to my high school principal's office. The numbers '203' are printed in peeling gold letters on the smudged glass. I rap on the door, knuckles on wood.

'Come in,' a voice yells from within. David Mullins, I assume.

I step into the office, which as I suspected, cannot rightfully be called a suite. There is hardly enough room for Mr Mullins' desk, the two small folding chairs pushed up against it, and the reams of paper covering his desk like a blanket of snow. Boxes clutter every corner and are stacked upon each other at odd angles like a child's building blocks, climbing towards the water-stained drop ceiling. At least I hope those are water stains. I can't be sure.

'You must be Vince Taylor. David Mullins.' He reaches across his desk to shake my hand. A firm handshake; his fingers wrapped confidently around my hand.

'Yes, I am. Thank you for agreeing to meet with me so quickly.'

'Seemed necessary,' he replies. His response is clipped, as if he's conserving words, forming unnecessary syllables a wholly invaluable use of his time. Yet, I find that I like him. I feel as though I can trust him on sight.

David Mullins is short and round with a protruding belly straining against black suspenders. His white dress shirt has a drip stain on the front, which he appears to have tried in vain to wipe away. His salt and pepper hair, heavy on the salt, is noticeably thinning, but his mustache is still bushy on his upper lip and is flanked by a pair of ruddy cheeks. If this private investigator thing doesn't work out, at least he will have a fair chance of landing a job as a mall Santa in a few years' time.

'Let me tell you a little bit about myself before we get into your … situation,' Mr Mullins tells me as I fold myself into one of the small metal chairs, my knees pressed up against the back of his desk. My ankle is throbbing after climbing the stairs and I'm just happy to be sitting down.

'I was a detective with the NYPD for over twenty years. Put away a lot of bad people. Learned a lot about what makes people tick. I retired from the force not because I wanted to, but because I had to. Young man's game, that detective work. And I have a bum knee. But that doesn't mean I can't still do some good in this world. I don't work like most of your run of the mill PIs. Not interested in cheating spouses and all that. Not my problem. What I'm interested in is real investigative work. For people that really need my help. And people that I think are worth helping.'

He stops speaking abruptly and I wait for him to continue, but he doesn't. Instead he looks at me expectantly. I suppose it's my turn to talk now.

'And you think I'm worth helping?'

'You're getting a hell of a bad rap in the press. Seen it plenty of times. Trial by public opinion. I'm interested in hearing your side of things. And then we'll see whether I think I can help you.'

'It's true that I had an affair with my intern. It was a terrible indiscretion, and—'

'Skip all that. I don't need to know about how much you love your wife and how sorry you are for screwing around on her, yada yada yada. Remember what I said about the cheating spouses? Not my problem.'

'Right. Sorry. Anyway, when Layla was killed, the cops imme-diately circled around me because of the affair. But I had nothing to do with her death. Nothing. I know the media is making it look like I did, but I swear to you I didn't kill that girl. And now I don't know how I can get out from under this, but it's going to ruin my life if I don't.'

'Okay.'

'Okay?' I'm not sure whether he's telling me to stop talking or agreeing to take my case.

'Okay, I believe you.'

'You do?'

'Yes. I can spot a liar from a mile away. I've been wrong a time or two, but I don't think I am with you. I think you're telling me the truth. And so I'll help you.'

I'm flooded with relief. Not because he's agreed to help me, which I sincerely appreciate, but because there is finally someone who believes my side of the story.

'What do we do now?' I ask.

'You give me as much information as you can about this girl, and I'm going to look into her. You better believe that the cops are digging through your past right now, looking for any skeletons in your closet, and so we're going to do some digging ourselves and find out everything we can about Layla. Because if you didn't kill her, that means someone else did. And in my experience, most people aren't murdered for no reason.'

He hands me a pen and paper and asks me to write down everything I know about Layla Bosch. Which is, embarrassingly, not a lot, but I forward him Layla's personnel file from KitzTech. Thankfully Eric copied me on the e-mail when he sent it to Detective Barnes last week.

'That'll give me a place to start,' Mullins says, looking at me expectantly.

I assume I've just been dismissed.

'Thank you again, really. I appreciate it.'

'Don't need to act like I'm doing you a favor. Wouldn't have agreed to do it if I didn't want to. And if you weren't paying. I'll call you with whatever I'm able to find.'

Chapter 26

Vince

DAY 6

I swing my arm as hard as I can, my racket colliding with the bright green tennis ball. It sails over the net and hits the surrounding fence with a satisfying clang. I lift another ball, the sun beating down on my head as sweat trickles down my back. The white linen shirt I'm wearing is nearly translucent by now. I squeeze the ball in my hand, my fingers digging into the spongy fuzz and the hard rubber underneath. I toss it into the air and swing my racket again. The racket whistles through the air and smacks the ball. *Thwack.*

I should probably find something more productive to do with my time, but I needed some way to burn off my nervous energy. I'm on edge waiting to hear from David Mullins, and even though Nicole and I spoke yesterday, the tension between us is still palpable.

When I got back from Mr Mullins' office yesterday I found a note from Nicole: '*Staying the night at Kathy's. Be back tomorrow.*' She got in this morning, a whirlwind of blonde hair and yoga pants as she rushed to get ready to teach today's classes. She was running late, and we skirted around each other while she quickly showered and dressed. I did my best to stay out of her way, hardly exchanging a more than a few words. She ran out the door heading for her studio, and, alone in the house, I felt as though the walls were closing in on me; as if the anxiety radiating off of me had seeped into the bones of the house. Our warm spacious home suddenly felt suffocating, the air stifling. I had to get out of there. And so here I am. Alone on my private court, taking my stress out on a bucket of innocent tennis balls.

I hear my phone ringing on the side of the court. I drop my racket, letting it clatter to the ground. It knocks over the bucket of remaining tennis balls and I watch them bounce merrily across the green asphalt, like bunnies scampering through a field. I ignore the mess and jog to the side of the court to answer my phone. The phone feels hot in my hand after roasting in the sun, and my fingers, slick with sweat, smudge the touch-screen, but I manage to pick up the call after a few tries.

'Hello?' I answer breathlessly, perspiration beading on the bridge of my nose. I run my hands through my hair, raking it away from my face.

'It's Mullins. Got some info for you.'

'That was fast!'

'It's my job.'

'Right, sorry.' *What is it about this man that makes me feel like a child eager to impress his teacher?* 'What did you find?'

'First of all, Layla Bosch did not attend the University of Pennsylvania like she claimed on her application to KitzTech. I pulled a few strings and was able to verify that no one by that name was ever enrolled in their Software Engineering program.'

'But she gave us a copy of her transcripts!'

'Not hers. They were doctored. The transcript she gave you was from someone named Fred Mattherson. She must have switched the names. Did a pretty good job of it too. Looks legit.'

143

'Wow …' I find that I'm speechless.

'I'm still doing some diggin' but I got one more thing for you so far. Old address. You want it?'

'Yes, please.'

David Mullins rattles off an address in Philadelphia while I scramble to type it into my phone.

'A basement apartment? Philadelphia?' I ask, confused.

'Need me to repeat the address?'

'No, it's just that Layla told me she grew up on a farm.'

'Not likely, unless cows rented the unit upstairs. Ha.' Mullins laughs, a choked, terse chuckle. 'Seems like she wasn't the most forthcoming and honest person,' he says, regaining his stoic composure.

'Right, thanks Mr Mullins. This was very helpful.'

'Mullins. No need for the mister. I'll let you know if I find anything else, but there's not much out there on this girl. Unusual for a girl her age these days. Usually have their whole lives on the Internet. Anyway, goodbye for now.' He ends the call.

It seems I didn't know Layla at all. But that's about to change.

Chapter 27

Allison

DAY 6

I try hard to suppress a yawn but it bubbles up within me, demanding to be released. Lanner, Kinnon, and I have been sitting in the conference room all day reviewing CCTV footage from the bodega across the street from Layla's apartment. The store owner keeps four months' worth of footage before it is automatically wiped over, but at this point I'll take anything I can get. The most difficult part of reviewing the footage is that we don't know exactly what we're looking for. Anyone who seems suspicious, anyone who seems to be paying particularly close attention to Layla's building, anyone who we see on multiple occasions that doesn't look like they belong ... all very vague. A shot in the dark.

'You guys find anything good yet?' I ask.

'Not yet,' Kinnon grumbles, an elbow propped atop the table, his cheek resting upon it. His eyes are bloodshot and he looks like he's seconds from sleep. 'I've seen Layla coming and going, but always alone or with Mindy.'

'Same here,' Lanner adds. 'Haven't found anything suspicious.

This old guy likes to pick his nose when he thinks no one is looking, but that's about it. Pretty sure the nose picker lives in the building anyway.'

'I was hoping we'd see Vince Taylor, to be honest,' I offer. 'No sign of him on my end though. Yours?'

Lanner and Kinnon both shake their heads. They haven't seen Vince either.

'Wait. I think I got something,' Kinnon says, sitting up straight. 'Look. Here.'

Lanner and I crowd around the tiny laptop screen and stare at the grainy footage that Kinnon has paused for us. Framed on the screen is a frozen black and white image of a tall, gangly man, with thick, square-framed glasses, a tuft of curly hair atop his head. He appears to be in his 20s, but it's hard to tell from the blurry image.

'Can we zoom in?' I ask.

'This is as close as I could get,' Kinnon explains. 'Quality on these cameras isn't the best, and don't forget he was across the street.'

'Well it's definitely not Vince,' I point out. 'Totally different build.'

Kinnon nods in agreement.

'Why did you point this guy out?' Lanner inquires. 'What did you see?'

'This is the third time I've noticed him standing outside the building, but he never goes inside. This time he's pacing back and forth, looking up at the building like he's waiting for someone, but he doesn't meet anyone. Watch.'

Kinnon hits play on the footage and indeed the man begins to pace nervously. I watch him take his hands in and out of his pockets, fidgeting, occasionally glancing over his shoulder, as he keeps watch on the front door of Layla's building.

'What's the date on this?' I ask.

'August fifth,' Kinnon replies.

'Almost three weeks before Layla was killed then.'

We continue watching the footage, huddled around the screen.

'Look, there!' Lanner exclaims. 'It's Mindy.'

There is no mistaking the mane of black curls on her head, the shuffling way she walks with her eyes trained down at the sidewalk in front of her, as if she doesn't want the world to notice her.

We watch the strange man look up at her and pause, his head tilted to the side, like a curious puppy. And then he walks out of sight.

'We need to finish reviewing the footage from the last three weeks, and then we're going to have to go back to the beginning. Go through all the footage again. Flag any sightings of this guy,' I say.

Lanner groans and throws his head back dramatically. He knows we're going to be in for a long night.

*

'Done,' Lanner announces, pushing his chair back from the table. He stands up and stretches his long arms, pulling each one across his chest in turn.

'I'm done too,' Kinnon adds.

'So am I,' I say.

The conference table in front of us is scattered with empty soda cans, crumpled napkins and the remains of a pizza that we dove on like vultures earlier in the evening.

'OK, let's see what we've got.'

I walk over to the whiteboard we set up in the back of the room. Each time one of us spotted the man in question, we added the information to the board, building a timeline of his visits to Layla's apartment. Overall, we've seen him four times over as many weeks.

I read the board aloud.

'Sunday July 21, 3.09 p.m.: Stands outside building for eight minutes. Does not enter.

Saturday July 27 10.11 a.m.: Stands outside building for seven minutes. Does not enter.

Monday August 5, 8.27 a.m.: Stands outside building for nine minutes, looking nervous. Seems to take note of Mindy. Leaves shortly after, not in same direction as Mindy.

August 23, 6.59 p.m.: Stands outside building for fourteen minutes. Watches Layla and Mindy leave building together. Follows in their direction.'

We're all silent for a moment while we consider the board, our heads fuzzy after spending the day glued to our computer screens.

'So,' Lanner begins. 'He shows up three weekends in a row. Then he sees Mindy, and doesn't show up again for three weeks.'

'Right, and that was the night before Layla died,' Kinnon adds.

'I don't know what to make of it,' Lanner says, a puzzled look on his face as he sweeps his eyes back and forth over the board.

'I'm not sure either,' I reply. The information swirls around my head, I see it strewn out before me like scattered puzzle pieces. I know there is something here, but I can't quite slot the pieces in place to reveal the full picture.

Kinnon looks at me expectantly, waiting for me to do my job and lead this investigation forward.

'Ok, here's what we're gonna do,' I say more confidently than I feel. 'Let's find the clearest freeze-frame we can get of this guy. One where you can see his face. And then we'll see if anyone in the area can identify him.'

Chapter 28

Vince

DAY 6

The Tesla flies down the parkway, quietly and smoothly, as I whizz past a large wooden sign, 'Welcome to Pennsylvania'. It was a two and a half hour drive from my house to Philadelphia. Surely by now Nicole found the note I quickly scrawled for her, *Running some errands, be back tonight*, not that she's tried to call. My phone sits dark and silent in the cup-holder to my left. I suppose it's a fair representation of our relationship right now though. My own fault. But I'm going to make things right no matter what it takes.

I thought the long drive would settle my nerves. It usually does. Our friends, or, I should say, wealthy acquaintances that we are forced to socialize with due to sheer proximity at certain events, have suggested on countless occasions that I really should hire a driver. As if the sight of me driving my own car is somehow unseemly in light of the balance in my bank accounts. My insistence on maintaining some semblance of a normal life is apparently offensive in certain circles. Oh well. I love driving, the feeling of

149

my tires connecting with the road, and I never wanted to lose who I am. Although, I suppose I did. Nicole was right. I have changed.

I can't help thinking about the day I proposed to her. The memory plays in my head unbidden, like a familiar song from long ago. I rented a bungalow in Montauk for a long weekend in May, just before the busy season began. It was still cool enough that we could meander along the sandy shorelines in shorts and light sweatshirts, enjoying the spray of the salty sea air on our faces. We spent four long and lazy days wandering the little beach town, among the brightly colored shops offering slow-churned ice cream, painted seashells, and shiny new surfboards. The aroma of freshly baked croissants greeted us each morning, and we spent the sunny afternoons nestled under a shady umbrella enjoying fresh oysters and frozen cocktails on Gosman's Dock, surrounded by the tinny sound of wind chimes blowing in the warm breeze and seagulls circling overhead.

On the last day of the trip, I booked us a tour of the famous Montauk Lighthouse located at the furthest tip of Long Island. We strolled through the tiny maritime museum, admiring the model ships, whale hunting artifacts, and photographs of days gone by, before we made our way up the narrow winding stairway leading to the top of the red and white lighthouse. As I walked up the stairs, I patted my pocket repeatedly to make sure I hadn't dropped the ring. I'd spent my last dime to buy it. When we reached the peak, we looked out at the wide expanse of sparkling blue water all around us, the Long Island Sound colliding with the Atlantic Ocean before our eyes. A misty gray fog swirled around the base of the lighthouse beneath our feet as I got down on one knee, with tears in my eyes and butterflies in my stomach, and asked Nicole to be mine forever.

That man, the man down on his knees begging the love of his life to be his happily ever after, could never have imagined hurting Nicole the way I have. The memory of happier times falls away from me now, like a ship slowly claimed by a dark sea. I lost sight of myself, but it's time to get back to the person I once was, the man Nicole made me want to be.

I pull up to the address Mullins gave me earlier this morning. It was only a few hours ago that I got his call, but yet it feels like it belonged to another lifetime: the one before I started tracking down Layla's past, before I took the first step towards taking my life back. I park the Tesla on a shady block, where kids have freed a fire hydrant and are dancing in its geyser-like spray. A rainbow reflects off of the escaped mist, and the children shriek and squeal with joy as they dart in and out of the cold water. It drips off the ends of their hair and rolls down their backs; summertime in a city. As I climb out of my car, I wonder for a moment if this was what Layla's childhood, her real childhood, looked like. Did she dance in rain that she made herself?

I approach the building Mullins directed me to on foot. A four-story town house, long ago painted red, with a sagging roof and fading shutters. Bars clutter the upper windows, and the curtains appear to be made of old bedsheets tacked to the window frames. A loosened gutter hangs listlessly from the roof, and a pair of worn sneakers dangles from the telephone wires cross-hatching the sky overhead. Far from the farm life Layla described. I feel a rush of renewed anger as I climb the front steps, the bricks wobbling beneath my weight. She lied to me. From the very beginning.

I press the buzzer for the basement apartment. None of the five doorbells are labeled with the names of the tenants, just the floor that they belong to. I'd imagine the tenants change often, this sad-looking house a transient arrangement. I have no idea if I'll find anyone here who knew Layla, but it's worth a try.

'Who's ringin'?' a deep raspy voice barks over the intercom. I believe it's a woman's voice but I can't be certain.

I'm momentarily at a loss for words. How do I explain who I am and why I'm here? I lean in towards the intercom, and explain as best I can.

'Hi, I'm looking for someone who may have lived here at some point. Her name is, was, Layla?'

The voice goes silent. Maybe I've struck out. Maybe there's nothing to find here after all. I'm just about to walk away when the voice blares over the intercom once again.

'Come in then. Back door.'

I walk around to the back of the building, picking my way around crushed soda cans, broken beer bottles, and discarded candy wrappers that litter the tight alleyway separating this building from the next. When I reach the back side of the building, I see a rusted fire escape climbing the facade. A child sits on the second-story landing eating a Popsicle, his feet dangling over the side, his shoe laces untied and hanging like tendrils. Beneath the fire escape is a small cement stairway leading to a dingy white door. That must be the entrance to the basement apartment.

'Come on, I don't got all day,' a woman says, craning her neck out the basement door. Her hair which was likely once black, is streaked with gray, and it hangs in matted tufts. Her dark eyes seem hollow and haunted against her pale, gaunt skin. The woman's fingers, long and thin, grip the side of the door and they seem to be nothing more than skin pulled over bone.

I follow her into the apartment and it's like I've stepped into another world, the dark underbelly of a life I never knew. The single room that makes up the basement apartment is shabby and worn, and clouded with smoke, the walls and ceilings coated with a brown film. In the center of the room is a stained couch with tufts of stuffing pushing its way out of the torn fabric. The couch has been pulled out to a bed, which dons graying sheets that are worn threadbare in the center and reek of sweat.

The woman sits on the edge of the bed and crosses her legs at the knee. She gestures for me to sit in a small wooden chair that's pushed up against the wall, clothes hanging off of its back.

She picks up a small glass pipe and takes a long drag. Marijuana, judging by the smell of it.

'It's medicinal,' she says, eyeing me through a curling cloud of smoke. 'Willing to share if you want though.'

She pulls the pipe away from her thin, cracked lips and offers it to me.

'No, thank you, I'm fine.' I try to sound polite and not repulsed at the thought of putting my mouth where hers had just been.

The smell in the apartment is nearly unbearable and I find myself suppressing the urge to burst towards the one small window at the other end of the room to gulp in fresh air. The window is cracked open, offering a view of asphalt and passing sneakers.

'You said you were looking for Layla?' the woman says, her eyes half closed as she gently sways in her seat.

'Yes, I—'

'Welp, sorry to tell you this, but you ain't gonna find her here. I dunno what kinda girl doesn't visit her mother, letting me rot away in this shit hole by myself, but there you have it. That's Layla for ya.'

Her mother?

'You're Layla's mother?' I ask bewildered. I would have thought her old enough to be Layla's grandmother, but her bedraggled appearance makes it difficult to estimate her real age.

'Sure am, not that she seems to remember that.' The woman huffs.

'I'm sorry, it's just that she told me—'

'I bet she told you I was dead or somethin'. Wouldn't be the first time. Only she wishes that was true.' The woman coughs into her arm, a phlegmy, wet cough. 'Ain't dead yet though.'

'She told me that she was raised by her grandmother. On a farm.'

The woman laughs now, a deep laugh that has her doubled over and sputtering for air between coughs. Her yellowed and rotting teeth on full display.

'Ain't no way. Her daddy ran off after she was born, didn't

have the stomach for all that crying and screamin', and my own mother wrote me off years ago. Far as I know, Layla never even met either of her grandmothers. A farm, ha! I raised that little ingrate myself, not that she ever gave me any thanks for it.'

I notice the woman scratching at her arm as she speaks. It's riddled with small red and purple dots. Needle wounds, track marks, if I had to guess.

'What did you say your name was again?' The woman leers at me now, suspicious.

I suddenly realize that I shouldn't tell her who I really am. It seems that she doesn't know that her daughter is dead, so I assume she hasn't seen the news yet, but when she does, I don't want her knowing that she was paid a visit by the prime suspect in her daughter's murder. I can only imagine the trouble that would cause me.

'My name … Jeff.' *It was the first name I could think of.*

'Well, Jeff. I'm Gemma. How'd you know my daughter?'

'Oh, we met at a bar. A while back. I was just looking to get in touch with her again, and this was the last address I had for her.'

'Surprised she'd give it. She hasn't lived here since she was sixteen. And even then, hardly spent any time here. Always thought she was too good for this place, too good for her only mother. If she only knew how much I gave up for her. I was going to be a famous singer, you know. I know I'm not much to look at now, but in my day I was really something.'

'I'm sure,' I reply, trying my best to sound genuine. 'When was the last time you heard from Layla?'

Gemma narrows her eyes, and points a bony finger at me. Her mood seems to swing back and forth like a pendulum.

'I don't know why you're snoopin' around here after Layla, but whatever it is, I don't want nothin' to do with it. I ain't seen that girl since the day she left.'

'Alright, ma'am, I'm sorry to have bothered you,' I say as I turn to leave.

Gemma follows me to the door. As I walk across the back lot, I hear her call after me. 'I'll tell you this much, if you're involved with Layla you better be careful.'

I turn around, wanting to ask what she meant, but she slams the door and I hear a lock slide into place behind her.

Chapter 29

Vince

BEFORE

'Are you sure you don't want to go somewhere else?' Layla asks seductively, a red straw held between her teeth. She steps towards me, and I can smell the whiskey on her breath, hear the ice rattling in her glass.

'Layla, not now. We're at a work function.' I can't seem to keep the irritation out of my voice, though, admittedly, I'm not really trying. She's drunk, sloppy, but she should know that we can't take risks like that. I take a step back from her and scan the room to make sure no one is watching us. We just finished developing a new app, Layla's app actually, and it's tradition that I take the whole team out for a happy hour as soon as it's released. From what I can tell, my employees seem to be taking full advantage of the open bar and are paying little to no attention to Layla and me at the far end of the bar. But you can never be too careful.

'Come on, Vince, you don't need to be so uptight all the time. Have a little fun, for once,' Layla pouts.

She's behaving like a spoiled and petulant child. Maybe it's the age difference, maybe I am just a grumpy old man who's forgotten how to have fun, but I have little patience for her neediness, her immaturity lately. It seems that Layla always finds a way to get what she wants.

Ever since Marta almost caught us in my apartment, I've been trying to put some distance between Layla and me. She told me not to worry about it, Marta didn't actually see anything, so who cares if she heard the shower running? But I do. I care. It was too close a call and made me realize how dangerous this game we've been playing really is.

I'd like to say that that time in my apartment was the last time I was with Layla, but truthfully it wasn't. As much as I've tried to avoid Layla, it seems that she is trying just as hard to find ways to be alone with me. Whether she's cozying up to me in the copy room, working late so that she can walk out to the parking lot with me, or hand-delivering memos to my office, Layla never seems to be too far away. I can't say for certain that she's doing it intentionally, but it certainly feels that way.

Earlier this week I was out to dinner with an important investor who was interested in learning more about the new video game branch, when Layla sauntered in draped on the arm of another man while wearing a tight red dress that left little to the imagination. I thought perhaps it was a coincidence that we ended up in the same restaurant, that perhaps she hadn't even seen me sitting on the other side of the room, but when the investor got up to use the restroom, Layla walked straight over to my table. She sat herself across from me and said, 'I'm sorry if this is a bit awkward for you, Vince. I wasn't expecting to run into you tonight.'

'Who's the guy?' I replied, nodding in the direction of the hulk of a man waiting for her at the bar.

'Oh, that's Adam. He's just a friend. That doesn't bother you, does it?'

'Not at all,' I lied. I could feel the jealously churning in my gut. Layla wasn't mine to possess, I knew that I was in absolutely no position to tell her that she couldn't sleep with other people, but I still felt territorial. 'It's none of my business who you choose to spend your time with.'

Layla smiled, almost pityingly. 'Right, I know. But call me later if you find yourself available.'

As she rose from the table, I thought to myself that her dress was far too short for a dinner with a friend. Especially a muscular, male friend with a chiseled jawline.

My investor returned to the table and we finished our meals, but I couldn't help but steal glances in Layla's direction. She sat on a bar stool, her long, toned legs crossed in front of her, smiling adoringly at her 'friend' and my jealously only grew. I watched as she threw her head back in laughter at something Adam had said, touching his arm lightly and nuzzling her stiletto-clad foot against his leg. I was practically seething with anger.

By the time my meeting was finished, Layla had left the bar. I called her immediately and told her that I'd booked us a suite at the Heatherly Hotel. She met me at the hotel, still in that skin-tight red dress that showed off all of her perfect curves, and I reclaimed what was mine.

The thing is, I can't stop wondering if Layla knew I'd be at that restaurant. If she showed up with Adam to make me jealous, to lure me into sleeping with her again after things had started to cool off. It certainly would have been easy enough for her to find out that I had an investor meeting on my calendar that evening. Did I walk straight into a trap? And now that I've fallen in, how can I get out?

Layla's hand brushes against mine, pulling me from my thoughts. 'Layla, I told you. We're at a work event. This isn't appropriate.'

'Not appropriate? I'll tell you what's not appropriate, Vince. You sleeping with me while your wife is at home! Making me fall for you when you knew you would never leave her!'

'Lower your voice,' I hiss. Layla is drunk and wobbling on her feet. I find it decidedly unattractive. Nicole would never lose her composure like this. Sure, Layla seemed fun and adventurous at first, but now I can't seem to recall why I ever thought that this was what I wanted. 'And I didn't make you fall for me, I was honest with you from day one. You knew what this was, you knew I was never leaving Nicole.'

'Tell yourself whatever you need to,' Layla replies, a hardness, an anger in her eyes that I've never seen before. She slams her glass down on the bar and walks out.

I see Eric glance in our direction and quickly avert his eyes.

This can't go on any longer. I'm going to end things with Layla for good.

Chapter 30

Allison

DAY 7

Lanner pulls up in front of the now familiar brick building. We figured that Mindy would be our best chance of identifying the man on the CCTV footage. It seemed that he recognized her, and so maybe she'll recognize him too.

Mindy agreed to meet us at her apartment on her lunch hour. She's an executive assistant, she explained, and her office is only a few blocks away. She'd rather meet in the privacy of her apartment, which is fine with me. With the exception of the heat, this building, the one our mystery man seemed so very interested in, is the perfect place to start tracking down his identity.

'I brought you some water this time,' Lanner says as we begin to ascend the stairs towards the fourth floor. 'You know, so I don't have to rescue you again.'

'Thanks. You're a real hero.' I tease him, but Lanner really is a great partner. He looks after me in ways I don't even look after myself.

Sweating and embarrassingly out of breath, I knock on Mindy's door. Lanner, on the other hand, doesn't look phased by our hike up the stairs in the ninety-eight-degree heat. Maybe I should consider Josh's offer for a membership to Lift after all.

'Hi, Detectives,' Mindy responds as she eyes us through her chain-locked door. She unfastens the chain and invites us inside.

Once we're all assembled on her couch, Lanner produces the photo of the man we saw on the CCTV footage outside of the building.

'Thanks for meeting with us,' he begins. 'We know you don't have too much time before you have to get back to work, so we'll try to make it quick. Do you know this guy?'

'Where did this picture come from?' Mindy asks, taking the photo from Lanner.

'We picked him up on the CCTV footage from the bodega across the street. Have you seen him before?'

'I … yes. I have …' Mindy seems dazed, the color draining from her face. 'Did he have something to do with what happened to Layla?' Her voice is rising, panic setting in.

'We don't know yet. Just wanted to see if we can identify him first and then we'll go from there,' I explain calmly. 'Can you tell us who he is?'

'He's … his name is Mike.'

'How do you know him?' I prod.

'We … went out. Like, on a date.'

'Did you go out with him more than once?' *Maybe it was Mindy he was watching, not Layla. But I don't want to frighten her, not until we know for sure.*

'No, it was just the one time. I thought we hit it off and then he never called again. Typical. Men are so immature … No offense, Detective.' Mindy smiles at Lanner, her cheeks glowing a rosy red.

He winks at her. 'None taken.'

'Can you tell us Mike's last name?' I ask, getting this interview back on track.

'Gentry. I think.'

'When did you two go out?'

'Mid-August, I don't remember the exact date, but hold on. I'll check my texts.' Mindy scrolls through her phone. 'Ok, it looks like we started talking on the night of August fifth, and then we met up for drinks on the following Saturday, August seventeenth.'

August fifth. That was the same day that this man spotted Mindy in the early hours of the morning.

'Where did you meet him?' Lanner asks.

'Date Space,' Mindy says, blushing again. 'I told you how Layla recommended I give it a try? Well I did, and I met Mike there. We talked in the chat space for like, hours, and it seemed like we were really hitting it off. I remember that he wanted to meet up pretty much right away, but I was being a little cautious, so I just kept talking to him in the chat for a while. But after a week or so of chatting in the app, like, all the time, I agreed to meet him for a drink and we exchanged numbers so we could meet up.'

'Where did you two go?' I ask.

'This bar down the block. It's called The Saloon. We hung out there for, like, three hours, and I thought it was going really well, but I never heard from him again after that.'

'Did you two talk about Layla at all?'

'Come to think of it, yeah, we did. A little. We were talking about Date Space and how we met there, and I told him that my neighbor and good friend, Layla works for KitzTech who developed Date Space, and she was the one who recommended I try it. Looking back, I thought he was just really into technology, but I guess he sort of did ask a lot of questions about Layla and her job. He was asking a lot of technical questions about what she did and stuff, and I really don't know the first thing about computers and so I said I'd ask her next time I saw her, and … oh God, I mentioned that I had plans to go to dinner with her the following Friday, that would have been the twenty-third, the day before she … died. Did I do something wrong? Was this my fault?' Mindy begins to cry, gulping, wracking sobs that shake her tiny frame.

'No, Mindy, you didn't. We don't even know if Mike had anything to do with what happened to Layla. And even if he did, you couldn't have known.' I rub her back gently. *Was that the right thing to do?* I'm not a very emotional person in general. I'm not prone to crying, and I find that I have no idea what to do when other people break down in front of me. You'd think after so many years on the job I'd have this down by now, but I never know if I'm doing the right thing. Should I offer comfort? Should I give people space? I feel like I'm always tripping over my feet in these situations. Thankfully Lanner steps in and saves me.

He gets down on one knee in front of the sobbing Mindy and hands her a clean tissue from the box on her end table.

'Here, it's ok,' he tells her. 'We're going to find out what happened to Layla, and when we do, it will be because of all the help you've given us. You've been a great friend to her.'

'Thank you,' Mindy says, lifting her eyes and dabbing at her tears. 'I just really miss her.'

'I know you do,' Lanner replies. 'There's one more thing you can do to help us now. Can you give us Mike's phone number?'

Mindy scrolls through her phone again and rattles off the number. Lanner types it into his own phone and presses the call button. He's greeted with an automatic message:

'*The number you have dialed is no longer in service ...*'

'Damn,' I say.

More helpfully, Lanner asks if we can look at their text exchanges instead. Mindy readily hands over her phone.

'There's not much here except your arrangements for when and where to meet.'

'I know,' Mindy explains. 'We mostly talked through the app, so the messages wouldn't be on my phone.

'Can you log into Date Space and see if Mike's account is still active?' I ask. 'Maybe we can track him down that way.'

'Sure.' Mindy rushes off to grab her laptop off of her tiny, round kitchenette table. She flips open the top and begins to type.

'His username was "MGentry123" but our chat space is closed, so I can't get into any of our old messages. They all delete after you close the chat, which I did when he never called after our date. Let me look up his profile though.' Mindy continues clicking away at the keyboard. 'Um, it looks like he deleted his account. I'm, like, so freaked out. Was he stalking Layla or something? How could he just disappear like this?'

'He didn't disappear,' I say. 'He's out there somewhere and we'll find out where.'

*

'Alright, where to now, boss?' Lanner asks as we walk back out onto the sidewalk. He mops the sweat on his brow with the back of his hand.

'Let's take this photo around to some of the local shops. It's a long shot, but maybe he stopped in at one of these stores and someone remembers him.'

We start at the bodega and work our way down the block. We stop in at a convenience store, a florist, a deli, and a barber shop, but no one seems to recognize the man in the photo. Our last stop is to the coffee house on the corner called Coffee Clutch.

'Excuse me,' I say, approaching the young woman behind the counter with a black apron tied neatly around her waist. She looks to be in her early twenties, her honey-blonde hair twisted back into a messy bun. 'I'm Detective Allison Barnes with the NYPD, and I just had a quick question for you.'

'Of course, Detective. What can I help you with?' The woman wipes her hands on her apron as she walks around to the front of the service counter. I notice that her name tag reads 'Beth'.

'We wanted to know if you recognize this man.'

Beth takes the photo from my hand and examines it closely.

'Actually, I might. It's hard to tell because the photo is a little blurry, but there was a guy that came in here a few times this month. I remember him because he always ordered a cappuccino, which is, like, kind of a pain to make when it's busy in here. Not that I mind, it's like, my job and all. But I remember him specifically because he always seemed so jittery that I thought to myself that maybe he didn't need the extra caffeine. And then he'd sit in here, like, forever, always looking out the window like he was waiting for someone, but he never met anyone.'

'That's really helpful. Did he ever tell you his name?'

'I don't really remember, but I could maybe find his credit card information for you if you know what days he might have been here?'

I give Beth the dates that we know Mike Gentry, if that is his real name, was in the area based on the CCTV footage, and the approximate times. She hustles into the back room and a few minutes later brings us back a box full of receipts.

'I called my boss, the owner, he said it would be okay to give you guys all of our receipts for those four dates you gave me, but he'd like them back for his records and stuff after.'

'Sure, no problem. Please tell him we appreciate it.'

We thank Beth for her help and leave, with the box of receipts tucked under Lanner's arm.

'Gonna be another long night, isn't it?' he says, rolling his eyes.

'Sure is,' I agree.

Chapter 31

Vince

DAY 7

I woke up this morning with a sense of foreboding hanging over me like a fog. I don't know for certain why I'm feeling this way, but I tossed and turned in bed in the early hours of the morning, perspiration breaking on my brow. I know something is coming my way, a dark storm looming on the horizon.

Now I'm sitting on my back patio, sipping my morning coffee, waiting for the ground to fall out from under me. Nicole walks out of the house, a warm breeze blowing around her. She has her favorite tea cup in her hand and I can smell the peppermint mingling with the fresh morning air. I feel myself relax in her presence. Maybe that's what has been bothering me, sleeping away from Nicole, being so distant from her, both physically and emotionally. I feel unmoored without her. She's been my anchor, my constant, for so many years.

'Good morning,' I offer. I feel as though I'm approaching a fawn in the wild, treading gently so as not to frighten her away.

'Good morning,' she replies, her tone clipped.

'I missed you last night.' *Was that too much? Too far?*

'Did you see my note? I was at Kathy's. Got in late. You were already asleep.'

'You and Kathy have been seeing a lot of each other lately.'

'She just broke up with Shawn, so she's been a mess. She's really going through it.'

'I'm sorry to hear that. I liked Shawn.'

'Shawn was a jackass.' Nicole's icy blue eyes go cold. 'Turns out he was cheating on her. Figures you two got along.'

Shit. I really put my foot in my mouth, but I couldn't have known. Nicole used to keep me in the loop about all the gossip amongst her friends, and even her clients. We used to talk into the late hours of the night catching up on all the tiny details about each other's lives. When did that end? I can't remember now.

'Sorry. I didn't know.'

'So as it turns out Kathy and I have had a lot to talk about these days.'

I can't seem to get out of my own way.

'So where were you yesterday?' Nicole asks. I'm grateful that the topic has moved away from cheating spouses, but I hate having to lie to her again.

'I was scrambling to line up some last minute investors for KitzTech. I thought maybe I could reach out to some old connections to see if I could save the video game branch.'

'Did it work?'

'No. Unfortunately not. And so now I really am going to have to leave it in Darren's hands.'

'It's probably for the best right now. I thought you said you were taking some time away from KitzTech anyway?'

'I know. I just had to give it one last try.'

Nicole's phone buzzes on the table, her screen lighting up.

'It's a client,' she says. 'Hang on.'

'Hello, Claudia … Oh, I'm so sorry to hear you have to cancel your session, would you like to reschedule? I'm available—Oh.

Right. I see … No, I didn't see that … Yes, I'll go look now. Thank you for calling.'

'What was that about?' I ask.

'Claudia Mumford. Do you remember her? She's one of my regular clients and she just canceled the remainder of her sessions with me. Evidently there's a new *World View* article out this morning.'

I feel my hands begin to shake. I wedge them between my knees to steady them.

Nicole clicks around on her phone and I watch her jaw fall as she scans the screen, her eyes growing round.

'I can't … I can't even read this,' she says with disgust as she shoves the phone across the table at me, tears filling her impossibly blue eyes. She pushes away from the table and storms into the house.

Alone once again, I pick up the phone with sweaty palms and begin to read.

Murder Victim Accuses Vince Taylor of Sexual Harassment
By Kate Owens for *World View*

As first reported by World View, *Vince Taylor (age 39), CEO of the popular technology development company, KitzTech, was allegedly involved in an illicit affair with his young intern, Layla Bosch (age 23), in the months leading up to her death on August 24, 2019. Taylor is now the prime suspect in the investigation into Layla's murder and has been questioned by the police on multiple occasions. An arrest has not yet been made.*

For those who have not been following this high-tech scandal, World View *previously reported that Layla Bosch kept a diary detailing her affair with Taylor and her fears that his feelings were becoming too intense for her liking.* World View *is now in possession of what we believe to be a never before seen page from the young victim's diary. It was provided to* World View *by an anonymous source, and reads as follows:*

'August 22, 2019.

Well, I finally did it. I told Vince that I wanted to end things. I wasn't comfortable with what was going on between us anymore, and I told him that it had to stop. He's become so possessive, so jealous lately, and his angry outbursts frighten me. I don't want to live in fear of him anymore. But it seems like I have no choice.

When I told Vince it was over, he went totally insane. He said if I wouldn't be with him, he would ruin me. He'd make sure I never found another job, and he'd tell everyone about how I made inappropriate advances towards him. ME! After he's the one that's been pursuing me for months! I never would have thought he was capable of something like this, but now I know that he is. I've seen a side of Vince lately that I never knew was there; a dark and dangerous side.

I really need this job. I spent my last dime moving to New York to work at KitzTech and I can't afford to leave now. I have nowhere else to go … especially if I don't leave KitzTech with a glowing recommendation from Vince, which he's very well aware of. But Vince said if I want his stamp of approval I'm going to have to earn it. He told me to meet him at a hotel this Saturday to prove to him how badly I want this job. I don't know what to do.'

If what Layla wrote in her diary is true, then it seems that she was planning to meet Vince Taylor the very night she died.

Was Taylor forcing his intern to continue a sexual relationship against her will? Was he involved in her death? Check in with World View *for updates on this scandalous investigation.*

The article is accompanied by a photo of me screaming in anger, my fist raised above my head. It looks like it was taken as I was driving out of my office parking garage. Probably the day that group of photographers blocked my car, taunting me. I look at the image of myself, my mouth open in anger, my eyes hard and cold. I look like a monster. And there I am, in full color, next to the same photo of Layla that's been published with each article, forever angelic in death.

I drop the phone and it clatters to the table.

The ground has fallen, the earth is shaking. I sensed it coming, the way an elephant feels the first subtle vibrations of an impending earthquake long before the earth rips in two, and yet I was powerless to stop it.

I run into the house to find Nicole. I have to tell her that this isn't true. I hope she knows that. No matter how much I may have strayed from the man she first met, the man she married, I hope she knows that I would never force a woman to be with me in that way.

'Nicole!' I shout from the kitchen, the patio doorway still open behind me. 'Nicole!' She doesn't answer. I continue calling her name as I run up the stairs towards our bedroom, her bedroom now. I take the stairs two at a time, my ankle still tender and I bound off of it.

The door to the master bedroom is closed. I knock gently.

'Nicole, I can hear you in there. Please let me in. Just talk to me.' No answer. 'Please, nothing in that article is even remotely true.' Still no answer. 'Nic, I'm opening the door. We need to talk about this.'

I want to respect her boundaries, but this can't wait. I push open the door to find a large suitcase opened wide on the bed as Nicole grabs armfuls of clothes from her closet and stuffs them inside.

'You said there would be no more surprises, Vince. You promised me.' I can hear the fury, the disappointment, in her voice, but she doesn't stop packing, even for a moment, as she admonishes me.

'I already told you everything!' It's a lie, but it's one well-rehearsed. Even I'm starting to believe it myself. 'I can't help it if that ridiculous tabloid insists on printing lies!'

'I want to believe you, Vince, I really do. But you're making that very difficult. Were you planning to meet Layla the day she died?'

'No.' *Yes.*

'Then why would she write that in her own diary?'

'How would I know?' I can hear my voice rising with hysteria.

'Don't yell at me. You did this, Vince, *you*. And I can't live with you anymore. I know we're supposed to be keeping up appearances, but I just can't be under the same roof as you for one more second.'

'Nicole, please. I know no one else believes me right now, but I need you to. Your opinion is the only one I care about. You know me! I would never do those things that were printed in that article!'

'I don't know what I believe anymore, Vince. I really don't.'

Nicole slams the lid of the suitcase shut. Clothes trail out the sides like a dog's tongue on a summer day. She begins to zipper it, but the over-stuffed clothes snag the zipper. She pulls at it forcefully, but the zipper won't budge. I watch as she collapses in frustration and begins to sob, face-down on top of the suitcase.

'Don't leave,' I plead softly.

'I have to. I can't be near you right now.'

'Where are you going to go? The apartment?'

'No. I don't want to go there. That's *your* apartment. There is too much of you in it. I'll call Kathy and see if—' Nicole sniffles.

'No, you stay. This is your home. I'll go. This was my fault. I should be the one to leave.'

I grab a duffel bag off the top shelf of my walk-in closet and begin to pack. I don't need much, I'm going to stay at the apartment and I have everything I need there, but I feel like I have to go through the motions. This feels like such a monumental moment in our marriage, the day I moved out, that it deserves the deference of packing a bag.

'I'll call you tomorrow, okay?' I ask hopefully as I sling my duffel bag over my shoulder.

Nicole nods, wiping tears from her eyes.

'I never wanted things to go this way,' she says.

'I didn't either. I'm sorry I got us here.'

I turn to leave without looking back. I'm afraid that if I do, I'll fall to my knees and beg her forgiveness, beg her not to make me go, beg her to forget all of this and love me again, the way she once did. But I can't. It wouldn't be fair to her.

'I love you,' I say as I close the door behind me, my voice barely a whisper. I'm fighting to keep my own tears at bay. I can't be sure whether she heard me, but there is no reply from my wife.

Chapter 32

Allison

DAY 8

My alarm blares and I strongly consider throwing it across the room. Instead I hit the silence button and pull my pillow over my head with a groan to block out the mid-morning sun streaming in through my bedroom window.

Lanner and I spent most of the night poring through the box of receipts from Coffee Clutch. I had no idea so many people drank cappuccinos. We narrowed our list down to five men who placed orders within a few hours of the times 'Mike Gentry' was spotted outside Layla's apartment and paid with a credit card. As suspected, none of them were actually named Mike Gentry. It would seem he gave Mindy a fake name. Poor girl.

Weary and exhausted, Lanner and I handed the list of names to Stu this morning, and we went home to finally get some rest. I hope that while we were catching up on our sleep, Stu was able to dig up some information on the men on our list which might help us figure out which, if any of them, is our mystery man. It occurred to me that none of these cappuccino-lovers might turn out to be the guy we're looking for, but I'm hoping luck is on our side for once in this investigation.

I quickly shower and then dress in a pair of tan dress pants and a loose white blouse. The ensemble is something my grandmother might wear, but at least it will keep me cool. It's supposed to be over one hundred degrees today. Which, in a city made largely of cement and asphalt, feels more like one thousand degrees.

*

'Good morning, Sunshine,' Stu greets me as I finally make it to my desk. He and Lanner are crowding around my workspace waiting for me, Stu in my chair and Lanner sitting on top of the desk. I'm eager to hear what Stu found on our list of potential new suspects, but I wish I'd had a moment to breathe before jumping into it, at least put my bag down, maybe even freshen up. Sweat is trickling between my shoulder blades, my blouse clinging to my skin.

'Yeah, yeah, good morning,' I grumble.

'Well, you're cheerful today,' Lanner teases, bumping his shoulder against mine. 'Nice outfit too.'

'Thanks.' I pretend not to notice the sarcasm dripping from his voice. 'Anyway, unless we're now the fashion police, how about we discuss the investigation?'

Lanner laughs, and Stu pulls out his tablet as I drag another chair over to my desk.

'Ok,' he begins. 'Here's what I found on each of your guys. The first is Gerald Banter. He's sixty-eight years old; lives about a block away from Coffee Clutch.'

'So he's out,' I say. 'Too old to be our guy. We're looking for someone in his twenties, maybe thirties.'

'That narrows things down quite a bit then. The next two guys on your list are aged fifty-five and forty-eight respectively.'

'That means we're down to two,' Lanner adds.

'Yes,' Stu continues. 'You're left with Anthony Valant, age twenty-six, lives in Astoria, and Thomas Barnett, age twenty-four, lives in Brooklyn.'

'Can you check to see if either of them have Friend Connect accounts or any other type of social media? Maybe we can get a picture,' Lanner inquires.

Stu smiles widely. 'I'm way ahead of you. I did all of that while you two were getting some shut-eye this morning. Here ya go.' Stu turns his tablet around so that the screen is facing towards Lanner and me.

'Meet Anthony Valant. Looks to be an electrician, loves football, owns an English bulldog.'

I study the image. His muscular shoulders and dark slicked-back hair don't seem to match the wiry, curly-haired man we saw on the CCTV footage. 'Let's see Thomas.'

'Thomas Barnett. Saved the best for last. Computer programmer. Loves, well … computers, former intern at KitzTech. Left there about two years ago. I think it's safe to assume he wasn't offered a job after his internship because he appears to be unemployed at present, and by the look of things, living with his mother.'

There he is. Mike Gentry is Thomas Barnett.

'You could have led with the KitzTech connection …' Lanner remarks.

'I know, but then I wouldn't have been able to give you my whole presentation.' Stu smiles and leans back in his chair (my chair), his hands folded behind his head. He looks rather pleased with himself.

'This is amazing, Stu, really. You're the best of the best.'

'I know,' he says with a wink as he gets up from my chair. 'I already forwarded you his current address.'

Lanner and I prepare to leave. We both know that we need to go talk to Thomas Barnett immediately.

Layla was killed over a week ago, and we finally have a solid lead to follow. Although I feel the familiar rush of adrenaline that I always get when chasing down a lead, I still can't help but feel like Vince Taylor is at the center of all of this. There has to be a connection there that I'm missing. Layla and Thomas Barnett didn't work for KitzTech at the same time, but it can't be a coincidence that Layla and her stalker both worked for Vince Taylor at one point.

'You guys heading out?' Kinnon asks as he approaches my desk, just as I finish pulling my car keys out of my bag.

'Yeah, why? What's up?'

'Chief McFadden wants to talk to you.'

This can't be good.

'What's going on with this investigation, Barnes?' the chief demands. His brows are furrowed, a deep ridge forming in the center of his forehead.

'We have a new lead, a man we spotted on CCTV outside the victim's apartment. We just identified him and we're about to go question him now.'

'That's all well and good, but that's not what I meant. Have you read the news lately?'

'Honestly, no, Sir, I haven't had a chance. Lanner and I were tied up—'

'Let me sum it up for you then. *World View* printed another article. With another page from that damn diary. Seems the vic's boss was harassing her after she called it quits with him, pressuring her into sleeping with him. And they claim that she planned on meeting Vince Taylor the night she died. Were you aware of this?'

I wasn't aware of that. Though if she was meeting her lover that would certainly explain why Layla was wearing a skimpy red dress and stiletto heels in the park the night she was killed.

'No, I—'

'Please don't make me take you off of this case, Barnes. I thought you could handle it, but if you can't keep on top of the investigation, I'll be forced to ask someone else to take the lead.'

'I'll keep on top of it, Sir.'

'Good. Please see that you do.'

The Chief waves me out of his office. Once in the hallway, out of his line of sight, I lean against the cold concrete wall and release a breath I didn't realize I was holding. This interview with Thomas Barnett better go well.

*

'Thomas Barnett?' Lanner barks authoritatively as he pounds on the door of Barnett's home. He lives in Park Slope, Brooklyn, a fairly affluent area, in a neat little brownstone across from a quiet park where an old woman sits on a bench tossing bird seed to a flock of greedy pigeons. The Barnetts, Thomas and his mother Gwendolyn, according to Stu, occupy the entire three-story home. It must be worth a fortune.

'NYPD, please open the door,' Lanner tries again.

'Just a moment,' a sing-songy voice replies before a petite blonde woman pulls opens the front door. Her slender frame is wrapped in an emerald green sundress, which perfectly accents the deep green hue of her eyes, and gold earrings dangle from her ears, twinkling in the sunlight. Her hair is neatly styled and she smells of expensive perfume. I like her on sight.

'What can I help you with, Officers?' She smiles kindly, a warm smile that reaches her eyes.

'We're Detectives Allison Barnes and Jake Lanner with the NYPD and we were hoping to speak with Thomas Barnett about a young woman who was killed recently.'

The woman seems genuinely shocked. 'Thomas is my son, but I'm certain he doesn't know anything about a … murder. He would have mentioned …'

'If it's all the same to you, we'd still like to speak with him if he's available.' Lanner turns on his most charming smile.

'Oh, yes, yes, of course,' the woman falters. She reacts to him the same way she might a lost puppy. The instinct to help him is almost immediate. *That's some trick*, I think to myself.

'Please, come in,' the woman continues. 'I'm Gwen, by the way. Take a seat and I'll go fetch Thomas for you.'

'Works like a charm,' Lanner whispers to me, a conspiratorial grin on his face, as Gwen escorts us into her living room.

She directs us to a cream-colored leather sofa while she walks toward the back of her house, presumably to find her son. The fabric is cool and as smooth as butter beneath my fingers. I look around the rest of the room. It's decorated tastefully in shades of cream and white, and a black and white photo of a horse hangs in a gold frame over the sleek leather sofa we're sitting on. Every surface gleams, and the floors smell of fresh polish. How does she keep this place so clean? Where is the clutter? Josh and I live in such cramped quarters that there is no way to keep the detritus of daily life out of sight. Our tiny kitchen table is used for eating meals, storing our keys, holding our mail, and even as a home office when needed. Someday I'll be the kind of person who owns a couch that doesn't double as a laundry basket and whose countertops sparkle. I'm just not sure when that day might be.

Gwen ushers her son into the room. I notice the way he shuffles his slightly pigeon-toed feet along the hardwood floors, and how he walks with his eyes downcast, as if he's actively avoiding making eye-contact with us. He clearly didn't inherit his mother's easy, affable charm. She glides toward us, chin held aloft, and I wonder if that type of confidence comes with wealth, if knowing that you hold a secure place in the world allows you to move through it with a fluid grace.

'This is my son, Thomas. Thomas Barnett,' Gwen offers.

Thomas looks up briefly, looking first at Lanner, then at me. He picks at the skin on the side of his thumb which already appears red and raw. A nervous habit, most likely.

'Hi, Thomas,' I begin gently. 'We wanted to ask you a few

questions about a young woman who was killed last week. We thought perhaps you might have known her.'

Thomas remains silent, his gaze still avoiding my own.

'Her name was Layla Bosch. Does that name sound familiar to you?'

It takes Thomas a moment to respond, and when he does, his voice cracks and waivers. 'No, not really.' He clears his throat. 'I mean, no, I've seen her name in the papers, but I didn't know her personally.'

'You've never met her before?' I ask, more pointedly.

'No. Never.'

'Well, here's the thing Thomas,' Lanner steps in, his usually gentle voice taking on an authoritative edge. 'We have video footage of you loitering around in front of her apartment on several occasions just before she went missing, and so we think that maybe you did, in fact, know her.'

Thomas looks over at Gwen, whose jaw has fallen open. Thomas's eyes dart rapidly between his mother and Lanner. 'I—'

'Thomas, don't say another word. Officers, unless my son is under arrest, I think we should speak to a lawyer before he answers any further questions.' Her warm, kind eyes have grown stern. A mother bear protecting her cub.

'No he's not under arrest at this time, but—' I begin.

'Excellent, then you can speak with our attorney.'

Chapter 33

Allison

DAY 8

'I guess I came on a little too strong with the kid back at the house,' Lanner says as he rubs the back of his neck and watches Thomas Barnett fidget in his seat in interview room one. Barnett is now flanked by his mother and his attorney, Glen Beringer, who sports a custom-tailored suit over a crisp white shirt. Beringer is no stranger to us; he's a well-known criminal defense attorney, revered for his talent in sending rapists, drug dealers, and murderers back onto the streets. It's clear that Barnett's mother spared no expense in retaining legal counsel for her wayward son.

'He seemed so on edge, I really thought he'd crack at the first sign of pressure,' Lanner explains.

'Probably would have if his mother wasn't there to stop him. You made the right call.'

Lanner nods. His shoulders seem to relax with my reassurance.

'Alright,' I say. 'We let him sweat it out long enough. Let's get in there.'

Lanner and I walk into the interrogation room and close the door behind us. Lanner drops himself into one of the metal chairs across from Thomas Barnett. He leans back causally, his arms crossed against his chest. I sit in the chair beside Lanner, my hands folded on the table in front of me. I know his strategy; I can read it on him without so much as a word exchanged. We know that if Lanner frightened Barnett earlier, he's not likely to open up to him now. The bridge is burned. We expect that Barnett will be reeling during the interview, looking for a kinder, softer, ally. And I'm hoping that will be me.

'Nice to see you again, Thomas,' Lanner says with a grin.

Barnett looks up at Lanner quickly. His eyes darting back to the table in front of him where he continues to pick at the side of his thumb. I notice a bright red drop of blood beading on his pale, white skin. The sight of it makes him shudder.

'Ok, Detectives. Let me say this first,' the attorney, Beringer, begins. 'My client is here voluntarily, to clear his name before you two get carried away and rope him into a murder investigation that he has absolutely nothing to do with. Certainly wouldn't be a first for this department.'

Beringer is a shark, his silver-gray eyes hard and sharp, as he assesses his prey. He is surprisingly decent-looking for a man who is likely nearly twice my age. He has wide shoulders and an imposing stature, combined with distinguished gray hair that sits in a well-trained comb-over. I might look twice if I saw him in a bar. A silver fox with a Rolex on his wrist. But in this room, I can't forget that he is a predator.

Lanner rolls his eyes. I look at him in mock disappointment. 'Ok, Counselor,' I reply. 'We just had a few questions for your client.'

Beringer nods, but he still appears distrustful. I suppose that's his job.

'Thomas, you told us earlier that you didn't know Layla Bosch, is that accurate?'

'Um, yeah, I didn't really know her. Like, I saw her around, but I didn't know her, you know? I never spoke to her or anything.'

'Is this you? Standing outside of her apartment building?' I ask, producing the photo from the CCTV footage.

'Detective,' Beringer interrupts. 'My client is willing to concede that he was in the vicinity of Miss Bosch's residence on more than one occasion. However, as I'm sure you will see on your videos, he never approached her or interacted with her in any way. In fact, he was in a romantic relationship with another woman in her building. The fact that my client sometimes visited that area of Brooklyn and occasionally visited a coffee house surely isn't evidence of murder.'

'They must make a really good cappuccino,' Lanner scoffs. Beringer glares at him.

'About that romantic relationship,' I continue. 'We spoke with Mindy and it turns out that you gave her a fake name and number. Seems sort of counterintuitive if you were hanging out around her building hoping to see her again.'

'I wasn't waiting to see her. I was, I was just getting coffee.' Barnett's voice waivers.

'See, that doesn't make sense to me,' Lanner replies. 'We have video footage of you pacing back and forth in front of the building, sometimes for up to fifteen minutes, before you went to get your little cappuccinos.'

'Maybe he was deciding on his order,' Beringer says with a smug grin. This time it's Lanner's turn to glare.

'I'll tell you what I think you were doing.' Lanner leans forward in his seat now, spreading both of his large hands on the table in front of him. 'I think you were waiting to see Layla. I think you were obsessed with her but you knew she was out of your league. You were too intimidated to approach her, and so you followed her instead. Lurking around her building like some kind of creep. I think you were getting a feel for her schedule, following her, so that you could finally get her alone. And then what happened Thomas? Did you follow her to Central Park? Did she reject you?'

'No, no! It wasn't like that!' Barnett shouts. He looks startled, as if the sound of his own voice took him by surprise.

Beringer places his hand possessively on Barnett's shoulder. A signal that the kid should shut his mouth. 'Nice story, Detective. Too bad it isn't based on any actual facts.'

But Lanner isn't ready to give up. 'Was that it, Thomas? Were you in love with Layla?'

'No!'

'I've seen pictures of her. She was pretty irresistible, wasn't she, Thomas?'

'It wasn't like that!' Barnett looks like he's nearing tears. He's about to crumble.

'So why don't you tell us what it *was* like,' I offer. I'm giving him a chance to tell us what happened to Layla on his own terms.

But he doesn't take it. 'I can't, I … I didn't know her!' Barnett whines. His mother hands him a tissue. The poor victim.

'Then why were you stalking her?' Lanner demands, his voice nearing a roar as his hands press down onto the table in front of him, the tips of his fingers turning white.

'It wasn't her! It was Vince!' Barnett shouts. He falls back into his seat, as though a pressure valve has been released. A balloon deflating before our eyes. His attorney scowls at him. He'll probably be charged extra for trying his patience.

'What was Vince?' I ask gently. Lanner got him to boil over, but now that the weight of his confession is off of his shoulders, we need to take a softer approach to keep him talking.

'It was Vince I was in love with, not Layla. Like I told you, I didn't even know Layla.'

'You knew Vince from when you worked at KitzTech?'

Thomas nods. 'I was an intern there a few years ago. That's where I met Vince. He's, well, have you met him? It's hard to explain. He just has this magnetism, this charm about him.

183

Everyone loves him. And he was so nice to me, even though I was just an intern. A nobody. He made me feel special. And I guess that's when I realized I was … I am …'

'Gay?' I suggest, warmly.

'Yes. I'm gay.' Barnett seems to deflate even further once he says the words out loud.

I glance over at his mother. Her jaw has fallen open once again. A lot of surprises for her today.

'I've never said that out loud before,' Barnett says shyly. 'But I am. I'm gay. And I was in love with Vince Taylor. Maybe I still am. I don't know. I don't think he killed that girl, you know. For what it's worth.'

'You should have told me, sweetheart,' Ms Barnett says. 'Being homosexual, that's nothing to be ashamed of. I would have accepted you and loved you no matter what.'

I momentarily feel a wrenching sadness for this young man who felt like he had to harbor this secret, to hide his own identity. And I'm sure this isn't how he envisioned coming out to his mother. But I can't let the sentiment derail the momentum of the interview. I need to press forward.

'Did something happen with Vince while you were at KitzTech? Is that why you weren't offered a position after your internship?'

'I *was* offered a job, actually.'

Once again Ms Barnett seems to have been taken by surprise by her son's revelation.

'But I turned it down,' Barnett continues. 'I was afraid of the feelings I was having for Vince. It was all new to me then. I didn't know what to make of it. And so I turned down the job hoping these feelings would go away once I was away from Vince. But they didn't go away. In fact, I think they only got stronger after I left KitzTech.'

'How did you come to be outside Layla's apartment then?'

'I'd follow Vince sometimes. I know it wasn't the right thing to do, but I think I was just trying to understand myself. To

184

understand what drew me to him; what it was about him that made me question everything I thought I knew about myself.'

'And you followed him to Layla's apartment?'

'No. But I saw them together a few times. I figured out pretty quickly that they were having an affair. They tried to be discreet, but I knew. It was just the way they were together. The way she looked at him, the way they'd stand a little too close to one another. They were in love. I could tell. And so I just wanted to find out more about her. About what Vince saw in her, about why he'd risk his marriage, his reputation, for her.'

Barnett swallows hard. 'That's why I went to her building. I followed her home from KitzTech one day. That's why I went out with Mindy too. I was just trying to learn more about Layla. But I never approached her, I never even spoke to her, I swear.'

'Oh, Thomas,' Ms Barnett says, wiping tears from her eyes.

'That's really something,' Lanner says. 'But I don't think you're telling us the whole story.'

'I am! I told you everything!' Barnett sounds panicked now. He's desperate for us to believe him.

'See, now I'm thinking you were jealous of Layla. Because Vince wanted her when he didn't want you. Is that why you killed her, Thomas?'

'NO! I didn't kill her! I didn't!'

'That'll be enough, Detective,' Beringer interrupts. 'My client has told you everything he knows, and so unless you have any evidence that puts him with your victim in Central Park on the night she was killed, or, hell, any evidence that he ever even met her, we'll be getting on our way.'

'I just have one last question, Thomas, please,' I implore. 'Where were you the night of August twenty-fourth?'

Barnett looks to his attorney who nods curtly, giving him permission to reply.

'I was at home all night. With my mom. We watched a movie. *The Breakfast Club.*'

185

'He certainly was,' Ms Barnett chimes in. She nods her head in agreement while patting her son's hand reassuringly.

'We'll be leaving now,' Mr Beringer announces. Ms Barnett stands, smooths out her dress, and slings her purse over her shoulder. She lifts her son by the elbow, helping him out of the chair. He seems drained after our interview, a boxer stumbling out of the ring.

Mr Beringer leads his clients out of the room. As he passes, he says, 'Do let me know if you'll be making an arrest. Though I should hope you'd only do so if you find some actual evidence.'

The door to the interview room slams shut behind him.

'Looks like the little creep has an alibi,' Lanner says.

'I'm always suspicious of alibis given by wives or mothers,' I reply.

Chapter 34

Vince

DAY 9

I slowly open my eyes. They're dry and gritty, and my head is pounding. My ankle is too, come to think of it. I probably should have it looked at, but I know I won't. There's no point anymore. My ankle is the least of my problems.

It takes me a moment to remember where I am. My apartment. I have no idea what time it is. Not that it matters. I have nowhere to be. The blackout curtains are drawn and the television murmurs quietly in the background. I must have fallen asleep on the couch at some point.

I sit myself up and my head swims. I'm hit with a wave of dizziness that forces me to fall back down onto the couch. I drag a hand across my face. My brow is sweaty and my chin is rough with stubble. My mouth feels dry and wooly, my tongue like sandpaper. I need some water. I try sitting up again, more slowly this time. I bang my shin on the coffee table, causing an empty wine bottle to fall over with a hollow clatter. That's right, now I remember. I had a few glasses of wine last night. Or, rather, a full bottle it would seem. My mind flashes back to the late hours of the night, and I see myself dumping the last remnants of the bottle into an already brimming glass. No wonder my head feels like it's splitting in two.

I drag myself to the kitchen and pour a glass of water. I take it back into the living room and hit the switch to open the automatic shades that cover the enormous glass windows. I squint in pain as my eyes struggle to adjust to the bright sunshine which now streams into the darkened apartment. Dust motes lazily dance before my eyes in the growing streaks of sunlight, like suspended glitter. When was the last time Marta was here? I need to remember to cancel her cleaning service for this week. I can't let her see the apartment in this state, the overturned bottle seeping blood-red liquid onto the coffee table, my discarded wine glass stained with the sticky rinds of my last glass, my clothes in a rumpled pile on the floor. I can't let her see *me* in this state. It suddenly occurs to me how desperately I need a shower. My clothes, a pair of boxer shorts and an undershirt, smell sour and it turns my stomach.

I look down onto the street below me. People bustle quickly along the sidewalk. Some wearing suits and carrying briefcases, others with skateboards slung over their backs. One man stands at the entrance to Central Park, a hat turned upside down at his feet as he plays the saxophone, eyes closed in rapture, while he tries to move jaded New Yorkers with the sound of his soulful melodies. A small girl tosses some coins into his upturned hat before trotting off down the sidewalk to catch up with her mother who, by all appearances, had no time to slow her pace for something as trivial as music. The world is in a rush. As it always is in this city. As I have been for the last ten years. I used to belong to that world, the one of business meetings, deadlines, and harried importance. But now, I don't belong to any world. I am lost. Marooned. Stranded and alone. Maybe Layla was right. Maybe this apartment is a castle, and I am a prisoner locked away in the highest tower, forced to watch the world move on without me.

Layla. She was the start of all of this. I think of the last time I saw her. Of the words we exchanged, of the rage I felt when I said them. *I want you out of my life.* Not for the first time, I wish I'd never laid eyes on Layla Bosch. She will be my undoing.

I hear the distant sound of a phone ringing. I sprint back towards the couch, tossing the pillows and tangled blankets out of my way. It might be Nicole calling. I haven't heard from her since yesterday afternoon, since I walked out of our home. I'm desperate to hear her voice, and a small part of me is holding out hope that she's calling to tell me to come home, that she's ready to talk to me. I find my phone lodged between two couch cushions and I snatch it up quickly, hurrying to answer it.

'Hello?' I answer desperately.

'It's Mullins.' *Right, the private investigator. Of course it wouldn't be Nicole calling.*

'Hi, sorry. Thought you were someone else.'

Mullins grunts before getting on with the purpose for the call. 'Finished looking into that Bosch girl for you. Dropped out of High School at sixteen. Got her GED. No evidence that she ever went to college.'

Most of what I knew of Layla turned out to be a lie. I think back to the last words Layla's mother said to me: '*If you're involved with Layla you better be careful.*' What was she trying to tell me? What kind of trouble was Layla caught up in? What was she running from?

'You still there?' Mullins asks, pulling me from my thoughts.

'Yeah, I'm here.'

'I was sayin', there's hardly any trace of this girl. In my experience, those are the people who don't want to be found.'

'Thank you again for looking into it. I appreciate the help.'

'Bill is in the mail.' He ends the call as abruptly as he does everything else.

I boot up my laptop and cringe as I check in on the *World View* website. I exhale with relief as I search for my name and find that they haven't printed anything new about me today. I click on one of the old articles, the first one reporting on Layla's death, and stare at the photo of Layla. Her thick hair shines in the midday sun, her smile is bright and warm. She was young, beautiful, and full of life. *But who were you, Layla? Who were you really?*

My e-mail inbox pings with a new message. It's from Darren. I remember now that he tried to call me a few times yesterday, but I ignored the calls. I was well into my bottle of wine by then, lamenting the damage I've done to my marriage, and I couldn't deal with Darren too. I click on his e-mail now, my stomach already in knots.

Mr Taylor,

The Board is saddened to have to deliver this news to you, but in light of the continuing negative media attention surrounding you at this time, KitzTech finds itself in a precarious financial situation. In the best interests of the company and its investors, we have, unfortunately, voted that you will need to resign as CEO of KitzTech effective immediately. We did not come to this decision lightly, but we feel that it is a necessary action in order to prevent any further financial losses.

That being said, we appreciate the years of service and dedication you have put into KitzTech, and we will allow you to retain your financial stake and shares in the company, as a silent investor. We hope that you will continue to serve as a valued shareholder, but we cannot allow you to continue to serve KitzTech in a public role at this time.

Sincerely,
Darren Hamish
CFO, Board of Directors

My company, my life's work, ripped out of my hands in a few type-written lines. The bottom has officially dropped out of my life, and yet, I feel numb. Perhaps the impact of what's just happened, the complete overhaul of the landscape of my world, has not yet set in, or perhaps it's because I've already lost something far more valuable than my company: my relationship with Nicole.

For years I've prioritized work over my home life. I built KitzTech into an empire while I let my marriage wither on the vine. When Nicole needed me most, while she was struggling with the grief of our infertility, I turned to work to bury my own grief. In a way, throwing myself into my job was my way of coping with my own sadness, but I should have been there for Nicole. I should have taken time away from the office, Nicole should have been my priority. But I was arrogant, foolish. I took our marriage for granted, and I trampled on the vows I once made to her. It wasn't until both my company and my marriage were hanging in the balance that I realized how much more she should have mattered.

I delete Darren's e-mail without responding. I cannot find the energy to form the words, or maybe there's just nothing left for me to say. I am no longer the high-powered CEO, the ruthless businessman, that I was just a mere week ago. That man wouldn't even recognize me right now.

But I need to save any fight I have left in me for Nicole. I may not have been the best husband to Nicole, in fact, I've been a rather abysmal husband of late, but I will not give up on her now. Someone is targeting me, systemically destroying my life and hers. I owe it to her to put a stop to it. I need to focus.

I walk into the master bathroom and turn on the waterfall shower. An image of Layla in this very shower, the warm water trickling down her smooth skin, pops into my mind unbidden. I shake my head as if I can loosen the memory from my mind.

I step into the shower and let the water cascade down my back, washing away my hangover. I spread the shampoo through my hair, massaging it deeply into my scalp, and my mind slowly starts to slide back into focus, like the twist of a photographer's lens. I need to think about who has the most to gain by ruining me and the life I've built. Who would benefit the most by making sure I take the fall for Layla's death?

My first thought is Darren. He's coveted my position as CEO for years now. But how badly did he want me out of the corner office? It dawns on me for the first time that he may have known about my affair with Layla. We thought we were being discreet, but in hindsight maybe it was obvious. I know Eric saw us arguing at that happy hour event, maybe he put the pieces together: the late nights, the long lunches, the impromptu 'meetings' that never found their way to my schedule. He could have told someone about his suspicions and the rumor spread through the KitzTech office like the roots of a poisonous tree.

And then again, there's Jeff. I cannot shake the feeling that he has feelings for Nicole. And it seems too coincidental that *World View* suddenly started receiving anonymous tip-offs just after I confessed the affair to Jeff. Plus, I still think that may have been him lurking around Nicole's studio in the woods the other day. But even if we've grown apart over the years, Jeff was once my best friend. How far would he go to orchestrate the end of my marriage?

Maybe I'm being paranoid. But is it paranoia if someone really is out to get you?

I step out of the shower and towel off the rivulets of warm water. I dress in a pair of soft gray sweatpants and a white T-shirt, and as I run my fingers through my damp hair, I can't seem to keep Layla's mother's voice out of my head: '*If you're involved with Layla, you better be careful.*'

I need to find out what Layla was involved in; what trouble may have followed her to my doorstep. It may be the key to everything, to saving what's left of my life.

Chapter 35

Allison

DAY 9

The wheels of Lanner's car hug the winding roads of Loch Harbor. The town itself is built atop a bluff beside a sandy white coastline. The area is densely wooded but as we meander down the tranquil roads, I can see snippets of the sparkling blue ocean below, calm under a clear azure sky. Sailboats bob atop the still, glassy water of the Long Island Sound, and from here they look like a child's toys. I roll down my window and I let the fresh air swirl around me. It smells of dampened pine, tinged with the salt of the sea.

As the ocean wind rushes through my hair, I find myself wondering if Vince Taylor owns a boat. I could picture him lounging on the bow of a yacht, hands folded behind his head, barefoot and carefree. Or maybe he's more of a sailboat kind of guy. He might glide through the Harbor beneath a billowing sail, a living Polo advertisement in white pants and a navy blue knit sweater. He certainly looks the part with his perfect smile, square jawline, and that ridiculous sea-swept hairstyle that seems to be his signature look. I hate that I secretly find him attractive. But then again, who wouldn't? He's double-take handsome. Even if he did murder his mistress …

Although I still have my doubts about Thomas Barnett's alibi for the night of Layla's death, every path we take in this investigation seems to lead back to Vince Taylor. After the most recent *World View* article accusing Vince of sexual harassment, we need to speak with him again. The newest diary page was handed over by Kate Owens, but once again the only prints on it were Layla's. I'm hoping that by showing up at Vince's house we can catch him off guard. Even if we do have to wait for his attorney, he won't be as well-rehearsed as he would be if we asked him to come down to the station on his own terms.

Besides, I need to prove to Chief McFadden that I'm fully investigating the new allegations printed in *World View*. He needs to see that I'm on top of this investigation. It's been over a week since Layla was killed and I still don't have any solid evidence. The clock is ticking before the Chief has had enough and takes this case out of my hands.

'You seeing these houses?' Lanner asks, astonishment in his voice.

'I'm not sure you can even call these houses.'

'Manors then? Estates? Whatever they are, they're damn impressive.'

He's right. It seems as though every home we pass is more grand than the last. They're not flashy, boastful, the way some of the newer mini mansions are that have been popping up on the outskirts of New York City. These homes are stately, dignified. Their ivied walls and towering pillars a testament to their distinguished history.

'I think this is it,' Lanner says. He rolls to a stop in front of a wrought-iron gate which stands guard between two stone pillars. The remainder of the property appears to be surrounded by a stone wall.

We climb out of the car and I watch as Lanner presses the buzzer on the intercom box next to the gate.

'I don't think it's working,' he explains. 'Doesn't seem to be connecting.'

'Maybe they unplugged it. Probably sick of reporters banging down their door.'

The intercom suddenly crackles to life, making me jump. We're basically out in the wilderness. I'm a city girl. This is far too much nature for my taste. For all I know, there could be bears wandering around.

'Is someone there?' a soft voice asks through the static of the intercom system.

That must be his wife.

'Yes, we're Detectives Lanner and Barnes with the NYPD,' Lanner replies, leaning into the speaker. 'We're here to speak with Vince Taylor.'

The intercom goes silent. I wonder whether maybe she's disconnected it again.

'Please come up to the house,' the woman continues after a pause.

The great iron gates slide open before us. Lanner and I take one look at the long drive leading towards the house and get back into the car. It's far too hot to traverse the distance on foot today.

Lanner drives up to the house and parks in front of the large wooden doors that stand at the entrance to the house. We unclip our seat belts and find ourselves too stunned to move for a moment. The house before us is incredible. Beyond the fact that it's massive, it is architecturally mesmerizing with its great sloping roofs, numerous balconies, and arched windows. The entire structure looks to have been built from natural stone, making it appear to be at one with the untamed beauty surrounding it. The elderly oak trees, mature pines, and brilliant array of wildflowers seem to show a polite reverence to the astounding house they share their land with.

The door creaks open and a petite woman stands in the enormous entrance. The first thing I notice is her long white-blonde hair that hangs loose over her shoulders. She is slim and graceful, fine-boned and fair-skinned. She is breathtakingly beautiful, an otherworldly creature with eyes like glacial ice. I recognize her from the *World View* photos; this is Vince Taylor's wife.

Nicole Taylor could not be more Layla's opposite. Is that what Vince saw in Layla? Did he stray to the dark and unfamiliar curves of her body? Did he covet the one thing he doesn't have tucked away in his fairytale woodland mansion?

'Come in, Detectives,' Nicole says as she steps aside to allow us to enter into the palatial entryway. My entire apartment could easily fit in the Taylors' foyer. Polished stone floors shine underfoot and a resplendent crystal chandelier dangles from the vaulted ceiling above, the fine crystals glistening like falling snow.

Nicole leads us into a sitting room where white gossamer curtains seem to float from the high ceilings and the morning sun casts a hazy glow. She invites us to sit on a tufted suede sofa which is set before a shiny glass coffee table and two matching accent chairs. A stone fireplace, its grate cold and dormant, sits in the corner, a black and white photo of a young Vince and Nicole on their wedding day on the mantle above.

Nicole perches on the edge of one of the chairs. 'I didn't want to explain over the intercom earlier, but Vince isn't here.'

'When do you expect him back?' Lanner asks.

Nicole shifts in her seat. 'I, um, I don't know exactly. He's … not living here at the moment.' I can see tears rising in her eyes.

'I can imagine this is a difficult time for you,' I say gently. Vince may not be here, but there's no harm in seeing what his now estranged wife may have to say about him. You never know what's going to be useful in an investigation.

'It is.' She nods. 'Those things they're saying about Vince in the papers. It's just awful. Not that I think he would ever … do those things … hurt that girl. But it's been very difficult to see nonetheless.'

'I'm sorry you're going through all of this,' I reply.

'Thank you.' Nicole swipes a stray tear from under her eye.

'Was that how you learned about Vince's … infidelity? In the papers?'

Nicole nods again. 'Unfortunately it was.'

'Wow,' Lanner adds. 'Real nice guy.'

I shoot him a look. We can't push her too hard. If she sees us as the enemy she could easily ask us to leave.

'He is, you know. You may not believe that, but I married a good man. He's made some mistakes, but if you knew him the way that I do, you'd see.'

I walk over to the mantle, Nicole watching me curiously as I cross the room. I study the framed wedding photo more closely now.

'May I?' I ask.

'Sure,' Nicole says.

I gently lift the frame from its resting place. 'This is a beautiful photo, you two look so happy.'

'We were.' Nicole smiles, a look of nostalgia on her face.

Now that she's started talking about her relationship with Vince, I want to keep the momentum going. I want to understand what their marriage was like, whether Vince would have killed his mistress to protect it.

'It was such a beautiful day. We were married on the beach. A small reception with just our close family and friends but that was all we needed.'

I smile warmly.

'Things were so different then. Before all of … this.' Nicole gestures at the grand home around her. It's filled with a quiet, tasteful opulence, all the trappings of a charmed life. 'Not that I'm complaining. I love our home, our lives. I know how fortunate we are. It's just that things seemed so much simpler before. When Vince and I were first dating.'

'What was he like then?'

'Oh, he was wonderful. He didn't have much back then, but he always made sure I knew how much he adored me. It was little things, you know? Bringing me bouquets of wildflowers to the art gallery I worked at, booking little weekend getaways here and there. We'd go wine tasting, or to see Broadway shows. I'm not sure theater was Vince's thing really, but he knew I loved it. He once surprised me with tickets to see *The Phantom of the Opera* because I'd mentioned that I'd never seen the show. He'd made reservations at a delightful Italian restaurant, and booked us a stay at the Heatherly Hotel. I knew it was probably beyond our means, but it meant so much to me that he'd gone to such lengths to do something so special for me.'

Nicole seems calm, almost happy, as if talking about the golden days of her relationship with Vince has awakened something that was long dormant inside of her, and has momentarily whisked her away from her current troubles.

'You two must spend a lot of time in Manhattan now, what with you having an apartment there,' I say.

'Funny, you'd think that would be true, but we really don't. Not unless it's for some sort of obligatory event. Now that we could afford to go to the theater every night, we never do. But I suppose it wouldn't be as meaningful anymore anyway.'

'Your apartment is right across from Central Park, right?' Lanner asks. 'I'm sure it's amazing.'

'It really is lovely. But it's really more of Vince's thing. I never really thought it was necessary that we have a second home. Vince wanted it for nights he had to work late, and I do stay there at times too, when we have to attend certain events, but I was more than fine staying at the Heatherly on occasion. It's just the two of us, you know, children just weren't in the cards for us, and so owning the apartment seemed like far more than we needed.'

'Is that where Vince is staying now?' Lanner risks.

Nicole's shoulders tense. Her eyes snap up to meet mine, as if she's only just remembered who she's talking to, why we're here. The time for nostalgia has ended.

'Oh, I … should I be talking to you about Vince? I didn't even think, I … I guess I got carried away … maybe I should call Jeff, Vince's lawyer …'

'There's no need,' I assure her. 'We came to talk to Vince, but since he's not here, that's quite alright. We can get going.'

'Alright, I'm … right, okay, I'll show you out.'

Nicole stands up quickly. I may have gotten her talking about her husband, but now the spell has been broken. I know we won't get anything further from her today.

Nicole escorts us to the front door and pulls it closed behind us.

'Well that was a waste of time,' Lanner grumbles as we climb back into the car. 'Drove all the way out here to find out what a wonderful guy Vince used to be before he started banging his employees.'

'True, but at least we know where he's staying now. I'd bet anything he's at that apartment based on the way Nicole reacted when you questioned her about it.'

*

I essentially fall through my apartment door when I finally get home. The traffic on the way back from Loch Harbor was brutal and we wasted most of the day scowling at the bumpers of the cars in front of us. Well, I did. Lanner seemed happy as a clam singing along to the radio. I don't think he knows he's an awful singer. I've told him many times, but unfortunately he doesn't seem to have believed me.

'Hey, babe, long day?' Josh says as I drop my things on the kitchen table. I may not have all the wealth and fame that the Taylors have, but I do have Josh to come home to. In this moment, I could not be more grateful for that.

'*Very* long.'

'Come over here.' Josh waves me over to the couch where I sit down next to him. He begins to rub my shoulders and I can feel the tension of the day draining away beneath his strong fingers.

'You're amazing, do you know that?' I ask.

'I do, but I'm glad to hear that you know it too.' I can hear the smile in his voice. I don't tell him how much I appreciate him nearly enough.

'Wanna tell me about your day?' he questions.

'The Chief is expecting results on this murder investigation and I spent most of the day sitting in traffic after interviewing a suspect's wife who didn't tell me anything of any use.'

'That sounds awful.'

'Why don't you tell me about your day instead?'

Josh begins to tell me about his day at Lift. He's running a fitness challenge and it's gaining traction. Some minor celebrities have even agreed to help him promote it. He's been putting this together for weeks and I'm glad to hear that it's going so well.

'Wait!' Josh exclaims. 'You have Friend Connect now! You can join the page and see how it's all coming together.'

'I wouldn't even know how to do that …'

'I'll do it for you.' Josh holds out his palm and I hand him my phone. He taps at the screen before handing it back to me.

'There. You're now part of the virtual Lift family,' he says with a grin.

'Happy to be here,' I reply as I snuggle into the crook of his arm. Josh clicks on the television and we settle into a comfortable silence.

Josh wakes me some time later. The television now turned off and the apartment pitch black.

'We must have fallen asleep,' he whispers gently. 'We should get to bed.'

I groan and pull his arm back around me, but he's right, we should sleep in an actual bed.

I make myself get up to brush my teeth and dress for bed. Josh falls into our bed and he's asleep the moment his head hits the pillow. I, on the other hand, am now wide awake.

I pick up my phone looking for something that might distract me until I can fall asleep. I might as well see what this Friend Connect thing is all about. As soon as I login, I see my newest connection: Lift.

I click on the page and begin to check it out. There are screenshots of people's daily running routes (do other people really care about those?), posts about calories burned, and photos posted by the members, taken in Josh's gym. I continue to scroll mindlessly before I see a photo of a familiar face: Officer Matt Kinnon, arm outstretched holding the phone in front of him, ear buds dangling around his neck, and smiling broadly. And standing behind him, looking straight into the camera, is Layla Bosch.

Chapter 36

Allison

DAY 10

That can't be Layla, can it? Maybe I'm just sleep deprived and seeing things that aren't there. I click the photo to enlarge it and zoom in on her face. No, this is definitely a photo of Layla Bosch. I check the date on the photo. It was taken three weeks ago. About two weeks before she died. And so for three weeks, Josh failed to mention that my murder victim was a member of his gym. Surely he's seen her photos in the papers, her face has been everywhere. Why wouldn't he mention it to me? He basically lives at that gym, and let's face it, Layla is hard to miss. Unless … there's a reason Josh didn't want me to know he knew her.

I've been lied to in the past, but I thought Josh was different. I'm not going to be played for a fool. I shake him awake.

'What? What's going on?' he asks, startled and looking around frantically.

'This.' I shove the phone towards him, Layla's photo still on the screen.

Josh squints as his eyes struggle to adjust to the beam of light and information I've just blared in his face. 'You woke me up to show me a photo of Kinnon on the Lift page? I told you when he joined up.'

'No, not Kinnon. The woman behind him.'

'Okay … I'm not sure what you're trying to show me.'

'Do you know who she is?'

'Not a clue.'

'That's Layla Bosch. My murder victim. Her picture has been all over the papers!'

'No shit? She was a Lift member?'

'I wouldn't know, but there's a photo of her inside your gym. And oddly you never mentioned that you knew her.'

'That's because I don't.' I can hear Josh's voice growing defensive. 'And I don't appreciate being interrogated by my own girlfriend in the middle of the night.'

'So you don't know her then? Even though she's in *your* gym.'

'No, Allison. I don't know her. Do you have any idea how many members we have? I couldn't possibly know all of them. I can tell you that she's not one of my regulars, but if she came in a few times here and there, well, I probably wouldn't have noticed.'

'Look at her, Josh. Of course you would have noticed her.'

'It's starting to feel like I can't win this argument. I didn't know her, okay? That's all I can tell you.'

Josh snatches his pillow off of the bed and stalks off towards the living room.

'Where are you going?'

'To sleep on the couch.'

'Why?'

'Because, Allison, you're treating me like some sort of suspect. I thought you knew me better than this. I thought you'd know that I'd never hide things from you. I've never given you any reason not to trust me, but still you didn't even give me the benefit of the doubt,' he says exasperatedly as he walks out of the bedroom. 'I know you've had it rough in the past, but if you can't find a

203

way to let me in soon, I don't know how we're going to make it.' Josh slams the door behind him.

I sit up alone in bed, pondering whether I should go to Josh, apologize, or whether I should give him space to cool off. He was right, he's never given me any reason not to trust him, and yet I was so quick to rush to judgment. I have a tendency to write people off too quickly, to push them away before they have a chance to hurt me. Over the years I've built up a wall around myself and I think I've forgotten how to let it down. All I know for sure is that I don't want to lose Josh. I don't want to be alone in this bed permanently.

I must have fallen asleep at some point in the small hours of the morning because I wake to the sound of my alarm blasting on my nightstand. I get out of bed and poke my head out of my bedroom. Josh is already gone, his pillow long deserted on the couch. I cringe when I think about the way I behaved last night, the way I accused him of keeping things from me before I even took the time to ask him what was going on. I feel like an idiot. And I owe him an apology. I won't make the same mistake when questioning Kinnon.

*

'Hey, guys, what's going on?' Kinnon asks as he walks into the conference room. Lanner and I asked him to meet with us about the case. I showed Lanner the photo of Kinnon and Layla as soon as we got to the station this morning, and he agreed that we needed to question Kinnon about it. 'Just don't be too hard on the kid,' he'd warned.

'We wanted to talk to you about something, dude,' Lanner begins.

'Sure, what's up?'

'I found this photo on Lift's Friend Connect page.' I hand Kinnon a printed version of the photo in question.

Kinnon laughs. 'Are you guys messing with me? I know taking selfies in the gym is a little ridiculous, but check out those biceps! I had to share that with the world.'

'This isn't about your biceps.' I resist the temptation to add 'you idiot'.

'My shoulders then? Because they're looking pretty jacked too.' Kinnon mocks a body builder pose, his arms curled, his muscles flexed.

'This isn't a joke!' I'm losing my patience now.

'So much for not going hard on the kid,' Lanner mutters to me before turning towards Kinnon. He takes the photo from Kinnon's hand and lays it on the table. 'We're talking about her.' He points at Layla, her eyes dark and haunted in the grainy photo.

'Is that … is that Layla Bosch?' Kinnon stammers.

'Sure is,' I reply. 'And she's standing right behind you at the gym.'

'What are you trying to say?' Kinnon's voice quickly grows angry, defensive.

Lanner steps in to calm the situation. 'We're not trying to say anything. We just wanted to give you the opportunity to tell us anything you may not have told us before. Like, whether you ever met her at the gym, or anything like that.'

'I would have told you if I knew the murder victim on one of our active investigations,' Kinnon snaps. 'A lot of people work out at Lift, you know. Just because she happened to be standing near me doesn't mean I knew her.'

'She's a little hard to miss …' I prod.

Kinnon glares at me. 'And yet, somehow I did. This is some bullshit!' He slams his hands down on the table in front of him.

'Okay, okay, calm down. We believe you,' Lanner says, putting his hands up in a gesture of surrender. 'But we had to ask. I hope you understand.'

'Well if this interrogation is over, I have work to do.' Kinnon pushes his chair away from the conference room table and walks out without a second look at me or Lanner.

'What do you think?' I ask Lanner once Kinnon is out of sight.

'I want to believe him, I really do, I like the kid, but he was acting really defensive just now. Almost cagey. I don't think he's telling us the whole story.'

'I agree. If he'd just said he didn't know Layla, hadn't noticed her in the photo, that would have been one thing, but to explode the way he did … it's suspicious.'

'We'll keep an eye on him. It's all we can do for now.'

Chapter 37

Vince

DAY 10

Today is going to be a better day. I tell myself that, but I don't believe it. It's one of Nicole's things. '*Positive thinking for a positive outcome.*' But I know that more likely than not, today will just be another day in the string of miserable days that now makes up my life. I've lost the love of my life and the company I worked so hard to build. The fact that I no longer have KitzTech to turn to finally hit home last night. That company was my refuge for so many years. It was my constant, a predictable world that was entirely within my control. But now the empire is under new rule and I've been exiled.

My office was my safe haven from the hardships in the rest of my life, and now that I need it most, as my life is completely spinning out of control, it's been torn away from me. It feels so unfair. I steered KitzTech though the roughest of waters, and now that I'm no longer needed at the helm, I've been tossed into the sea to fend for myself. Maybe that's how Nicole has felt all this time, while I gave more of myself to that damn company than I did to our marriage, to her.

My phone rings on the nightstand next to my bed. I roll over and ignore it. I'm in a dark place and I don't want to speak to anyone right now. Except for maybe Nicole, but, of course, she hasn't tried to call. She wants nothing to do with me. I swat at the phone blindly without turning around and I hear it clatter to the floor. At least it's stopped ringing. I close my eyes and hope to fall back asleep.

I know that at some point I'll have to get up and figure out what to do about Layla. I need to find out what kind of trouble she'd gotten herself involved in, what, or who, she may have been running from. But I don't know where to start. Everything she told me about herself was a lie. I didn't even know her, this woman I ruined my life to be with.

My phone rings again. I can hear the vibrations against the hardwood floor, and the screen glows blue in the darkened room. The call ends and immediately starts again. I groan and lean over the side of the bed to check who's been calling. It rings furiously in my hand, Jeff's name on the caller ID.

'Jesus, Vince, where the hell have you been?'

'Sleeping.'

'It's almost noon! What the hell is going on with you?'

'Are you really asking me that? Literally everything in my life is in ruins right now.'

'Okay, well, not to add to the list, but you need to see the *World View* this morning.'

'Fuck,' I mutter as I roll out of bed to fetch my laptop.

'This one is bad, Vince. We can't just ride this one out,' Jeff continues as I wait for the *World View* website to load.

My stomach roils with anxiety, last night's wine sloshing about uneasily. When was the last time I'd eaten a real meal? I can't remember.

When the site appears on my screen, I'm immediately horrified. 'I'll call you back,' I mumble.

'Vince, we need to talk about—'

But I don't let him finish. I've already ended the call and let the phone fall onto the bed beside me. My eyes scan the computer screen but I can barely focus on the words. My head is spinning, my vision going blurry.

Rape Allegations Made Against Vince Taylor
By Kate Owens for *World View*

As first reported by World View, *Vince Taylor (age 39), CEO of the popular technology development company, KitzTech, was allegedly involved in an illicit affair with his young intern, Layla Bosch (age 23), in the months leading up to her death on August 24, 2019.*

World View has now been informed by a source close to the investigation, that this is not the first time Taylor has been under investigation for harming a young woman. In fact, a young girl, whose name World View *has decided not to print in an effort to protect her privacy, filed a police report against the then 21-year-old Vincent Taylor, accusing him of rape. Taylor was investigated but ultimately was not arrested for the alleged sexual assault of the underaged girl, who at the time was only 16. Interestingly, Taylor's wife, Nicole Taylor, is also significantly younger than the media mogul. It seems Taylor certainly has a type.*

This can't be happening. *Shannon.* I haven't thought about her in years. Would she really have gone to the press with the details of our past? I doubt it. And so I have to wonder how *World View* had access to that information. So few people know about what happened between Shannon and I, and I went to a lot of trouble and expense to bury the ancient police reports. The only people I ever told about Shannon were my father, and … Jeff. I never even told Nicole. *Fuck.* She's certainly going to find out now.

My phone rings again. I answer it quickly without checking the caller ID, assuming it's Nicole calling about the latest article.

'Hello? Nic?'

'Vince? It's … it's Shannon Hartley, er, Combs.'

'Shannon.'

'I hope it's okay that I'm calling. I got your number from your office after I saw the article in *World View* this morning. I had to pretend I was your groundskeeper needing to get in touch with you about an emergency plumbing repair.'

'That was very clever. It's usually pretty tough to get around my assistant, Eric.'

We both fall silent for a moment. The weight of the past hanging heavily between us.

'I just wanted you to know that it didn't come from me, the things in that article. I never told a soul about what happened between us all those years ago. My husband, my kids, they have no idea. And I never wanted them to. I'm so sorry I've put you through all of this.'

'It's not your fault, Shannon. You were just a kid.'

'No, Vince. I wasn't, not really. I knew what I was doing was wrong. That article, it made it sound like you're some kind of predator. It was never like that.'

'I know.'

'This *is* my fault, Vince. You met me in a bar, I lied to you about my age, you had no way of knowing I was … sixteen.' She says this last word at nearly a whisper. 'I shouldn't have lied to you. But even worse, when my parents insisted on pressing charges for statutory rape, I should have stopped them. But I didn't. I was so afraid of getting into trouble, that I never told them the truth. I didn't tell them where we met, and that I had lied to you about my age. I let them think you were the bad guy, that you'd pressured me, but you didn't, Vince. You were never anything but a gentleman to me.'

'Shannon, I don't blame you for any of this. Sure, I was upset with you at the time, but we're both adults now, and I understand that you were just a kid then. You aren't to blame.'

'I am, though. I never told you the whole story. And I'm so sorry that I didn't. But I want to tell you now. My parents found out that I had started taking birth control without their knowledge. They assumed I must have been sexually active, and they were right. I'd just broken up with my first boyfriend, Greg, when I happened to meet you at the bar that night. I was devastated over Greg leaving me after I'd lost my virginity to him. I thought you were cute, and that maybe an older, more mature man, wouldn't break my heart like my high school boyfriend had. But I knew you wouldn't be interested if you knew how young I really was, so I told you I was 19. Anyway, when my parents confronted me about the birth control, I didn't want to tell them I'd slept with Greg. They knew his parents and I was afraid they would humiliate me and call them. And so when they put me on the spot, I blurted out that I'd slept with you. I wasn't thinking, and as you know that wasn't even true. We did nothing more than kiss and hold hands during a scary movie. I thought that since my parents didn't know who you were they would just ground me and that would be the end of it. But they kept badgering me about who you were and where we met, and when I finally told them you were twenty-one, they immediately dragged me to the police station. I didn't realize at the time how much trouble the age difference would get you into. I let everyone think that I was an innocent victim when I knew that I wasn't. But I'm going to make this right.'

'You already did all you could. You recanted your statement back then. You told the police that we were never … together … sexually, and the charges were dropped. That must have taken a lot for you to stand up to your parents like that, and it cleared my name. I was never charged.'

'And yet, you're still dealing with the repercussion of my actions. I'm going to make a statement explaining what really happened back then. I'll go to the press and tell them the real story, and my role in it. I'll tell them about how I lied to you, and to the police. I'll say you never touched me in a sexual way,

211

which is why I recanted my story, and you shouldn't be held accountable for the consequences of my actions.'

'I appreciate that, Shannon, I really do, but I can't ask you to do that. The tabloids will print your name and then all of this will be out in the open. For you. For your family.'

'I don't care anymore. I want to do this. I need to.'

'Thank you, Shannon. Really.'

I end the call and fall back into the bed, draping one arm over my eyes. Shannon's statement might sway a few minds, but, like Jeff said, you can't unring the bell. Once the information is out in the world, there is no way to rein it back in. The world will have already made up its mind that I'm a monster preying on young women.

I have to talk to Nicole. I have to explain that what was printed in the *World View* article isn't the real story; it's not what it seems. I want to tell her what happened with Shannon in my own words, the way I should have from the beginning.

I quickly shower and dress. I need to get to Nicole.

I race down to the parking garage and start the Tesla. For once, luck is on my side and the traffic out of the city and into Connecticut isn't too bad today. My fingers drum impatiently on the steering wheel as I cross over the state lines and rehearse exactly what I'm going to say to Nicole to make her see that this was all a big misunderstanding.

I'm well into the imaginary conversation with my wife when my phone rings. The car's Bluetooth system picks up the call and asks, in its calm robotic voice, if I 'would like to accept a call from Nicole Taylor'. *Yes. Yes I would.* I know she may be angry with me, especially if she's seen the latest news, but I can't help but feel relieved that she's finally calling. At least it's an indication that she's willing to talk to me about it.

I can hear Nicole sobbing the instant the call connects. 'Vince, I … you need to … I'm …' The panic in her voice echoes through the car.

'Nic, I can't understand you. You need to calm down and tell me what's going on. Is this about the article?'

'It's … I can't … you need to come home. NOW.'

'I'm already on my way. I'm about five minutes out from Loch Harbor. I'll be there as soon as I can, Nic. Just hold on.'

I don't know what exactly has her so upset, but she's said all she needs to. Nicole needs me and I'm coming as fast as this car will take me. I thought she'd never need me again.

I jam on the accelerator jerking back in my seat as my tires screech against the warm asphalt. I whip around the familiar curves of the roadway leading into Loch Harbor, the wooded landscape blending into a blur of green outside my windshield. I round a tight turn kicking up a spray of gravel into the woods along the road, the car swerving to steady itself. I will myself to slow down, telling myself that I'll be no good to Nicole if I careen off of the road before I reach the house.

I finally reach my front gates after what feels like a lifetime, but was likely just a matter of minutes. I pound on the steering wheel as the gates slowly slide open before me. As soon as they open wide enough to fit the car, I push through, scraping my side mirror along the metal gate.

I race up the driveway and throw the car into park outside the front door. I clamber out of the car and I'm about to run up the front steps, when movement in the woods adjacent to the house catches the corner of my eye. I whip around to find out who, or what, is on my property, when I see a familiar figure: a man wearing a black hoodie, the hood pulled tight over his head. I can't see his face, but I'm fairly certain this is the same man I chased off of the property a few days earlier, the man who was spying on Nicole in her studio. Is this what has her so upset? So frightened? Did she see a dark and shadowy figure outside of the house and call to me for help? I will not let her down this time. I will protect her, protect our home. I won't let him get away again.

I sprint toward the man, who starts to run into the woods. My ankle is screaming at me to stop, but I'm not listening. I'm blind with rage and I have my target in my sights. I run after him as quickly as I can, ducking under tree branches and leaping over the patches of dense undergrowth. The man briefly looks back at me, his face nothing more than a quick blur, but he must see that I'm gaining on him because he begins to run even faster. I can feel my legs pumping, my heart pounding. I'm gaining on him now, I can hear both of us breathing heavily, one of us with fury, the other with fear.

The hooded figure stumbles on an exposed tree root and is forced to slow his pace. This is my chance. I spring off of my injured ankle and lunge towards him. I grab him by the waist and wrestle him to the ground. I pin him underneath me as he covers his face with his arms to protect him from the blows that he must know are coming.

I raise my fist into the air and prepare to strike a man for the first time in my life. I've never been a violent man, but right now I cannot stop what he has set in motion. I'm driven by a primal need to protect what is mine. I land the first punch striking him in the side of the head. He moves his arms to protect his injured temple, and I hit him again, this time my fist colliding with his jaw. The man is yelling something, but I cannot hear what he's saying. Blood is roaring in my ears, I am no longer in control. I hit him again, a sickening crack, as blood begins to trickle from his nose.

The sight of the deep red blood snaps me out of my rage-induced trance and I let up just long enough to hear him shout: 'Stop! NYPD!'

Chapter 38

Allison

DAY 10

What the hell was he thinking? I keep replaying the events of the morning over and over again in my head; pulling up to Vince Taylor's house to find him on his doorstep, his arm protectively wrapped around his wife's shoulders.

'You need to arrest him!' he ordered, pointing across the drive to Kinnon who sat on the curb, shoulders hunched over with blood dripping from his nose. 'I found him sneaking around my property, spying on my wife. And it wasn't the first time either!'

I looked over at Kinnon. 'Is this true?'

'I wasn't spying on his wife, I was—'

'Actually, maybe it's best if you stop talking for now,' I directed, holding a hand up to stop his words.

'I want to press charges against him for trespassing,' Vince continued. 'I've already placed a call to my attorney.'

'We'll handle it, Mr Taylor.'

I scowled at Kinnon. 'Get in the car. Now.'

'Aren't you going to handcuff him?' Vince demanded.

'It's not necessary. I assure you that we will look into this incident.'

Kinnon walked to my car, kicking up gravel in the driveway like a sullen child.

'What the hell were you doing on Vince Taylor's property?' I shouted the second the car doors closed behind us. I'd gotten a call from dispatch earlier that morning that one of our officers was involved in an altercation on private property. When she told me it was Kinnon, and whose property he was on, I volunteered to handle the situation myself. I wanted to keep this incident as quiet as possible. But inside the car, alone with Kinnon, I can be as loud as I'd like.

'I want to speak to my attorney first.'

'You have to be kidding me.'

'No. I'm not.'

We drove back to the station in an uncomfortable silence. I was angry enough to wring his neck. I don't know what he was doing on Vince Taylor's property, without any kind of warrant, but he has jeopardized our investigation.

Now he's seated in interview room two, whispering conspiratorially with his disheveled attorney. Kinnon's attorney, Arnold Finch, is a tall, gangly man with scruffy hair and an even scruffier suit. His tie is tucked into his shirt and one of his shoelaces is untied and frayed at the ends. I hope for Kinnon's sake that he's savvier than he appears.

'What the hell was he doing out there?' Lanner asks me as we wait for the okay to enter the interview room.

'I don't know. Wouldn't tell me without his attorney.'

'This can't be good.'

'No. It can't.'

Kinnon's attorney finally pokes his head out of the room and lets us know that they're ready to answer a few questions.

'I'll take the lead,' Lanner suggests, which makes sense given that he and Kinnon have more of an established relationship. I nod in agreement.

Lanner and I sit down across from Kinnon and his attorney. It feels so much more adversarial than our discussion in the conference room only yesterday.

'Kinnon, we just need to know why you were at Vince Taylor's house today,' Lanner begins. 'I'm sure this is all some sort of misunderstanding, but we need to straighten it out before it gets out of hand.'

Kinnon looks over at his attorney who gives him a nod, directing him to answer the question.

'I was taking photos of Taylor's wife.'

'Why in the hell would you be doing that?' I all but yell. Lanner looks over at me raising one eyebrow. I know I was supposed to let him take the lead, but the words seemed to fly out of my mouth before I could stop them. What Kinnon did was just so colossally stupid.

'I wanted to sell them to *World View*.'

I feel my jaw drop, before I quickly close it again, clenching my teeth in anger.

'Why would you do that?' It's Lanner's turn to ask now, but he does so much more calmly than I had.

'I needed the money. I've run myself into a little bit of trouble. I have this gambling debt, and …'

Kinnon's attorney looks over at him. A subtle warning.

'Well, the details don't matter. All that matters is that I'm in debt, and I needed to get out of it. I figured *World View* would hand over some quick cash for photos of the wife.'

'Was today the first time you've done that?'

Kinnon hesitates a moment. 'No, it wasn't,' he finally confesses. 'I went there a few times. The first time I was trying to get a photo of Vince, but he spotted me. I ended up with a picture of Nicole Taylor in a bikini though. It got me a few bucks and held me over for a while. I didn't plan on going back; I was going to find another way to pay off what I owe, but that didn't go to plan. I still had more debt than I could handle, so I tried again to get a photo of Vince a few days ago. But he saw me and chased me off the property before I could get anything. I went back this morning to give it another shot, and well, this time Vince caught up with me. Guy is faster than he looks.'

I'm biting my tongue so hard that I'm surprised I haven't yet tasted blood. I want to scream at him for interfering with our investigation just to make some quick cash, but I agreed to let Lanner handle the questioning and so I have to try to let him do that.

'Did you give anything else to *World View*? Maybe Layla's diary pages?'

'No! No, that wasn't me! I swear!'

'So it was only the photos? You never leaked any other information to the press?'

'Well, I … I … when I couldn't get the photos I needed, I leaked the info about the old statutory rape report. But I swear that was all they got from me. You guys have to believe me!'

'We want to believe you, Kinnon, we really do, but you must know how bad this looks. Especially after we found that photo of you standing next to the vic yesterday.'

Kinnon's attorney looks shocked, his eyebrows in high arches, his mouth forming a perfect 'O'. I assume Kinnon forgot to mention the photo to him, the same way he forgot to mention its existence to us for over a week.

'Look, I recognized her from the gym, okay? I saw her there a few times and, like, of course I noticed her. She was hot as hell. I even tried to talk to her once, but the girl was cold as ice. Wouldn't even give me the time of day. I didn't want to mention it earlier because I didn't want to get kicked off the case. And what does it really matter anyway? It's not like I knew a single thing about her. I didn't even know her name until she turned up dead.'

'It matters because you lied to us. Had you been honest up front, maybe you could have still worked this case, but you weren't. And now we're finding it hard to trust you.'

'Hard?' I finally interject. 'It's more than *hard* to trust you, Kinnon. I'm finding it impossible. First that photo turns up, then you get into a wrestling match with our prime suspect while trespassing on his property, and now we find out that you lied to us about knowing the victim too. It makes me question what else you've lied about. Honestly, I think you have those diary pages too.'

'I don't! Check my apartment if you want to!'

'Whoa now, let's discuss this,' Kinnon's attorney interrupts.

'No, we don't need to discuss it,' Kinnon protests. 'I have nothing to hide. Check my apartment. You'll see.'

*

Lanner and I have been wading through Kinnon's disgusting apartment for hours and have not found anything aside from sweaty socks, balled-up tissues, and cereal bowls with the crusty remains of Kinnon's breakfasts stacked up in the sink.

'I can't believe a grown man would choose to live like this,' I remark as I push some dirty laundry across the floor with the side of my shoe.

'It's really not shocking that he's single,' Lanner replies.

'No sign of those diary pages though. We'll have a team comb through here and see if there are any signs that Layla was ever in this apartment, but I suspect that she wasn't.'

'Kinnon is pretty screwed either way.'

'That's for sure. Chief already pulled him off the case and he'll be suspended while Internal Affairs looks into this mess.'

'Let's get out of here,' Lanner suggests and I'm more than happy to follow suit.

We make our way back to the station, and as soon as I step inside, Chief McFadden calls me into his office.

'This investigation is turning into a complete circus,' he remarks before I even have a chance to close the door behind me.

'I know, Sir. I had no idea what Kinnon was up to.'

'Internal Affairs will be dealing with him. But this is an utter humiliation for this office, Barnes. The press is going to have a field day with it. We need to make an arrest as soon as possible so that we don't look like complete buffoons.'

'Understood, Chief.'

The pressure is on.

Chapter 39

Vince

DAY 10

My knuckles are raw where they collided with skin and bone. I shudder at the thought of what I'd nearly done, of the level of rage I'm capable of. I never knew that I had it inside of me, bubbling and brewing beneath the surface. I nearly killed a man today. Had I not heard him shout that he was a cop … I'm not sure I ever would have stopped hitting him, not until he was a bloody pulp beneath my hands.

Nicole brings me an ice pack and lays it gently over my swollen hand.

'Thank you for coming when I called,' she says gently.

'You don't need to thank me for that. I'll always be here for you, Nicole. Always.'

She nods as she sits down next to me before casting her eyes towards her lap. 'I just don't know where we go from here.'

'I don't either. But I want to figure it out. Together.' I lay my good hand over hers. Her small, familiar hand beneath mine feels like home.

She hesitates a moment before pulling her hand back into her lap. 'I do too. But it's going to take some time for me to get there. I never wanted things to turn out this way, but I don't know how to trust you anymore.'

I choke back the emotion welling up in my throat. I don't blame her for losing faith in me, but it stings to hear her words nonetheless.

'Can you stay? Just for tonight?' she asks. 'I don't want to be alone in this house right now.'

'Of course.' It's a start. At least she still feels safer with me around. And being here, under the same roof as Nicole, gives me hope that there's still a chance for us yet.

'I guess having all of these spare bedrooms will finally come in handy,' she says.

She must have seen the spark of hope ignite and needed to manage my expectation of a fire. She may be ready to share a roof, but not a bed. 'Right. I'll go put some of my things into one of the guest rooms then.'

She nods and leaves me to it.

I walk upstairs to the master bedroom and take the pillows from my side of the bed.

I miss this room, sharing it with my wife. It's painted a bright white and our fluffy white duvet is tucked neatly over the bed. Floaty white curtains frame a picture window that looks out over the glittering pool and into the woods beyond. The only splash of color in the room comes from a painting of blue poppies which hangs on the wall above the bed. I smile as I recall the day I bought that painting.

After I rented my first KitzTech office space, above the art gallery where Nicole worked, I was looking for any excuse to see her again. I knew she was far out of my league, and I was too shy to simply walk up to her and ask her on a date, so when I saw a flyer for an art exhibition to be held at the gallery downstairs, I immediately knew I'd be attending. I put on my best suit that evening and walked into the gallery as nervous as a child on the first day of school. I immediately spotted Nicole chatting to another attendee. She was smiling brightly, a mouth full of perfect white teeth, and her eyes were dazzling even from across the room. I took a glass of champagne from a passing waiter and quickly knocked it back. I thought I saw Nicole looking over in my direction and I didn't want to appear as out of place as I felt, and so I nervously busied myself looking at a painting of some bright blue flowers resting in a glass vase. I knew nothing about art, I still don't truthfully, but that particular painting caught my eye. It was lovely in its simplicity, and the blue of the flowers reminded me of Nicole's incredible eyes.

'It's exquisite, isn't it?' Nicole asked, materializing at my side.

'It is.'

'They're Himalayan blue poppies. One of my favorite kinds of flowers.'

'I'd like to buy it.' I blurted out. I had no idea how much the painting was going to cost me, or how I was going to pay for it, but I knew that I had to have it – that it would always remind me of Nicole, and that I someday hoped to share it with her.

Nicole seemed surprised. 'Oh, I didn't realize you were a collector.'

'I'm not,' I admitted. 'I don't know much about art at all, to be honest. I just find this particular painting to be beautiful.'

'That's so refreshing. That really is the purpose of art, isn't it? To bring something beautiful into our lives? I think many people have lost that perspective in the scrambling to possess it.'

Eight hundred dollars later, I was walking out of the gallery with this painting I could barely afford and Nicole's phone number. It would still take weeks for me to work up the courage to ask her out on a proper date, and a month more still for her to agree to go out with me, but this painting is where it all began.

I shake off the memory of happier times as I walk out of the bedroom we once shared with my pillow tucked under my arm. I toss it into the nearest nondescript guest room before heading back downstairs.

When I reach the kitchen, I see Nicole out by the pool, her feet swishing in the water, rippling its glassy surface.

Maybe I'll bring us some lunch. Maybe we can have a moment of normalcy before I tell her about the Shannon thing. She'll see that I'm not the person the papers are making me out to be, she *knows* I'm not.

I open the refrigerator and pull out some leftover sandwiches wrapped in shiny foil, a bowl of hummus, and some fresh vegetables. Yes, I can envision it now. We'll sit down for lunch, just as we always do, and then I'll calmly and rationally explain what happened with Shannon all those years ago, how it's all been twisted and distorted to look like something it never was. Nicole will understand. She has to.

My mouth is watering as I collect the food and my stomach rumbles in anticipation. I haven't eaten a real meal in days.

I grab the platter of food, and some plates and silverware, and I bring them out to the patio. The pool is shimmering under the scorching sunlight, the cool water luring me to its edge, begging me to dive in. Maybe if lunch goes well, we might even go for a swim afterwards. I smile to myself. Yes, there may be hope for Nicole and I yet. I won't give up on us.

Nicole turns around and rises from her seat by the pool.

She looks at the meal I've brought us, at the places I've begun setting at the table, and I see the corners of her mouth fall.

'Vince, I don't know what all of this is about but—'

'It's about lunch. I thought maybe we could eat, talk. Have a start at setting things right between us.'

'Look, I appreciate what you did earlier with that … man. But just because I need you here tonight doesn't mean I've forgiven you.' There is no anger in her voice anymore. There is no more fight left in her, only hurt, only the hollow sound of a broken woman. 'What I read in *World View* yesterday, about that girl, Vince, that's unforgivable.'

'That's what I wanted to talk to you about!' I feel the words falling out of my mouth, a desperate jumble. 'I can explain—'

'Right, Vince. I know. You can always *explain*. You're never to blame. Everyone is lying except you, right?' Her words are barbed with sarcasm. 'But the thing is, Vince, I don't even know when you're lying anymore. I used to be able to tell, know you. You couldn't even get away with telling me you got caught in traffic when you'd come home late. I always knew when you'd really just lost track of time and forgotten to leave your office on time. But now, *now*, I find out that I never really knew you at all.' She hugs her arms around herself. 'That last article, it changed everything.'

'This is all wrong. Nothing ever happened between me and that girl back then. Her parents thought it did, and they made me out to be some sort of *predator* and—'

'The same sort of predator Layla accused you of being.' Nicole's words seem to hover in the air between us after she speaks them. The evidence is damning. I know it is.

'But I guess she was lying too, Vince?' Nicole asks. It's spoken as more of a statement than a question. She's made up her mind about me. She's lost her faith, her trust, in me, and I don't know how to win it back.

My wife looks at me now, her pretty blue eyes locking on mine. It feels as though she's looking right through me, as though she's searching for the man she once knew, hoping, and failing, to find him there. It feels like a stab to my heart to see how far I've fallen in her eyes.

My mind races to find the words, the perfect words that will clear the fog of doubt that's formed between us, that will allow her to see the truth, but I can't. 'Nic, I … I …'

My phone begins to buzz in my pocket.

I ignore it. Now is not the time.

But Nicole must have heard the buzzing too. 'Shouldn't you see who's calling?' she asks.

'No, we need to talk about this.'

'But what if it's the police? What if they have more questions about what happened here this morning?'

I sigh and pull out my phone. It's Eric.

'Hey, Eric, this isn't a great time.'

'I think it might be urgent. Some guy named Robert keeps calling the office asking for you. He said he knows something important. About … the investigation.'

'Give him my cell number.'

Eric ends the call and within a matter of seconds my phone begins to ring again. An unknown number.

'Hello?'

'Is this Vince Taylor?'

'Yes, it is. Who is calling, please?'

'My name is Robert Henderson. And I just needed to ask you: Was it really her? Natalie?'

'Natalie? I'm afraid I don't know anyone by that name.'

'That girl in the papers. The one they think you killed. I knew her too. Except she told me her name was Natalie.'

Chapter 40

Layla

BEFORE

Vince Taylor. God, he's perfect. I remember the first time I saw him, staring back at me from the cover of *Forbes* magazine. Its glossy pages full of privilege and promise; advertising the kind of life I'd never lead – not without someone like Vince Taylor on my arm. I ran my fingers over the edges of his face, his strong jaw, his kind eyes, his half-cocked smile.

No, he wouldn't be like the others. Vince was different, special. But to make this work, it was going to take a hell of a lot of planning. And that's fine. I've never been one to shy away from a challenge. Even though I never finished high school, I've always had the uncanny ability to learn anything I need to survive rather quickly. It's not like I had a choice. It was either learn on my feet or end up like my mother. I was meant for more than that. I was getting out of that basement apartment one way or another. And so I became a chameleon, changing my colors as needed. I've been a waitress, a real estate agent, an executive assistant, and most recently a 'sales representative' hocking used cars. Frankly, the job felt a bit beneath my intellectual abilities, but it served its purpose. Every morning I plastered on a fake smile and pushed those dilapidated clunkers on the middle-class dolts who would probably never be able to afford something new and shiny. They had to settle for the unsightly castoffs of the upper class. That will not be me. My life will be different, because I will make it so. I'm not lacking for ambition, and I'm willing to put in the work to get to where I want to be.

I'm not perfect though. I can admit that. After I saw that photo of Vince, I became a bit obsessed. I began to envision my life as Mrs Taylor. I read pretty much everything there was to read about him, his company … and his wife. She was always on his arm. His frigid ice queen, smiling stiffly as if she didn't appreciate that she was standing on a red carpet in a designer gown. I bet she never wore the same one more than once. She probably tossed them aside, as unceremoniously as used tissues. I'd do things differently, better. I'd appreciate my unlimited bank accounts and trips to the Mediterranean on my private jet.

But all of this daydreaming of a better life kind of got in the way of my plan with Robert Henderson. *Robert Henderson, Henderson Used Cars, nice to meet ya.* God, he was an imbecile. A caricature of an actual man. A nobody outside of the nowhere town in the middle of Ohio where he owned his used car 'empire'. The commercials alone, the low-budget homemade embarrassments that they were, should have been enough to send me running towards something better. But I suppose he was a stepping-stone in the right direction. He was practice for the real thing. You can't just go after a man like Vince Taylor without a little practice. Yes, that's what Robert was. A test run. I shouldn't be too hard on myself, that thing with Robert was my first long-term plan. He was the first one that was supposed to be more than just a quick cash-grab to get me by, to the next city, to the next man. And I was doing alright out of it until I got too distracted with Vince.

I started getting sloppy, impatient. I pushed Robert too hard and he started to panic. Worried that his fat, frumpy wife was catching on to our affair. I had to resort to blackmail, which, though it wasn't my original plan, worked quite well. All I had to do was sleep with that doughy, middle-aged idiot one last time, make sure I got it on tape, and before I knew it he was draining his pathetic bank account, basically shoving his life's savings at me hand over fist if I promised not to share it with the world. I didn't get as much as I was hoping for, but I wasn't in a position to be picky. Anyway, it was enough to get me to New York and cover my rent in a shitty apartment for a few months while I figured out how to get myself a job at KitzTech.

That part was a stroke of genius, if I do say so myself. These college kids, they're so eager to please. All I had to do was create a fake job listing for a 'Prestigious software development company, offering a competitive compensation package' and the résumés and transcripts came flying into my inbox. I guess all that money spent on higher education doesn't actually make you any brighter. After that, I just had to sit back and decide who I was going to be. I chose a transcript from someone named Fred Mattherson: software engineering major at the University of Pennsylvania who did well enough in his classes to make me look like a competitive applicant, but not *so* well that anyone would think to double check that my achievements hadn't been exaggerated. It was perfect.

My only hesitation was that I'd have to use my real name this time. I'd never done that before. But KitzTech, unlike Henderson Used Cars, was a legitimate corporation that might run a background check. It was a risk, but it was for Vince Taylor, so I had to take it.

And would you believe it worked? They actually offered me an internship. It was a lot of work learning the basics of computer programming on my own, on my crappy, second-hand laptop, but it had to be done. I had to know enough to get by. I didn't have to be the best, my programming skills were not exactly how

I planned to impress Vince, but I had to be decent enough not to be fired before I could put my plan into action.

Now that I had a spot at KitzTech, I set my sights on learning everything I could about Vince Taylor. I needed to know how to get to him. I'd already read everything I could dig up on the Internet, but I needed more. I needed to know who he was as a person, what was going to have him groveling at my feet.

I signed up for Date Space thinking maybe I could find Vince there. I knew he was married, but let's be real, they're all looking for something on the side. I should know. I've been on the side more times than I care to count. But to my surprise I didn't find him there. Which only served to make me want him more. I do love a good challenge, and it made me think that once I had him firmly under my thumb I wouldn't have to worry about him straying again. Not that I suspect he would. I plan to give Vince everything a man needs to keep him happy. In my experience, all men are looking for a woman who will do the things their wives won't. But he'll soon find out that there's nothing I won't do to be the next Mrs Taylor.

Date Space wasn't entirely useless though. In a stroke of luck, which is a notably rare occurrence in my life, I stumbled across someone named Jeff Mankin. I'm not sure why he was so eager to connect with me. I didn't exactly use the most flattering photo of myself. It was suggestive enough, but you couldn't even see my face. I couldn't risk Robert, or any of the others, catching up with me and spoiling my shot at Vince. But I guess all Jeff needed was a little cleavage and he was sold. I would have ignored him, as I did with every other pathetic slob who sent me Date Space requests, but Jeff had one thing that redeemed him. His profile photo was a shot of him with his arm slung around the very man I was hoping to find: Vince Taylor.

It was pitifully obvious that Jeff's profile picture was nothing more than a thinly veiled attempt to ride the coat-tails of his friend's celebrity. Although one would think he'd realize that standing next to Vince only served to make him look shorter, heavier, and more boring. The lackluster sidekick that no one would have given a second thought to if he wasn't standing next to someone who mattered.

I guess I shouldn't complain too much about Jeff though. He really was instrumental in my efforts to learn more about Vince. It was all too easy. All I had to do was strike up a conversation, stroke his ego for a while (*Wow, you're a lawyer? That's sooo impressive!*) and then subtly start introducing questions about his friend. Jeff was only too happy to talk about Vince. Which made sense, given that his friendship with Vince was basically the most interesting thing about him.

Aside from bragging about how close he and Vince are, all he did was prattle on about his job, his condo on the beach, and his glory days of playing college baseball. Does he really think women want to hear about any of that? Hint: they don't. Or at least I don't. Maybe there is some brainless halfwit out there without a thought in her own head who would be content to twirl her hair and listen to Jeff Mankin blather on about the cases he's won. But I'm not that girl. The only time he managed to hold my attention for more than twelve seconds was when he was talking about Vince, which, thankfully, was often.

He told me all about how they met as kids when they were on the same baseball team. Though Vince outgrew his sporty phase (fine with me as I'd rather not be made to watch football every Sunday once we're married), he and Jeff remained close friends. After a few weeks of chit-chat with Jeff, while somehow managing to avoid actually meeting him (how many migraines can one girl fake?), I had put together a rather thorough cache on Vince Taylor. I knew his favorite restaurants, movies, and books. I knew that he loved French fries and hated mustard, that his favorite color was red, and that he, unlike his friend, was modest about the extent of his wealth, choosing to live a more reasonable lifestyle despite his unlimited means. (Well, we'll make a few adjustments once he's with me.) But more importantly, I learned that Vince longed for children and that his wife has thus far failed to provide them. I knew exactly how I was going make him mine.

But learning about Vince wasn't enough. I also needed to know about his current wife. I needed to know what drew him to her – what he liked in a woman, what was going to make me irresistible to him. Drawing this information out of Jeff was much easier than I anticipated. The man was like an overgrown puppy, wagging his tail, so eager to please in the hopes that I'd someday reward him with an actual date. Or, Jenna Norwell would since that's what I told Jeff my name was. To be fair though, I dangled the prospect of sex like a carrot whenever he seemed to be losing interest. ('*I can't wait to meet you in person. I keep thinking of all the things I want to do to you …*') But when I brought up the topic of Nicole Taylor, he couldn't say enough about her.

I brought it up subtly: 'You and Vince must spend a lot of time together since you're so close. Do you hang out with him and his wife? What's she like?' and Jeff was chomping at the bit to sing her praises.

'Oh, Nicole is incredible. She's brilliant but understated, stunningly beautiful but modest, and just the sweetest, kindest woman you could ever meet.'

I wonder if Vince knows that his friend is in love with his wife. It was pretty obvious to me given the way he was gushing over her. Probably for the best though. Nicole will have someone to turn to when Vince leaves her, and Jeff will probably welcome her with open arms. The information I got from Jeff was precisely what I needed though. Vince is essentially married to a Disney princess. So he likes sweet and innocent? I can do that.

I could probably take a few notes from that boring little mouse, Mindy, who lives in the apartment next to me. She has it in her head that we're going to be 'best friends forever'. She's constantly asking me to hang out. In my real life, I wouldn't give the likes of Mindy a second glance, but for the time being I guess going out with her is better than sitting alone in my apartment. Besides, I do like the extra looks I get when I'm out with her. Standing next to mousy Mindy only highlights how much prettier I am. I think she's noticed it too. Oh well, I'll be cutting ties with her the second I'm with Vince anyway.

I've been at KitzTech for a few days now. I've tried to lie low while I got a feel for the lie of the land – which interns will trip over themselves to help me if I bat my eyelashes a few times, where to get the good coffee, and what Vince's daily routine looks like.

I decided that today is the day. Today is the day I'm going to go introduce myself to Vince Taylor. My stomach is in knots. I feel like a schoolgirl passing a note to her crush, which isn't like me. I don't get nervous. There is no need for nerves when you have a carefully laid plan. But Vince is the big league. This has to go off flawlessly.

I bought a new dress with some of the remains of Robert Henderson's nest egg, and it fits me like a glove. It shows off everything I have to offer without giving away too much. I still look demure, professional … just … genetically blessed. (Which I am.) I went light on the makeup today, making my eyes look as big and round as I could, with some light blush and innocent pink lipstick which matches perfectly with the mani/pedi I treated myself to last night. For the final touch, I sprayed on some sugary sweet perfume and brushed my hair to a high shine. I could definitely pass for a Disney princess.

I smooth my hair one last time and pull open the door to Vince Taylor's office. This is the beginning of everything.

Chapter 41

Layla

BEFORE

(One month later)

I need to get this plan back on track. Progress has been unexpectedly slow, which is shocking given how Vince's jaw nearly hit the floor the first time I sauntered into his office. That dress was worth every one of Robert Henderson's pennies. I expected that Vince would pursue me after that, like the others did. But to my annoyance, he took some more persuading.

It took me two full weeks to get him alone in a room. Even if it was just the copy room. Not exactly sexy, but sometimes you have to play the cards you've got. I decided to play the damsel in distress, hoping that would catch his attention.

It was clear by then that looks alone were not going to be enough for this one. I knew he was special. Vince was going to take a little extra finesse. He wasn't as shallow as the others who needed nothing more than the most basic carnal fulfillment. No, Vince was smarter, deeper. But I can read people, understand them, well enough to figure out exactly what he needed. Vince needed to be needed. He wanted to be a knight in shining armor, he wanted someone to take care of. As a woman who's taken care of herself for pretty much her whole life, the role of 'helpless farm girl lost and all alone in the big city' was going to take some Academy Award level acting, but I think I pulled it off well.

I had to make up some sob story about being orphaned at a young age and a dead grandmother that never existed. It's not like I was going to tell him about my pathetic, junkie mother. She might as well be dead anyway. For all I know, she might be. But the lie worked. Well, that, plus stealing that little twit Brian's idea for some absurd video editing application. Why must people put their whole lives on the Internet? Sorry, Brian, but it had to be done. Vince needed to see that I was more than just a pretty face; he needed to know that even though I was all wide-eyed and innocent, I wouldn't embarrass him in front of clients if I was the one on his arm.

And before I knew it, Vince was escorting me around Manhattan, taking me to investor meetings and showing me the city. When he suggested *walking* down Fifth Avenue I nearly broke character and asked if he was fucking kidding. Had he seen the heels I was wearing? But, never a quitter, I sucked it up and hobbled down the streets of New York, past the glittering shop windows full of all the luxuries I'd soon be able to own. I placated myself by making note of the most expensive heels, purses, and shining diamond bracelets that I could find knowing I'd be coming back to buy them soon with Vince's credit card.

I thought that was going to be it, that we'd have a beautiful, romantic afternoon, maybe retire to a five-star hotel, or even the penthouse apartment I saw featured in a real estate magazine. But then Vince took me to the Circle Line.

The oversized ferry boat, packed with gawking tourists slathered in sunblock, smelled like low tide and rotting fish. I was with *Vince Taylor*. Why weren't we seeing the city from a private yacht? But once again, I had to endure it, reminding myself not to lose sight of my goal. There would be plenty of time for yachts and penthouses later. I closed my eyes and pretended we were sailing out to a private bungalow over the crystal clear water of the Maldives. I ignored the fact that my feet were throbbing from traipsing all over the city like a peasant, my hair, which I'd gone to great lengths to style that morning, was now a complete disaster, and that my bare arms were shivering in the cold. This doe-eyed innocent act was getting old really fast. But my sacrifices paid off.

Vince soon wrapped me in his jacket, which smelled of lux-uriant, expensive cologne, and all I had to do was look at him after that, and his lips were on mine. God, he's an incredible kisser. Just as I imagined he would be. For a moment, I almost forgot where we were.

The first kiss is always the most difficult. But I generally find that once that barrier is broken down, men, even the ones who once claimed they were most devoted to their marriage, lose all inhibitions. In for an inch, in for a mile.

But that's not how it's been with Vince. For some reason, after the kiss we shared on that dreadful boat, Vince seemed to go out of his way to avoid me. I couldn't let the momentum die. I know how men are: out of sight out of mind. And so, I've made every effort to make sure he sees me in the office. I will not be forgotten about. I've found little ways to touch him, my fingers grazing his as we pass in the halls, finding ways to be alone with him in the copy room or in line at the café, wearing outfits that I knew would catch his eye. I had to dip even further into my savings, but the new wardrobe was essential. I'd made progress with Vince and I didn't want all of this to have been for nothing.

It did work to some extent. Vince hasn't been able to keep his eyes off of me. I see the way he looks at me, desire in his eyes, but I need to take this to the next level. It's been months and I'm getting tired of waiting for him to do this on his own terms. I don't need the guy to fall in love with me, though that would be a welcome bonus. I just need him to sleep with me … Enough times for me to fall pregnant with his baby.

Tonight I'm going to stay late and corner him in his office. Once I have him alone, I'll make sure he gets the message. I'll climb right into his lap if I need to. I put on a new pair of black lace panties this morning, and the fabric feels like silk against my skin. It really is worth the extra expense to own nice things. I've been tingling with anticipation all day, knowing these panties were hidden beneath my skirt, just waiting for Vince. I'm going to do whatever it takes to make sure he sees them tonight, because once he does, I know there won't be any turning back.

Chapter 42

Vince

DAY 10

My hands are shaking by the time I end the call with Robert Henderson. His words swirl in my head now, like echoes from another world. *'She wasn't who you think she was.' 'You weren't the first.'*

I feel as though a curtain has been drawn, a smoke screen cleared, and I am finally seeing Layla clearly for the first time. I can see now how I was drawn to her like a sailor lured by a siren's song, only to find myself dashed upon the rocks. The sweet lies she whispered in my ear were carefully designed to ensnare me, and I walked right into her meticulously laid trap.

My breathing becomes shallow, a pain in my chest grows into a crushing heaviness. I've never had a panic attack before, but I'm fairly certain that I'm having one now. Despite my awareness, my body's physiological response is beyond my control. I gasp for air as I lean against a window frame, gripping it with both hands for fear that if I let go, I will be washed away into nothingness.

The scene outside my window is calm, serene. The natural world unaware of my plight. The late afternoon sun is slowly sinking towards the horizon, a golden haze flooding the forest as the fevered orange sky burns off the last of the day's scorching heat. Rays of sunlight reach through the trees in long shafts like outstretched arms. It is as if the light itself is trying to reach me, to pull me back from the brink, but I am just beyond its grasp, doomed to fade into the shadows.

I sink to the floor, my knees pulled up to my chest, and I let my head fall between them. I feel my breathing slowly begin to regulate, my heart slow its hammering pace.

I need to talk to someone about all I've just learned about Layla. I need to tell someone the truth before it buries me alive. I find that the only person I want to talk to in this moment is Jeff. I was wrong about him, and I feel ashamed for ever having doubted him. It wasn't Jeff who has been lurking around my house, spying on my wife. After so many years of friendship, my loyalty, my trust, should not have been so easily swayed. I owe Jeff an apology, but more than that, I owe him the truth.

*

'Wait, so this guy, Henderson, just called you out of the blue?' Jeff asks, shock evident on his face.

We're sitting by the pool, each of us perched on a sun lounger, a glass of whiskey in our hands, under a brilliant cotton candy sky. The sun is setting into twilight now. The harsh burning orange of the afternoon sky has faded into soft gradations of pink and blue which melt into an ethereal purple glow overhead. Under different circumstances it would be a beautiful evening. I hear the ice tinkling against my heavy crystal glass as I swirl the dark brown liquid inside and wait for Jeff to process what I've just told him. Layla wasn't who she claimed to be.

'Yup. And the story he told me sounded all too familiar. He met this woman, she was going by Natalie then, but it was definitely Layla. He recognized her from her photo in the papers.'

'It makes sense now why there aren't any other photos of her floating around on social media or anything. She was probably afraid to be recognized.'

'I think you're right. But we take photos of all of the interns at the summer barbecue for the KitzTech website. I guess that one was unavoidable.

'Anyway, Natalie got herself a job at Henderson Used Cars. From the sound of things, the company is a pretty big deal out in Ohio. Layla, er, Natalie, probably thought she was catching a big fish. Too bad she didn't know that Henderson's wife was the one that owned their home and the car dealership, having come from family money.

'Regardless, Natalie wormed her way into Robert Henderson's life and then came onto him, making him feel like a million bucks. I haven't seen the guy, but the way he tells it, Natalie was far out of his league and about half his age. He told her he was married and held his ground at first, but after months of working in close quarters with her one thing turned into another.

'He felt awful for having betrayed his wife and tried to end things, but Natalie wasn't having it. She blackmailed him with a sex tape that he had no idea existed up until that moment. She threatened to expose the affair to his wife unless he paid her off. Henderson, knowing he would lose his marriage, his home, and his business if his wife found out about his infidelity, gave her as much as he could scrape together without tipping off his wife, about twenty thousand dollars in cash. Natalie was furious that he didn't have more to give, but he never heard from her again. Apparently he's been living in fear that she was going to turn up demanding more money when her savings ran dry. But then he saw her picture in the papers after my story made the national news, and he knew he had to warn me.'

'Do you think Layla was even her real name?' Jeff asks.

'It was. We ran a background check when we hired her. Plus, I met her mother.'

'You, what? When?!' Jeff exclaims.

I tell him about my meeting with David Mullins, my trip to Philadelphia, to the basement apartment where I met Layla's mother, and her last words to me: '*If you're involved with Layla, you better be careful.*'

'At the time I thought she was warning me that Layla was in some kind of trouble, but now I understand that she was warning me that Layla *was* trouble.'

'Vince, this is insane! You had no idea what Layla was really up to?'

'I didn't, but I should have. There's a lot I haven't told you.'

I take a sip of my whiskey, the ice melting quickly in my glass. 'The night that Layla died, I told you that I was working late. But that wasn't true. I was … I was supposed to be meeting Layla at a hotel.'

'What about the security records you gave to the police? With documentation of your fingerprints scans at KitzTech?'

'They were falsified.'

'Jesus, Vince …'

'I didn't know what to do. *World View* was already printing all of that garbage exposing the affair before I had a chance to tell the police my side of the story, and by then I thought that if I told them I was supposed to be meeting her at a hotel, they would have crucified me. I knew how bad it would look, and so I tried to cover my tracks.'

'Did you see Layla that night?'

'No, I swear to you that I didn't. She never showed up to the hotel. Which was strange, because she was the one that arranged the meeting. About a week before she … died … I tried to end things with her. She followed me out into the employee parking lot and I told her I was never leaving Nicole and that she and I were through. But Layla wasn't having it. She was irate, screaming

241

at me that I'd regret my decision. At the time I thought that she meant that I'd regret ending our relationship, but now I think it was more than that. I think she was threatening me.'

'How did you end up agreeing to meet her at a hotel?'

'She approached me again two days before she died. She found me in my office this time. I'd been going out of my way to avoid her after the incident in the parking lot. She told me she had something to talk to me about and that it was important, but I wasn't hearing it. I was absolutely furious that she would approach me at the office like that. Someone could have overheard us; people are always coming in and out of my office. I told Layla that she needed to leave and that she was never to call me again. She begged me to hear her out and promised me that she'd leave KitzTech, and my life, if I'd just meet with her one last time in our usual place, the Heatherly Hotel. She said she had something to show me, something I'd want to see.

At the time I thought it was just a ploy to get me into a hotel room so she could talk me into continuing our relationship. She'd become rather clingy in the preceding weeks, unpredictable too, and so I agreed to go because I wanted to keep her happy and quiet. I couldn't risk her exposing my infidelity. But now, I'm thinking that maybe she wanted to meet with me because she was planning to blackmail me, the way she had with Robert Henderson.'

'If the cops ever figure out that you falsified those security records, it's going to be real bad, Vince. We're going to need a backup plan. We'll need to prove that you were at the hotel all night, and not wandering around Central Park killing off your mistress. Did you use a credit card? Order room service?'

'No, I was trying to keep a low profile. I used a fake name, paid cash.'

Jeff lets out a disappointed sigh. 'I'll scope it out and see if they have any CCTV cameras on site that might have picked you up. But a swanky place like that gets a lot of high profile guests, so I'd doubt it. You should have told me all of this sooner, Vince. Not just as your lawyer, but as your friend. I would have helped you through this. Why didn't you come to me?'

This is the part of the conversation that I've been dreading the most. It was difficult to tell him the truth about Layla and where I was the night she died, but telling him that I lost my faith in him is going to be even harder.

'I didn't know if I could trust you. I think I became a little paranoid with everything going on. I was convinced that you had feelings for Nicole and that you may have been working against me.'

Jeff, the attorney with the quick tongue who always has something to say, grows silent. And I've known him long enough to know that this means there's something he doesn't want to tell me.

'I *was* just being paranoid, wasn't I?' I ask.

'I never did anything to come between you and Nicole, Vince. And I never would. You're my best friend and I'd never do anything to hurt you. But I also can't truthfully tell you that I've never felt anything for Nicole. Since the first time you introduced her to me, I've had something of a crush on her. Can you blame me? She … well, she's incredible … beautiful, smart, kind …

'I think I was a little jealous when you two found each other. It wasn't just because it was the end of our bachelor days, but because as much as I talk a big talk about loving my no-strings-attached lifestyle, I wish I had someone like Nicole to come home to at the end of a long day.

'I know I've told you this before – you're so lucky to have her, Vince. But what maybe I haven't told you enough, is that she's lucky to have you too. You may have made mistakes, I don't think either of us will deny that, but at the end of the day you're a good man and the best friend I've got. If anyone deserves someone as amazing as Nicole, it's you. I would never, ever, do anything to jeopardize what you two have together.'

'Thank you for being honest with me.' Jeff may have just admitted to having feelings for my wife, but I feel closer to him than I ever have. For the first time in a long time, we've both laid our cards on the table. We've confessed our darkest truths, and I feel as though I can trust him again, the full and complete way I did when we were kids.

We both take long gulps of our drinks, pulling the last watery remains from our glasses.

'You want another round?' I ask.

'No, I think I should call it a night,' Jeff replies as he pushes himself up from his chair. 'I'm glad you told me the truth. Let's just hope Henderson was wrong and that Layla doesn't have any other surprises in store for you.'

Chapter 43

Layla

BEFORE

I'm losing him. I can feel it. Something changed in Vince after the night we spent together in his penthouse.

That penthouse … wow, it was amazing. Unlike anything I've ever seen. All polished marble and arched windows overlooking Central Park. And that's only his *second* home. The moment I passed through the red velvet ropes and stepped into the building, I could almost feel what it would be like when this was all mine. The doorman would greet me every morning, '*Good morning, Mrs Taylor, shall I have your driver bring the car around?*' as soon as I stepped out of the private elevators which only services the most elite of the residents. I could all but hear my designer stiletto heels clicking on the shining stone floors as I'd make my way through the lobby, onlookers unable to take their eyes off of me, wondering who I was and how I'd gotten so lucky.

But the fantasy is starting to fade, growing hazy around the edges. Vince has been so distant these last few weeks. The only reason I could imagine for the sudden change of heart was that his damn maid walked into the apartment while I was in the shower. I don't know why he made such a fuss over it. It wasn't like she'd seen me or anything. And even if she had, she's the help. It's not her place to judge. When I'm in charge, letting Marta, Mary, whatever her name is, go is the first order of business.

That is, if I'm ever in charge. I have to admit, Vince is not making it easy for me to get back into his good graces. Which is rather unfair considering *he*'s the one that forgot to cancel the maid. Why should I have to pay for his mistake? I've tried everything I could think of. I wore my sexiest outfits into the office (which everyone except Vince seemed to take note of), I sprayed on that sickeningly sweet perfume he's so fond of, and I've been abundantly clear that I'm available for whatever … needs may arise. But he hasn't taken the bait.

I tried that thing with Adam too. I thought that maybe if Vince saw me with another man it might reignite the fire between us and thaw the growing coldness I've been feeling from him. It *was* rather brilliant. Although at first Vince acted like a child pretending he hadn't seen me sitting at the bar with that dumb hunk of a man I'd found online, I knew that he had. He seemed distracted during his meeting, unable to take his eyes off of me in my new red dress. He was basically green with envy. And I played it up. Throwing my head back in laughter and touching Adam's arm, as if that oaf had anything even remotely interesting to say. Vince looked like he might keel over.

When I saw his client get up from the table, I made my move. I walked straight over to Vince's table and put on my sweet and innocent act, making it sound like it was some kind of unfortunate, awkward coincidence that I'd run into him on my date. (Which, of course, it wasn't. I checked Vince's appointment book when Eric stepped away from his desk. I knew exactly where he'd be that night.) Vince ate it up, and he couldn't call me fast enough once his meeting was over.

I was hoping he'd take me back to the penthouse again, but he did the second best thing and took me to the Heatherly Hotel. I could get used to that kind of five star luxury. The duvet was a fluffy white cloud and the room service, served under shiny silver domes by bellhops in white gloves, was exceptional. And we made love. If you can call it that. It was something more wild, raw. A passion ignited in Vince that I'd never seen before. It was as though all of his inhibitions had finally been lifted. He was a man set free, a beast awakened, and he was ravenously hungry for me.

After a night like that, I was sure we'd be back on track. But to my surprise, when I saw Vince at work the following day, he acted as though nothing had happened. As if I was something that could be used and tossed aside, the way a child might an old, broken toy that he'd grown bored of playing with.

I let it get to me more than I should have. I realize that now. I lashed out, lost control. I wanted to make him feel my pain, to hurt him the way he hurt me. But I think I went too far. I drank too much at the office happy hour. I let my voice grow too loud and Vince freaked out that someone was going to hear us and figure out what we'd been up to. That was really the nail in the coffin. If I'd thought Vince was cold before, after that night, he was pure ice. He wouldn't so much as glance in my direction.

I was forced to corner him in the employee parking lot. It wasn't my proudest moment. I reminded him of how good things had been between us, how good it could be again. I put my hands on his waist, letting my fingers trail towards the zipper of his pants. I envisioned sliding into his sexy black car next to him, and finding another luxury hotel for the night. But Vince wasn't interested in what I was offering, in fact, when I looked up at his face, he looked horrified. I was humiliated. I could feel my cheeks burning.

Vince grabbed me by the arm and pulled me off of him. He got into his car and peeled out of the parking lot as if it was on fire. And to make matters worse, when I turned around, that pathetic intern, Brian, was standing there watching the whole thing. I couldn't be sure how much Brian had seen, so I turned on the waterworks just to be sure he'd keep his mouth shut for the time being. I knew he wasn't my biggest fan after I'd stolen his idea for the intern pitch contest, but I was willing to bet that a decent-looking woman had never given him the time of day before, and if I cried on his shoulder he'd probably do just about anything I asked of him. Brian spotting us wasn't part of my plan, but I guess I can use him to my advantage later if I need to.

Chapter 44

Allison

DAY 11

I lay my head on my desk feeling the cool metal on my forehead. The day's heat is no match for the air conditioning in the squad room. I hear it growling in the ducts overhead, but the soaring temperature outside is clearly winning out.

It's been eleven days since Layla Bosch's body was found and I'm no closer to finding her killer. I know in my gut that Vince Taylor was involved somehow, but I can't seem to prove it.

And that incident with Kinnon has only made matters worse. The pressure is mounting to make an arrest and I've got nothing. My first case as lead detective is a total failure. I won't be surprised if Chief McFadden hands it off to someone else by the end of the day today. But I can't just lie on my desk all day. If I don't have any new leads, it's time to re-examine the old ones.

I gather up my folder on the Bosch investigation and walk over to Lanner's desk. He's busy on a call and holds up one finger, indicating that I need to wait a moment. He knows I'm not the patient type, so he's probably not surprised when I start tapping my foot and pretending to check my non-existent watch as he wraps up his call.

'About time,' I say as he clicks the receiver back down on his desk.

'You're a pain in the ass,' he chides.

'I know. But I want to go over the Bosch file with you. I'll set us up in the conference room.'

'You have anything new?'

'No, and that's the problem. There has to be something here that we're missing,' I reply, waving the case folder. 'There just has to.'

Lanner follows me into the conference room where I spread the contents of the folder onto the table.

We spend the next several hours reading through every last shred of evidence, time and time again. It feels as though all links of the chain are present and accounted for, but we have no way of connecting them.

'Let's go over what we have again,' I suggest.

'Okay,' Lanner begins. 'First we have the coroner's report. He puts the vic's time of death at approximately 9.30 p.m. Cause of death was blunt force trauma to the back of the head. No sign of sexual assault.

'Vince Taylor, who was having an affair with the victim, has an alibi for the evening, and provided security records showing that his fingerprints were scanned at KitzTech headquarters, putting him there from 6.26 p.m. until 10.43 p.m.

'Then we have the report from CSI from the crime scene. According to their report, the blood spatter patterns shows that the vic was struck one time on the back of the head while she was standing on a jogging path in Central Park.

'There is no CCTV in the area of the park where the murder took place. And the only useful CCTV footage we found was from the bodega outside Layla's apartment where we identified Thomas Barnett. He too has an alibi for the night of the homicide, though it was a questionable one given by his mother. And there is also the unsettling fact that he had an obsession with Vince Taylor. I still think he could have killed Layla Bosch out of jealousy because Vince had chosen her over him.

'Then we have the issue of the missing diary pages. We know Kinnon was selling photos to *World View*, and that he knew the victim from the gym, but he claims the diary pages didn't come from him and we didn't find any others in our search of his apartment.'

I nod. 'It's not much to go on. I also looked through our notes from our interviews. In addition to Taylor and Barnett, we had Brian Geller who came in to tell us that he witnessed Taylor being aggressive and hostile with the victim in the KitzTech parking lot one week before she turned up dead.'

'Right, and let's not forget the interview with Nicole Taylor, though she didn't have much to say, other than that Vince wasn't always a cheating, lying bastard.'

There's something about the interview with Nicole that still isn't sitting right with me. I can't put my finger on what it is, but something she said is softly seeking my attention, like a cat gently rubbing against my leg.

'Can I see the notes from Nicole's interview again?' I ask.

'Sure,' Lanner replies, passing me the typewritten page.

I scan the familiar lines one more time and I finally see it.

'Look.' I point down at the page. 'She mentioned the Heatherly Hotel twice during our conversation with her. It must have been a special place for her and Vince. Do you think he may have taken Layla there too?'

'Used the same hotel for trysts with his wife *and* his mistress? Wouldn't be the brightest move, but who knows, he may have.'

'Let's take a trip over there and see if anyone remembers seeing him with Layla.'

*

I wipe the sweat off my brow with the back of my hand before we enter the cool lobby of the Heatherly Hotel. I wonder to myself what kind of people are regulars at a place like this. Inside the marble-covered lobby, bellhops in red jackets scamper to and fro, dragging luggage behind elegantly dressed women and men swathed in expertly tailored suits.

To the right of the main entrance is an old-fashioned bar with assorted bottles of liquor artfully arranged before a mirrored wall which sparkle below soft overhead lights. The bar itself, a deep cherry red, is polished to a high sheen. A few customers are enjoying an early happy hour, sipping colorful cocktails from thick glasses. I spot at least two purses that are worth more than I make in a month casually draped over the backs of the plush red seats lining the bar. At the back of the bar is a sign, written in curled gold lettering, advertising a gentleman's cigar lounge. I feel as though I've stepped back into the 1920s' into an atmosphere of glittering luxury and elegance.

As I'm taking in the scene at the bar, imagining what it might be like to be Vince Taylor puffing expensive cigars in the gentleman's lounge, Lanner strides up to the front desk and asks to speak with the on-duty manager.

I hear the receptionist, in her chipper customer service voice, tell him that the manager, Dale, will be right with us. I join Lanner at the front desk and pull up a photo of Vince Taylor on my phone as we wait for Dale.

'What can I help you with, Detectives?' a portly man with graying hair in a black suit asks as he walks up to us and extends his hand.

'You must be Dale,' I reply, shaking his hand firmly.

'That's me. Dale Haverstad.' He offers me a warm smile.

I have to wonder how much of the 'happy to help' attitude around here is genuine and how much if it just comes with the territory of working in a high-end hotel where guests won't tolerate the help appearing as if they are anything less than thrilled at the opportunity to serve them.

'We were wondering if you'd ever seen this man in your hotel.' I show him the photo of Vince.

'We here at the Heatherly try to respect our guests' privacy. We have many guests who value anonymity and—'

'I understand, Mr Haverstad,' Lanner interrupts. 'If you'd prefer, we could come back with a warrant and some officers in blue uniforms. But I suspect your elite clientèle might be less than pleased at the intrusion.' Lanner winks.

'Oh … I … no that won't be necessary. Between you and I, yes, I've seen that man here before. I recognized him the first time he came. I'd seen his picture on the cover of *Forbes* magazine, so I knew he was Vince Taylor. But he signed in under a fake name, paying in cash, and so I assumed that he didn't want to be recognized. We have a lot of celebrities who come in here looking to escape public attention, and so I didn't think much of it.'

'Did you ever see him with a woman?' Lanner asks.

Dale's face burns a crimson red. 'I … yes. Just once. A brunette. Pretty young thing. I try to stay out of the guests' business but, well, I couldn't help but notice her.'

I pull up a photo of Layla on my phone. 'Was this the woman you saw him with?'

'Yes, that's her.'

'Do you remember the fake name he used to check in?'

'I think I do. Vinny Gambini. I remember because that's the name of the character from that movie, *My Cousin Vinny*. I found it humorous. I'm a big fan of Joe Pesci.'

'Can you check to see when the last time … Vinny Gambini … checked in?'

'Certainly. Just give me one moment here …'

Dale steps behind the reception desk and hit a few strokes on the keyboard. 'Ah, here we are,' he says. 'Mr Gambini checked in for a one night stay on August twenty-fourth at eight o'clock in the evening.'

'And you're sure this was Vince Taylor?'

'I'm absolutely certain of it. I checked him in myself on that particular evening.'

'Was he with anyone that night?'

'Not that I recall, but I can't be certain.'

'Thank you, Mr Haverstad, you've been very helpful.'

'Excuse me, Sir!' A woman in a royal-blue dress, a pashmina pulled over her shoulders, exclaims. She's waving her arm in Dale's general direction. Her lips are pursed and her foot is tapping impatiently on the gleaming floor of the lobby.

Dale scuttles off to attend to his demanding guest and Lanner and I turn to leave.

'Guess Vince Taylor's alibi isn't so airtight after all,' Lanner says.

'I knew he was lying to us. He's been hiding something from day one. Let's just hope this is enough to get us a search warrant.'

*

Lanner and I sit by the fax machine waiting for a copy of the warrant to come through. After finding out that Vince lied about his alibi for the night Layla Bosch was killed, we were able to convince a judge that we had probable cause to search KitzTech's electronic data and she signed off on a warrant allowing us to access the metadata to their security records.

I didn't have the faintest clue what 'metadata' was, but we requested it upon Stu's suggestion. He explained, in that 'I can't believe you don't know this' way of his, that 'Metadata is a set of data which gives information on other data.' He must have noticed that I was still puzzled because he went on to explain, in less complicated terms, that the metadata will show us if and when the KitzTech security records provided to us by Vince Taylor were accessed and if anyone altered them.

'It's coming through!' Lanner shouts animatedly. I pull the signed warrant from the fax machine, the paper still warm under my fingers.

'Let's get this over to KitzTech right away.'

Chapter 45

Allison

DAY 12

I've always wanted to be a detective. My father was a detective, and my grandfather before him. And so you'd think I would have had a clear understanding of what the job would entail. But I guess I had loftier ideas. I naively pictured it being more like a Sherlock Holmes story. I envisioned myself scouring crime scenes looking for the muddy footprint or the stray hair that would crack the case. And there is some of that involved, but in reality, a lot of my job involves sitting in front of a computer.

I've lost track of the number of times I've refreshed my inbox this morning waiting for an e-mail from Darren Hamish, the acting CEO of KitzTech. He was served with the warrant last night directing him to turn over the metadata pertaining to KitzTech security records for the night of August twenty-fourth. Not that I'll know what I'm looking at once I get them though. That'll be Stu's department. So I guess my role here is just to deliver the digital evidence to someone who might be able to see it as the proverbial muddy footprint. Not exactly the stuff dreams are made of.

And yet, when that little red icon pops up advising me that I've received a new e-mail from Darren Hamish, I nearly fall out of my chair in my haste to open it.

'Stu!' I call excitedly. He's been hanging around the squad room all morning just waiting for this moment. 'I got the e-mail!'

Stu comes rushing over, his eyes wide with delight. This is like Christmas morning for him.

'Let me get in here,' he says, shooing me out of my chair. Stu adjusts his wire-rimmed glasses and sits them neatly on the bridge of his nose.

'What does it say?' I ask impatiently.

'Hold your horses. It's going to take me a little time to comb through the data. Go get yourself a cup of coffee or something. I'll call you as soon as I have something.'

I think I've been dismissed. I guess he doesn't want me hovering over his shoulder peppering him with my novice-level questions while he works. Fair enough.

I walk toward the back of the station, to the break room that's next to McFadden's office. I check the coffee maker, but all that's left in the pot is a splash of burnt coffee, the grinds clinging to the pot like dried sediment. It reminds me of low tide. I don't know why I even bothered to check. No one ever cleans this thing properly, and consequently the coffee tastes like sludge. I suppose I didn't need the caffeine anyway. My nerves are already on edge as it is.

I grab a granola bar instead and bite into it without checking the expiration date. I'm certain that I don't want to know. I chew the stale breakfast bar while pacing the break room, resisting the temptation to shoot back over to my desk to ask Stu if he's found anything yet.

I really should eat better. Josh is always lecturing me on

providing my body with proper fuel. But I never find the time to prepare healthy meals. It's far more common for me to grab something quick that I can eat on the go. I exercise enough to make sure that I keep fit, but my body would probably appreciate the odd vegetable thrown into the mix of carbs and takeout. I should talk to Josh about arranging a meal prep schedule we could both stick to. Maybe something involving salads. *Josh.* There are a lot of things I need to talk to him about. I make a mental note to myself to apologize to him again tonight, to do something special to make him see how much I appreciate him.

'Thought I might find you in here,' Lanner says as he appears in the doorway. 'Stu sent you off, didn't he?'

'Yes, he did,' I admit.

'Bit bossy, that one. But he knows his stuff. If there's anything to find in that data, Stu will find it.'

I nod, and wipe a stray crumb from my lip.

'You're not eating one of those granola bars are you?'

I nod again.

'Barnes! They've been in here since the dawn of time!' He shakes his head in a mock shudder.

'Barnes! Lanner!' I hear Stu shout. 'You guys better come over here.'

I practically bowl Lanner over as I rush out the door and back to my desk. Lanner follows closely behind me.

'What have you got?' I ask, staring at the computer screen containing a jumble of numbers that I can't make head nor tail of.

Lanner seems far more relaxed than I am. He casually seats himself on my desk, his long legs splayed out in front of him. *Is that a male thing?* I've noticed it on the subway too, men spreading their legs wide, taking up as much space around them as possible. Is it simply to do with defending their personal space in a crowd? Or is it something deeper, something lurking in the collective subconscious of our society, that makes men able to move through the world with such confidence, such entitlement to claim the territory around them, while women are constantly reminded to make their bodies smaller, to take up less space in the world?

'You're going to be very pleased with this,' Stu says, pulling me from my contemplation. 'These records clearly establish that KitzTech's security log was accessed by someone on August twenty-sixth, and several lines of data were added at that time to show that after Vince Taylor left the building at 6.03 p.m., returned at 6.26 p.m., scanned his fingerprints to get into his personal office at 6.31 p.m., and left again at 10.43 p.m.. There was a trip to the men's room somewhere in there too.'

'August twenty-sixth was the day we interviewed Taylor at the station – when we started asking him for an alibi,' I say to Lanner.

'Yup,' he agrees, 'and this timeline is impossible because we know he checked into the Heatherly Hotel at eight o'clock, so he couldn't have been in his office at that time. Looks to me like he didn't want us to know he was at the Heatherly.'

'Stu, is there any way to determine who altered these records?' I inquire.

'No, all I can tell you is that they were definitely tampered with. But there is no way to determine who accessed the records from what I have here.'

'Thanks, Stu. You're the best.'

'I know,' he says with a wink. 'I'll leave you two to it.'

'Obviously Vince doctored these records,' I say to Lanner after Stu leaves us alone at my desk. 'Who else would have done it?'

'I agree. But let's take it to the Chief,' he suggests.

I knock on Chief McFadden's door.

'Come in,' he barks.

We step into the Chief's office and I'm relieved to finally have some good news for him.

'What's going on with your investigation?' he asks.

Lanner and I fill Chief McFadden in on our interview with Vince, his false alibi, and how the metadata showed that the security records were tampered with. We also tell him about our chat with Dale, the manager at the Heatherly.

'Arrest Taylor,' Chief McFadden responds curtly.

'Do you think we have probable cause, given that we can't prove that he was the one that altered the records and—'

'Detectives, make the arrest. What are you waiting for? A confession? We can't sit around waiting for more evidence to fall into our laps. That idiot Kinnon has brought too much attention to this case as it is, and we need to wrap it up. Now.'

'Yes, Sir.'

'You'll have a warrant by the time you get to Loch Harbor.' McFadden picks up his phone, punching in the numbers with one finger has he shoos us out of his office with one hand. 'Go.'

*

Lanner and I once again find ourselves driving through Loch Harbor, but the atmosphere has changed a great deal since the last time we traveled these roads. The sun has ducked behind a thick, dark cloud making the woods around us appear somber, ominous. The trees loom tall above us and seem to lean over the road; nature threatening to reclaim the man-made structure. The ocean below is a pale slate gray and I watch as the waves break in angry white crests; the sea is baring its teeth, reminding me of its power. There is an unusual chill in the air, and though I'm pleased to see the end of the heatwave that has been bearing down on us, I can't help but feel a sense of malevolence whispering in the cool breeze.

Lanner pulls up to Vince Taylor's front gate, the scrolling black ironwork towering before us. As we stand outside the imposing entryway, the first fat raindrop falls from above. I look up at the sky, a swirling pallet of gray, and another drop splashes onto my face.

Lanner looks down at his phone. 'Chief says we have our

warrant. Let's do this.' He presses the intercom button. Nothing. It seems to have been disconnected.

'How are we going to get up to the house?' I ask. I'm about to suggest that we wait in the car, when the gates before us slowly begin to slide open. I look up the driveway and see a sleek black car rumbling towards us.

'That's his car,' Lanner says. 'Perfect timing.'

We wait for Vince to pull through the gates, where he rolls to a stop next to us, sliding down a dark, tinted window.

'Detectives, what can I do for you this morning?' Vince says coolly. If he's shaken by our appearance at the end of his drive, he doesn't show it. 'I was just on my way out.'

'Please step out of the car,' Lanner orders. He takes a wide stance, keeping one hand on his holster.

'Is this … are you … arresting me?' Vince's eyes grow wide with shock. He looks like a trapped animal desperately assessing his means of escape.

'I said please step out of the car, Sir.' I'm reminded of how intimidating Lanner can be when he needs to be.

Vince seems at a loss for words as he puts his car in park and fumbles to open the door. He steps out onto the road wearing a pair of deep blue jeans and a black V-neck T-shirt pulled tight across his muscular chest. It seems to be his signature look. I can hear the gritty gravel on the side of the road crunching beneath the soles of his smooth leather shoes.

Lanner gives me a nod.

'Vincent Taylor, you are under arrest for the murder of Layla Bosch—' I begin.

'This is a mistake! I didn't kill her! I need to call my attorney! I—'

'Anything you say can and will be held against you in a court of law …' I continue to recite Vince's Miranda rights as I pull my handcuffs off of my belt. The cuffs, a bright flash of silver, only make Vince's eyes grow rounder. I can see his chest rising and falling in rapid succession, his breath becoming jagged and desperate.

I turn him around, pressing his stomach against his expensive black car and begin to clip the cuffs around his wrists. Just as the first cuff locks into place, the sky above us opens up. It is as though the heavens have torn and a torrential rain begins to fall.

By the time I lock the second cuff onto Vince's wrist and begin to lead him towards the back seat of our car, his hair is soaked through, hanging in stringy ropes, and water drips from the ends.

'Please don't do this,' he says as I duck his head into the car. 'I never hurt Layla. You have to believe me. She's not who you think she is.' His eyes lock with mine, they're full of a pleading desperation; a look I've seen so many times during my career. But there is something else there too. Vince's eyes hold a glint of something deeper, something far less common that takes me quite some time to place – sincerity.

I look in the rearview mirror to check on the now silent Vince Taylor as we drive him back to New York City where he will be charged with second degree murder. I can't see his eyes, only the crown of his head and a shield of dripping wet hair. It strikes me how different he looks now than he did the first time I met him: the man with the easy smile, the perfect hair, bold and brazen in his corner office. The Vince I see reflected back at me now seems much smaller, his shoulders fallen, his head bowed. Gone is the affable charm, the breezy confidence.

My gut twists and I feel bile rising into my throat. I don't know why I'm feeling this way, but I can't seem to shake the feeling. The look in Vince's eyes as I pushed him into the car haunts me for the rest of the silent ride back into the city, and I suspect it will for a long time to come.

Chapter 46

Layla

BEFORE

I can't sit here for another minute. Vince is strutting around the office like he doesn't have a care in the world, turning that quick smile of his on everyone except me. My cheeks burn with shame as I recall the way he rejected my advances in the parking lot last night. He hasn't even so much as glanced in my direction all day, and it's not like I haven't been trying to catch his attention. This dress alone should have been enough to set him drooling. It certainly set me back enough, and I'm running dangerously low on funds as it is. I wonder if I can return it. I run my hands over the smooth black fabric that hugs my hips as if it was made for me. Such a shame I can't keep it.

'How are you doing today, Layla?' Brian whispers to me conspiratorially, leaning in close to my ear. I can hear the pity in his voice and it makes me want to lash out at him, grab him by the throat and tell him to stay the hell out of my business. But of course I can't.

After he saw Vince and me in the parking lot last night, I have to keep him thinking that it was all a big misunderstanding. I can't have him blabbering all over the office about what he saw; I wouldn't want people figuring out the truth and spoiling everything. If Vince thinks I've been gossiping about what we've been up to, my chances with him are as good as gone.

'I'm fine, really,' I reply, smiling sweetly. 'Let's just forget it ever happened, okay?' I touch his arm gently and he seems to light up at my touch. *Loser*.

'Okay, if you're sure. It just seems so unlike Vince to get so mad over work stuff. He's usually so chill with everyone.'

'I know, I really messed up an assignment he gave me. He was, like, so pissed. I'm really embarrassed that you had to see that. But I talked it out with Vince this morning and it's all handled now. No need to worry.'

'Alright, good, I'm glad,' Brian replies, a slightly puzzled look on his face. You'd think he'd *want* me fired after that whole incident where I took credit for his app idea, but turns out Brian is a bit of a softie. No wonder it was so easy to walk all over him.

Mercifully, Brian walks away from my workspace leaving me with my thoughts. Maybe I should bring Vince a cup of coffee. Yes, he'd like that, and that way I can be sure he sees me in this dress before I have to bring it back to the store.

I make my way to the break room, teetering on stiletto heels while walking in this dress that clings to my thighs. I pour a cup of coffee, one scoop of sugar, no milk, just the way Vince likes it, and bring it to his office.

His door is, as always, open wide. I see Vince bent over his desk, looking handsome as ever. His sprawling corner office is full of soft morning light, and he's humming something to himself while he works. Did the fact that he rejected me in a deserted parking lot last night not affect him in the slightest?

I march into his office, coffee sloshing over the side of the paper cup. It trails down my wrist and splashes onto the white floor. I slam the cup down on his desk, more coffee spilling over the top of the cup and spreading in a dark blot onto the papers scattering his desk.

Vince looks up at me with a look of shock on his face. He hadn't even noticed I was standing in front of him until I spoiled his work. His eyes quickly shift from surprised to angry.

'What are you doing?' he hisses, looking past me towards the open door to check that no one has seen us together, the embarrassment that I am to him.

'I thought I'd bring you some coffee,' I reply with a scowl, gesturing at the mess spreading across his desk.

'You need to go.' He begins to mop up the spill. He doesn't even bother to look at me again. I've been dismissed, and the message is clear. Vince Taylor runs his world and I am no longer welcome in it. I was a mistake to him, something to be swiftly swept under the rug and forgotten about.

I feel my cheeks flush with shame again and I bolt out of his office as fast as I can in this dress that is far too tight and these heels that are far too high. I quickly walk past my desk, grabbing my purse out of the bottom drawer and make my way towards the lobby.

'Where are you off to?' I hear Brian calling after me. But I don't have the words to respond. I need to get out of here. I can't stand to be in this office any longer.

I walk straight out of KitzTech's headquarters and down the city block. The sidewalk is crowded with the lunch rush, important people in designer suits eagerly waiting their turn to hand over exorbitant amounts of money in return for a chopped salad and a kale smoothie. I don't know why I ever thought I could fit into this world. I don't know why I ever thought I could convince Vince to choose me.

I walk a few more blocks, my feet sweating and my shoes rubbing blisters onto my heels, feeling sorry for myself. I let myself feel the humiliation of Vince's rejection and the panic about what I'm going to do next. I'm running out of Henderson's money, and I can hardly afford the lifestyle I want on an intern's measly salary. It's not like I'm going to get a real job at KitzTech after my internship like the others. That was never the plan anyway.

I hobble to a stop. I don't know exactly how far I've walked, but my feet are aching and I'm sweating through the thick fabric of my dress. So much for returning it. Everything is going to shit.

I lean against the cool stone wall of the building behind me, taking a moment to collect myself. I need a new plan. I always have a plan. But this time I don't know where to start. I lean my head back in frustration and happen to notice the awning of the storefront I'm standing under. It's a small stationery store called Paper Cranes. I walk over to the display window, and sitting in the corner is a black leather diary tied with a thin leather strap. A new plan is forming.

*

It took me nearly a week to write enough entries in my new diary to make it feel authentic. I even switched up the pens I used each time, which I thought was rather ingenious. I now have emotional, heartfelt documentation of the love story of Vince and Layla … a story that took an unexpected dark turn when Vince became jealous and possessive, forcing me to continue a sexual relationship against my will.

It's perfect. I may not have a sex tape this time, but if Vince refuses to give me enough money to keep me comfortable and happy for a very long time, I'll threaten to sell my story to the media. Who cares if it's not the real story? This one is even better.

I could probably make a pretty penny if I got this diary into the right hands, but I'm a reasonable person. I'll give Vince a chance to pay me the hush money it's worth. The only problem is going to be getting him to agree to meet with me. He hasn't spoken a word to me all week. I don't want to do this at work, but he isn't leaving me much of a choice.

I brought my finished diary to the office with me today. It's tucked neatly in my purse just waiting for the right moment. I wait for Eric to leave his desk to pick up lunch and I slip into Vince's office, closing the door behind me.

'Layla, I don't know how many times I have to tell you that you can't be doing this,' Vince warns angrily the moment he sees me.

'We have something we need to talk about. It's important, I—'

'No. There is no "we". Can't you understand that? There is nothing to talk about. You need to leave. Now.'

'I was hoping it wouldn't come to this, but I have something you're going to want to see.'

'Whatever it is, I can assure you that I don't care.'

'Oh, but you will.'

'No, Layla it's over. I want you out of my life.'

We're interrupted by the sound of Eric settling back down at his desk. I was going to show him the diary, but I don't have time now. These things can't be rushed. I'll have to adjust my plans.

'You want me out of your life? Fine, Vince. Have it your way. I'll leave KitzTech, and I'll leave you alone for good if you will meet with me one last time in our usual suite at the Heatherly Hotel. You do that for me, and you'll never have to see me again.'

'Fine,' Vince hisses, his eyes darting to the door, no doubt aware that Eric could walk in at any moment. 'I'll meet you at the Heatherly and we can talk. And then this is over, Layla. I mean it.'

'Great. 8.30 p.m. Don't be late.'

'And after that,' Vince says through gritted teeth, 'don't ever contact me again.'

Chapter 47

Layla

BEFORE

I made the arrangements to meet Vince at the Heatherly Hotel tomorrow. I sent him a message over Secret Messenger confirming the details to make sure he won't be standing me up. I know he read it because the message disappeared, but he couldn't even be bothered to respond. He's making this decision so easy for me.

I think I'll wear that red dress he loved so much the night he saw me out with Adam. There's no harm in showing him what he missed out on, right? As I pull it out of my closet and hold it up in front of me, my phone alerts me that I have a new message on Secret Messenger from Vince. I open the message and read:

'*Change of plans. Meet me at Central Park instead. By the fountain.*'

So he still thinks he's in charge. Okay, Vince. I'll play your little game for just a while longer. He's about to find out that I'm in control now.

'*I'll be there,*' I reply. The message disappears only moments after it's sent, so I know Vince read it.

*

I pace up and down the jogging path that runs beside the fountain in the center of Central Park. I am, of course, wearing a pair of sexy black stilettos to complement my dress, and so meeting in a park was wildly inconvenient for me. But that won't matter soon. Thanks to Vince, I'll be rich enough that I won't ever have to be inconvenienced again.

Vince is late and it's getting dark. I'm beginning to lose patience with him. Does he think this is a game? When he sees the diary pages I brought, he'll know I'm not playing around. I didn't bring the whole diary, not yet, I only brought the last few pages – just enough to show him how bad things can get if he doesn't cooperate. I'll save the rest for leverage later, should I find he needs extra encouragement to make his payments on time.

Suddenly I hear movement on the path behind me. I turn around, ready to lace into Vince for keeping me waiting.

'You?'

Chapter 48

Vince

DAY 13

'Mr Taylor. Are you listening?' the judge bellows from behind his bench. His bald head shines under the florescent lighting of the courtroom and he reminds me of the bald eagle on the crest hanging behind him. *In God We Trust*. I'm not so sure that's true anymore.

I *am* listening. Or I'm trying to at least. But I'm in a daze. I feel disconnected from the scene around me and I'm slow to respond. This all feels so surreal, as if it's happening to someone else. I feel like a spectator watching a movie reel of my life and at any minute the credits will roll, the lights will come up, and I'll get on with the rest of my day. But I won't. Not really.

'Vince,' Jeff hisses in my ear. 'You need to enter your plea. Now.'

'I'm sorry, your Honor,' I mumble, reawakening.

'As I said, Mr Taylor. You have been charged with second degree murder in the death of Layla Bosch. How do you plead?'

'Not guilty. I plead not guilty, your Honor.'

The judge bangs his gavel, the sleeve of his black robe fluttering behind it. 'The defendant enters a plea of not guilty. Bail is set at one million dollars.'

Jeff begins to argue. Something about me being a pillar of the community and not posing a flight risk, but I'm no longer listening. I'm watching the bailiff approach, one hand on a set of handcuffs ready to cart me off to jail.

Jeff must have lost his desperate plea to send me home, because the bailiff snaps the cuffs over my wrists and abruptly grabs me by the arm, leading me out of the courtroom.

I knew this was coming, Jeff warned me it was a possibility, but I still feel shocked as the cold cuffs rub against my skin. As Jeff had suspected, the Heatherly doesn't have CCTV cameras inside the premises. Too many guests who value discretion. And the manager didn't remember seeing me again after I checked in for the evening. In theory, I would have had plenty of time to slip out and kill Layla after I checked in. I have no alibi. Of course I'm going to jail.

'It's going to be okay,' Jeff calls out behind me. But I don't believe him.

'Vince!' I recognize Nicole's voice, and I whip my head around to see her, but the bailiff jerks me back in line.

'Let's go,' he orders, tightening his grip on my arm.

*

I sit on the edge of my new government-issued bed, drumming my fingers atop the thin mattress. I don't know how I'm supposed to face the day in here.

My first night in jail was unlike anything I've ever experienced. As soon as I left the courtroom I was stripped of my suit, my shoes, even my socks, and I was issued a misshapen orange jumpsuit which looks to have been intended for someone twice my weight.

I was handed a thin gray blanket and a sliver of a pillow and locked in a cell the size of a closet. I don't know what I was

271

expecting, but I was woefully unprepared for the sound of the bars closing on my freedom. I suppose I'd never really given much thought to what it might feel like to be caged like a dangerous animal, a predator. I never saw this coming.

I laid on the flimsy mattress pad and stared at the chipping cement ceiling and tried not to think about who lived in this cell before me, where they may have ended up.

My cellmate's name is Larz. A large spiderweb is tattooed over half of his face and the only thing he cared to say to me was 'stay out of my way', which I imagine will be quite difficult given the close living quarters. I nodded in response and pretended to fall asleep.

But I didn't sleep. The sound of a prison at night is reminiscent of a dog pound. Men releasing desperate howls, groans, cries. The clicking of bars, the flushing of toilets, feet pacing the floor. I lay awake most of the night while Larz snored loudly, his bed creaking underneath his weight.

I've only been here for one night and I can already understand how prison permanently changes a person; how urinating in front of guards, constantly looking over your shoulder, and wondering when you may see the other side of those barbed-wire gates again can quickly break a man down and make sure he will never see the world in the same way. Wherever I go from here, even if I somehow find a way to get out of this mess, I know I will never be the same man I was before I stepped foot inside this place.

But Nicole is coming today. She'll arrange my bail, and at least I'll be able to await my trial from home. *My trial.* This is what my life has come to.

'Taylor. Visitor,' a guard barks.

He leads me down a long corridor and into the visitation room. He directs me to sit at a small, metal table that's been fastened to the floor.

Nicole walks into the room looking small and frightened. I wish she never had to see the inside of this place, I wish she never had to see *me* in this place. The impact of my indiscretions wash over me anew. I may not have killed Layla, but my choices led us down this path.

Nicole sits down across from me and puts her hands in her lap. She's picking at her nails nervously.

'Are you ok?' I ask.

'This place, it's just …' She looks around the room, a look of horror on her face.

'Yes, it's awful.' I instinctively reach across the table to comfort her.

'Hey!' a guard shouts, cracking his baton against the wall. 'No touching.'

I bring my hands back to my lap.

'I'm arranging for Jeff to post your bail today,' Nicole says.

'Thank you.'

'Are you alright? You look … awful. Sorry. I didn't mean it like that, you just don't look like yourself.'

'I know. I couldn't sleep.' She's right. I do look awful. I saw my reflection in the warped metal mirror this morning. My chin is shadowed with stubble, my skin looks gaunt and pale, and dark circles are spreading under my eyes, purple crescents that look like fresh bruises.

'I'm so sorry, Vince.'

'No, Nic, I'm sorry. I may not have been responsible for Layla's death, but I brought this into our lives.'

'Visiting hours are almost over,' the surly guard announces.

'I'll make sure Jeff posts your bail,' Nicole says as she stands to leave. 'You'll be home before you know it.'

'What are you going to do today?' I ask. 'Are you going to be okay?'

'Yes, I'll be alright. I'm going to meet Marta for lunch.'

'Marta? The housekeeper?'

'Yes.'

'I didn't realize you two were friendly.'

'There's a lot you didn't realize, Vince.'

Nicole turns her back to me, a cascade of frosty blonde hair, and I watch her, my mouth agape, as she walks away to freedom, the heavy security door slamming shut behind her.

Chapter 49

Nicole

DAY 13

Did Vince really think I didn't know about his affair with Layla?

It will be a long drive back to Loch Harbor, and I have nothing but time stretching out ahead of me. My mind wanders back to where it all began. To when I first learned that Vince had ruined everything.

I think I knew before he did that he was venturing down a dark and dangerous road. My husband, who would usually return from work exhausted and stressed, came home to me starry-eyed and blissful. He was like a love-sick teenager over that girl. I didn't know who she was, not then, but I knew I'd lost a piece of him that could never again be mine.

I figured it had to be someone he worked with. All those late nights, the long lunches where I'd call his office and Eric would advise me, embarrassment in his voice, that Mr Taylor was unavailable. I checked the company website to see who this mystery woman might be, and the moment I saw Layla I knew. She was stunning, with her chocolate-brown hair shining in the afternoon sun, her sweet smile, her youthful innocence that would have called out to Vince like a beacon in the night. He loves to be needed, my husband. And a girl like Layla, all doe-eyed naiveté, would have been almost irresistible to him. The way I once had been.

I watched as Vince transformed before my eyes. He was reawakened in her. Vince had been living as a hollowed version of the man I once knew. He'd never say the words aloud, but I knew it was due to my inability to provide him with the child he so desperately wanted. I wanted to be there for him, to support him through the loss I knew he must have been feeling, but I was so exhausted from wading through my own grief, that I hardly had the strength to rescue our marriage. We were drowning in quicksand, and it was every man for himself. But at least I knew he was there, in the thick of it alongside me. He was fighting the same battle in his own way, and there was comfort in that. Someone understood what I was going through.

But all of that changed over the course of a few months. Layla put Vince back together in a way I couldn't. He was no longer broken, a ghost who silently passed through the halls of our house, he was revitalized. His young mistress made a younger man of him. And that left me alone, to drown in the depth of my sadness.

Although I had my suspicions about Vince and his affair, I didn't know for sure. Not until Marta accidentally walked in on them together in the apartment. Marta and I have become friendly over the years. I once gave her some passes to attend one of my yoga classes, and what began as a kind gesture, developed into a friendship. It was something of an awkward relationship given that she was in my husband's employ, but every time I'd teach a class in Manhattan I'd be sure to save her a spot in the studio, and we'd occasionally go out for a cup of coffee afterwards.

A few weeks ago, I called Marta to ask if she'd like to attend an open-air yoga session I was planning to lead in Central Park.

She thanked me profusely for including her, but explained that she found herself in an uncomfortable position.

'I consider you a friend, but I know that Mr Taylor is also my employer. There's something I've been wanting to talk to you about but I've been so torn about what I am supposed to do.' She sounded upset, on the verge of tears.

'I consider you a friend as well, Marta, and whatever it is, I'm sure we can work it out.' I thought perhaps she'd broken something in the apartment. Some material, minor, thing that Vince would never miss in the sea of material, minor things he owns. But I could understand why she might be afraid to admit her mistake.

'I went to clean your apartment last week. It was a Tuesday and I always clean on Tuesdays. But when I walked in, I saw Mr Taylor there. He was not at work.'

'Oh, is that all? Vince probably had a late night at the office the night before and overslept.'

'No, no, there is more. Mr Taylor was already dressed for work, but I heard the shower running. And there was a woman's clothes on the floor.' I hear Marta swallow nervously and she rushed to fill the silence that had fallen between us. 'Maybe I shouldn't have told you. It's not my business what my employers do in their own apartments, and I shouldn't meddle. I could lose my job and—'

'It's okay, Marta,' I reassured her, 'you did the right thing by telling me. I won't tell Vince a word you said. I'm sure it was all just a big misunderstanding anyway.'

Marta sounded relieved, but that was a lie. I was certain that she hadn't misunderstood the situation at all. My suspicions had been confirmed.

I couldn't believe Vince would betray me that way. For ten years, he'd worshiped at my feet. When we first met, he all but begged for me to take a chance on him, the nobody computer nerd who could hardly afford his rent. But I saw something in him: a quiet ambition that I knew would take him far. He was brilliant, yet humble and unassuming, and under those glasses and fringed haircut, he could even be quite handsome. He just needed a push in the right direction. Vincent, as I knew him then, was on the rise and I made sure I was going with him.

I invested everything in Vince Taylor and the brand he was building. I helped to build him up, to carefully craft the public persona that garnered him all the recognition he needed to skyrocket to the top, while I let my own career fall to the wayside. I enjoy practicing yoga, but sometimes I feel like I haven't lived up to my full potential, like I'm wasting away teaching downward dog to the 'ladies who lunch' when I could have been so much more.

I have a master's in art history, and I once dreamed of owning my own gallery. I planned to travel the world curating an exquisite and interesting collection. I wanted to discover art that had something to say, that would make people see the world though a new lens. But being Vince's wife and supporting his career was so all-consuming that I never made time for my own dreams. Even when we built our house in Loch Harbor, I told myself there was still time. After I started a family, I could start the gallery. I could have it all. But I was kidding myself. Even if I'd managed to have the children I dreamed of, how was I going to run a successful art gallery in Manhattan and raise a family? We both knew Vince was never going to take a step back from his career. One of us was going to have to recede into the shadows to let the other shine, and it came as no surprise that the responsibility landed on me. I gave up my career ambitions, and let our lives revolve around Vince and his success.

Becoming a mother was going to be my reward for all I'd given up. I may not have had my gallery, but I knew that someday I'd have a little hand in mine. I'd have first words, first steps, first days of school. But in a cruel twist of fate, the family I'd sacrificed so much for wasn't meant to be.

And then, after everything I'd given up for Vince, after all the lonely nights I spent in our big, empty house while Vince followed his dreams and built his empire, he decided to take a mistress. It wasn't fair. Why should he have had it all, and get to have her too?

It seems that Vince forgot who he was when I met him, the boy in the makeshift office in Brooklyn. He's forgotten the way he once looked at me as if there was no one else in the world who would ever matter to him, as if he couldn't live without me. I was young and beautiful to him once too. But it seems that now that Vince has made it big, he feels entitled more: to someone younger, to someone who's beauty hasn't yet been dulled by marriage and infertility.

I wonder what he told her about me. Was I the nagging wife, the frigid shrew who couldn't, or wouldn't, keep him happy? Did he tell her about my failure to provide him with precious children who would carry on his legacy?

I was irate. I wasn't going to be the cliché first wife who got traded in for a newer model. Not after all the time and energy I'd put into Vince. I knew I had to do something to put an end to their affair, but I didn't know where to start.

I didn't want to confront Vince with my suspicions without solid evidence of what was going on. Especially since I couldn't tell him what I'd learned from Marta. I know my husband – he'd offer me his charming smile, the one he's perfected for the cameras, and tell me it wasn't true, that he loved me and he'd never hurt me. He'd sweep his infidelity under the rug, and I, wanting to believe him, would be left questioning whether I had imagined all the little changes I knew I saw in him.

I tried checking Vince's phone for evidence of his indiscretions. The passcode is our anniversary date, and it wasn't lost on me that he'd have to type it in every time he wanted to talk to his lover. But I never found any incriminating texts or emails. I'm certain that Vince was using that childish Secret Messenger app to talk to her so that their messages would disappear after they were read. He wouldn't want to leave a trail.

For weeks, Vince and I grew distant from one another. He

guarding his secret and I guarding mine. If he noticed the change, the cooling of our marriage, he gave me no indication. I was losing him to her and I didn't know how to stop it. But then, to my surprise, something changed all on its own. The late nights in the office slowed to a halt and Vince would come home edgy and anxious. I thought maybe there was trouble in paradise.

One night, only two weeks ago now, though it feels like another lifetime, Vince finally slipped up. He came home like a whirlwind, typing furiously on his phone with a scowl on his face. I watched from the kitchen as he threw his phone down on the sofa in what appeared to be frustration, and stormed off to his office. I knew I had to be quick. It would only be a matter of moments before Vince realized he'd left his precious phone behind.

I quietly sprinted over to the sofa and picked up his forgotten phone. I keyed in the security code and opened Secret Messenger. I'd hoped that Vince and his mistress had been in the middle of an argument, it certainly seemed heated enough, and that maybe she'd sent a new message that I could read before Vince returned – something incriminating that would give me the ammunition I needed to confront Vince about his affair. But what I found was even better.

Chapter 50

Nicole

DAY 13

'*Don't forget our little meeting tomorrow night. 8.30 p.m. Heatherly Hotel. I'll be expecting our usual suite. It's in your best interest to show up, Vince. Let's just say, I have something that's going to be worth bringing your checkbook for.*'

I read Layla's message again and again before it disappeared from the screen. Was she blackmailing him? Was that why Vince was so upset? I'd bet anything that husband of mine would pay her whatever she asked just to keep his dirty little secret under wraps. I wasn't letting that happen. She wasn't entitled to a single dime. Not from us.

We built this life, Vince and I. Vince may have started KitzTech, but I helped him make it what it is today. I was the one that insisted he change his image, that he bring his skills to social media. I was the one that made him an icon. And I never complained when I had to hang on his arm making all the right public appearances as the silent and dutiful wife. I was just a bit of sparkle, like an accessory, to complete his look.

I've earned the life we have just as much as Vince did. I gave up everything I ever wanted so that Vince could shine. And now Layla thought she could take what was ours? It wasn't enough that she'd taken my husband, now she wanted our money too? I couldn't let that come to pass.

I heard Vince stirring in the office, drawers opening and closing, and I knew I had to move fast. I quickly typed out a reply to Layla:

'Change of plans. Meet me at Central Park instead. By the fountain.'

I waited with butterflies in my stomach as the message faded away moments before Vince emerged from his office. I tossed the phone back down onto the sofa and picked up a book, quickly opening it to a random page. By the time Vince reached the living room, I looked as though I was deeply engrossed in a paperback.

'Have you seen my phone?' he asked.

'No I haven't, sorry,' I replied, not daring to look up from the page.

'Oh, here it is.' Vince picked up his phone and brought it back with him into his office, none the wiser that his plans were about to change.

The next day I obsessed all day over whether I was making the right decision meeting Layla. I taught a few classes, but my students could tell I was distracted. I messed up the order of the poses in our usual sun salutation and the women in my studio looked at me quizzically as if I'd lost the plot. I couldn't focus on my practice when Layla's words were ringing in my head: *It's in your best interest to show up.* She had to be holding something over Vince but I didn't know what it could be. I just wanted to talk to her, to try to make her see reason. And, to be honest, to show her that I was a real person whose life she was ruining along with Vince's. I'm not nearly as much of a pushover as my husband is, and I thought that of the two of us, I was more likely to show her that we won't be taken advantage of. I never meant for her to die.

That evening I dressed in a pair of tight black pants, and a low-cut, black, sleeveless top. I completed the outfit with a pair of spiked, open-toed booties in a deep black suede. It was embarrassingly difficult to decide what to wear to confront the woman my husband was sleeping with. Even though we'd be meeting in the park, and my outfit wasn't the most practical, I wanted her to see what Vince had at home. I wanted Layla to know that I wasn't some frumpy old housewife who'd let herself go. No, I wanted her seething with jealously. I applied my makeup, rimming my eyes with black eyeliner to make them stand out as much as possible, and I brushed my hair into a sexy high ponytail. I looked in the mirror, assessing the finished product. Thanks to all of my yoga sessions, I looked lithe and fit, and I thought the outfit made me seem edgy and dangerous, not the type of woman whose husband and money would easily be stolen. It would do.

I grabbed my purse, adding some extra cash to cover the tolls into the city. Our EZPass is linked to Vince's credit card, and I didn't want him to ever suspect that I'd gone into Manhattan to meet his mistress. And with that, I was on my way.

I got to the park early. The sun was low in the summer sky and the horizon was dappled with gold-rimmed clouds. I saw Layla before she saw me. She was wearing a tight red dress that left little to the imagination and she was teetering on stiletto heels as she paced back and forth along the path beside the fountain. My stomach turned as I imagined Vince slowly peeling that dress off of her young, curvaceous body. I looked down at my own outfit, and it no longer felt quite as sexy.

I debated turning around. I wish now that I had. I told myself that it wasn't too late. I could walk away and spend the rest of my life pretending I'd never heard the name Layla Bosch. But if I did that, she'd think Vince blew her off. I didn't know what she was holding over my husband, but I couldn't risk it coming to light, not without knowing what it was. I took a deep breath, held my chin up, and approached Layla, hoping I looked far more confident than I felt.

'You?' she said as I approached. She spat the word at me with disgust and a roll of her eyes. I was nothing to her. No one. A mere inconvenience. I suddenly felt foolish standing before her in the outfit I'd spent hours deciding on, the one I thought would intimidate this intruder into my marriage. It was clear that she'd never given me more than a passing thought.

'Yes. Me,' I replied, meeting her gaze.

She seemed to ponder my presence for a moment, biting her plump lower lip as if she was making a decision as to how to make the most of the fact that she was stuck with me instead of my husband.

'This isn't about you,' she finally said, dismissively.

'Like hell it isn't. This is *my* marriage, *my* life, that you've weaseled your way into.'

'Look, I don't have time for this. What is it that you want?'

'I want you out of our lives.'

'And I will be. As soon as Vince does what I asked of him.'

'It seems you think that you're in charge here, that you get to call the shots. But you don't, little girl. Not anymore. You think you can blackmail my husband? What were you going to do? Threaten to tell me all about your dirty little affair? Well I already know, so it's over, Layla. Give it up.'

'You think that's all I had on Vince? That I was going to tell his wife he'd misbehaved?' A vicious smile spread across her face. 'You've overestimated your worth and underestimated mine. And now you're both going to pay the price for that.'

I felt sick, but I wasn't going to back down. Not to this stupid, spoiled girl.

'What do you want, Layla? Is it money? Because I can promise you Vince isn't going to give you a dime.'

'Oh, I think he will. Once he sees this.' She pulled a few pieces of lined paper out of her purse, waving them before me as if she was wielding a knife.

'What is this?' I snatched the papers from her hand and began to skim the handwritten pages.

I felt tears pricking my eyes as I read all the vile things she'd written about my husband, about how he was violent and dangerous, forcing her to sleep with him against her will. I didn't want to believe it.

'This isn't true … it can't be.'

'Believe what you want,' Layla said flippantly, as she flicked her shiny brown hair over her shoulder with a perfectly manicured hand.

Vince wouldn't really do those things. Would he? That wasn't the Vince I knew, but I had to admit that I hardly knew him anymore. I didn't want to think that he'd become the person Layla wrote about, but a small voice in my head reminded me that I couldn't be sure. After all, I never thought he'd have an affair either.

'There's more where that came from too,' Layla added. 'You can keep those if you want. Show them to your husband. Let him know that if he doesn't pay me what they're worth, I'll sell my story to the highest bidder.'

'You can't do this!'

'Oh, but I can.' Layla laughed, a condescending chuckle. I hadn't shaken her. Not in the least. 'Let me know what Vince decides,' she said, turning on her heels and walking away from me.

I don't know what came over me in that moment, what dark thing possessed me, but I rushed at her, shoving her with both hands.

'You bitch!' she shouted, stumbling in her absurd heels.

Layla whipped around, a venomous glint in her eyes, and she pushed me to the ground. She was right, I had underestimated her. Where did a girl who looked as pampered as Layla learn to be so tough?

Layla towered above me, her shadow blocking the sun. Her hair fell around her face like a curtain as she leaned over me on the ground. I scuttled backwards, pushing myself up onto my hands. I could feel the grit and sand of the walkway digging into my palms.

'You tell Vince that he won't be getting rid of me this easily. After all, I'm carrying his baby.'

Layla turned to walk away, laughing viciously to herself, but I couldn't let her go.

She'd taken so many things that were supposed to be mine, but she couldn't have this. She couldn't have the child I was denied.

I was blind with rage. I wasn't thinking. I didn't plan to kill her. Not even as I picked up the rock that lay on the ground next to me. Not even as I swung my arm and watched it collide with her head. In truth, I didn't even remember hitting her. Not until much later. But I did. I killed that girl.

Her body fell to the ground in a broken heap, and I watched as the life drained out of her. Her glowing skin grew pale and the malice in her eyes evaporated into nothing. I know I should have felt something: horror, remorse, guilt, maybe even relief that she was gone. But in that moment, as I watched the last dregs of Layla's young life slip away, I felt nothing. Absolutely nothing.

*

I took the rock with me, and tossed it into the Long Island Sound somewhere along my drive home. I was going to do the same with Layla's diary pages, but something told me to keep them. I took them home and shoved them into a shoe box and hid it away in the back of my closet. But I knew that they were there, their venomous words haunting me.

After Layla's body was found, Vince was questioned in his office. I wasn't expecting that to happen. I hadn't really considered who would be blamed for her death, beyond the fact that I'd hoped it wouldn't be me.

I remember that I made my favorite lasagna recipe that night. I took comfort in the routine motions of cooking, layering the pasta and the cheese, putting everything in the right order, creating something warm and familiar. I needed it to distract me from the constant worry that the police were going to pound on my door at any moment, and I thought the meal would bring Vince and me together so that we could finally talk.

Over dinner Vince told me about the death of his intern, but he made it seem as though he hardly knew her. Did he not see what he was doing to us? Did he not see how his lies, his secrets, were the very thing that had broken us? Did he even notice that we were broken?

Even after death, Layla was destroying our marriage. I could picture her twisted smile, mocking me, taunting me. She had won. She'd driven a wedge into our marriage, buried a secret between us, that Vince would protect long after she was gone.

But sometimes Vince needs a push in the right direction to do what has to be done. Just like when he needed my guidance getting KitzTech off the ground. Maybe he just needed a little motivation before he was ready to tell me the truth.

That night I sent my first anonymous email to Kate Owens from an untraceable Gmail account to tell her that the dead girl in the park was sleeping with her boss, the CEO of KitzTech. Kate Owens was the perfect person to run the story about Vince. I remembered reading about her fallout with *The Minute* after her boss had sexually harassed her in the office. I knew she'd latch onto the story of the media mogul preying on his young intern.

After the news of the affair broke, all eyes were on Vince. I thought he would come clean with me after his secret was exposed for all the world to see. After all, he had nothing left to lose. I went to him in tears, finally able to admit that I knew about him and Layla … even if I had to pretend I read about it in *World View*. I thought that maybe in that moment Vince would finally confess everything, and we could begin to heal, to come together once again. But to my surprise, he continued to lie.

It came so easily to him too. The lies rolled right off his tongue without a moment's hesitation.

'Where were you the night that girl died?'

'I had to work late and then I spent the night at the apartment.'

I was giving him the opportunity to stop the lies and to give us a chance for a fresh start, but Vince didn't take it, choosing instead to pile more lies on top of our already strained marriage.

If he'd been honest with me in that moment, I may have told him everything. I might have confessed what I'd done to Layla. But of course that's not what happened. Instead, we both jealously guarded our own secrets until they became too big to contain.

As the days passed, the lies living between us began to distort my image of Vince. The more he lied, the more I began to believe that maybe the words Layla had written about him were true. I didn't know this man I was sharing a home with. We were strangers passing each other in the halls. I grew to resent him, to hate him, for what he'd done, for how close he'd come to ruining both of our lives. And I couldn't help but think about Layla's baby.

I wondered if Vince knew she was pregnant, if he really had grown obsessed with her after she'd given him the one thing he wanted most in this world, the one thing I could never provide.

I gave Vince so many chances to make things right and confess the truth, but he never did. And every time he chose to tell me a new lie, I gave more information to Kate Owens. I never told her that Layla was pregnant though. I was saving that last bit of information for when I needed it most.

Carrying my own secret wasn't always easy. I almost broke down and told Vince the truth several times. After Vince moved out, I called him in tears. The guilt of what I'd done, causing him to lose his position at KitzTech, was eating me alive. I was going to tell him everything that day. But when he got to the house, he got into an altercation with a cop who had apparently been loitering around in the woods. I never even knew the officer was there. With all of the commotion, cops traipsing all over the property, and Vince assuming I'd called him to rescue me from an intruder, the moment passed, and I kept my secret to myself.

When the next *World View* article came out, breaking information about a previous rape allegation, (information that they hadn't gotten from me), I felt validated. Maybe Vince really was the monster Layla described. Maybe what I'd done in exposing the truth about him wasn't so bad after all.

I wasn't trying to frame Vince for Layla's murder, not really. I just wanted him to feel the same pain he was causing me. I wanted him to feel ashamed for what he did. I wanted him to sweat. I never really thought he would be arrested for Layla's death because there would be no evidence that he'd killed her since, after all, he hadn't.

No one ever questioned me. Not even the police when they were in my house. They saw what they wanted to see: the sad, heartbroken wife. The one who couldn't possibly be as smart as her brilliant husband. That's the thing about being married to someone as intelligent as Vince – everyone is content to think you're an idiot by comparison. I didn't plan to tip them off about the Heatherly, but it was the day after Vince had moved out and I was feeling particularly vulnerable. After Vince left, I was all alone in our big empty house and I had nothing to do except obsess over the thought of Vince with Layla's baby in his arms. In truth, Vince had never even taken me to the Heatherly before. I've never set foot inside that hotel. But when the detectives began to question me, I couldn't resist offering them that little crumb.

I never dreamed it would be enough to lead to Vince's arrest. But, of course, I didn't know about the security records that Vince had already doctored. There were too many secrets between us. The situation spiraled out of my control, and before I knew it Vince was being led away in handcuffs.

I know I'm partially responsible for landing Vince behind bars, but all he had to do was tell the truth and none of this would have happened.

If only Vince had been honest with me. If only he hadn't given Layla the baby that should have been mine.

*

I finally make it back home, physically and mentally exhausted, and I check my phone for messages. There's one new text from Jeff: '*Issue posting Vince's bail. It won't be processed until Monday.*'

I picture Vince drowning in that orange jumpsuit. Today was the first time he ever looked small, vulnerable to me, and now he's facing a weekend in jail for a crime I know he didn't commit.

When Vince was first arrested I convinced myself that he'd be sent right back home. Surely they couldn't send him to jail; he was an innocent man. Maybe not in our marriage, but at least in the eyes of the law. When he didn't come home that night, I told myself he'd be set free soon. There wouldn't be a trial, what real evidence could they possibly have? I thought I could live with what I'd done, that all I had to do was wait for someone to figure out that Vince was innocent and send him home to me, and then everything could go back to normal.

But seeing Vince in that place today made me realize that I was deluding myself. I just wasn't ready to face what I knew deep down that I'd have to do. I see now that this has gone too far. I'm beginning to think that the police are never going to figure out that Vince is innocent. They've stopped looking, so sure are they that they have the right guy, and they aren't going to give up until he spends the rest of his life in jail. I have to stop prolonging the inevitable. I need to turn myself in.

I pick up the phone to call Detective Barnes. It's time she knew the truth. But before I have a chance to dial her number, the phone begins to ring in my hand, a familiar number blazing across the screen.

I listen to the voice on the other end, and in that moment everything changes.

Chapter 51

Vince

DAY 14

Nicole and Marta are friends? How did I not know? And what else is there that I don't know about my wife? I spent the entirety of last night thinking about how far Nicole and I have grown apart. I feel as though I hardly know this woman that I vowed to spend the rest of my life with. When did I start to lose her? I want to blame Layla, but I know it was before that. I was so wrapped up in my own life, that I left my wife to drift away. But this thing with Marta, it has thrown me for a loop. Is it possible that Nicole knew about the affair all along?

My stomach rumbles. My body is craving nutrition. I've barely eaten more than a few bites of food since I've been here. I constantly feel nauseous. And this morning was made even worse when I learned that my bail hadn't been posted. Jeff called to tell me that there was an issue processing the payment. 'Typical bureaucratic bullshit,' he'd said. But nothing about this feels typical to me. I pushed the dry eggs around my breakfast plate, unable to stomach a bite.

'Taylor. Visitor,' a guard calls.

I wasn't expecting anyone today. I hope that it's Jeff coming to tell me that he's worked some magic, bail was posted after all, and he's here to take me home.

I shuffle down the hallway and back into the visitation room, sitting impatiently as I wait to see if Jeff will appear.

But it's not Jeff who's come to see me.

'Nicole? I wasn't expecting you today.'

'I know, but I think we need to talk.'

'I think so too. There's something I have to ask you. It may sound crazy, but I need to know the truth, Nic. Did you—'

'I'm pregnant.'

Her confession has stunned me into silence. Suddenly it no longer matters what she knew and when. Nicole is pregnant. I'm going to be a father.

'Are you sure?' I ask, still feeling dazed.

'The doctor called last night. Just after I got home from visiting you.'

'Wow. Nic, this is everything we've always dreamed of.'

I want to reach out to her, to fold her in my arms and cry tears of joy with her. But then I remember where we are. We will not have the celebration we always envisioned we would when we heard this news.

'There's something else I need to tell you,' she says. I watch her squirm nervously in her seat before she straightens her spine, holds up her chin, and tells me the rest, her voice a whisper. 'Layla was pregnant too.'

'How … how do you know that?'

Nicole falls silent, but realization dawns on me now. Nicole killed Layla. She knew about my infidelity and she confronted Layla. There is no other explanation. I want to ask her more, I want to beg her to tell me what happened, but I can't. Not in here where the walls have ears.

Nicole looks at me knowingly. Her eyes searching mine.

Even without words, we're finally coming clean with each other. Between us finally hangs the truths we could never speak.

I know in that moment that I will take the fall for Nicole. We can't turn her in. Not while she's carrying the child we long dreamed of. Nicole will be the mother of my child, and I will protect her at any cost.

Chapter 52

Allison

DAY 14

'Cheers, Barnes!' Lanner shouts while raising his glass to mine. He clangs our pint glasses together, causing foam to slosh over the side of my glass and drip down my wrist.

'Cheers.' I smile and sip my beer.

'You okay? You don't sound as excited as I thought you would.'

'I'm fine, it's just been an exhausting two weeks.' I'm not ready to tell Lanner that I'm having second thoughts about Vince Taylor's guilt. I have no real reason for the change of heart, aside from the look in his eyes when I arrested him. It's not exactly evidence, yet I can't help the doubt churning in my head.

Josh puts his hand on my waist. 'Well, I'm really proud of you.'

I appreciate that he came out to celebrate with me tonight. Whenever we close a major case, the team goes out to celebrate at the local beer garden, and since this was my first case as lead detective, the whole crew came out for me. Even Chief McFadden stopped by. He didn't say more than 'Well done, Barnes,' before walking back out of the bar, but it meant a lot that he came. I invited Josh but I wasn't sure he would come, not after the way I'd treated him, basically accusing him of hiding evidence from me.

'Thanks for coming tonight,' I say, leaning my head against his chest. 'It means a lot to me.'

'Of course I'm here. I love you.'

I need to learn to trust that his love is real, unshakable. Josh was right, I need to start taking down the walls I've built around myself. I want to let him in, and I know it's going to take some time, but I'm trying. One step at a time.

'Did you hear the latest?' Lanner asks, oblivious to the tender moment he's just dashed. 'I heard Taylor is refusing bail. Maybe the guilt is getting to him.'

'He refused bail? Are you kidding? The guy is richer than God. He could probably pay that bail with his pocket money.'

'I don't know. Just telling you what I heard from my buddy in the District Attorney's office.' Lanner shrugs. 'Want another one?' He points to his empty pint glass.

'No, thanks. I think I'm ready to call it a night.'

Lanner looks surprised that I'm ducking out of my own party, but he doesn't question me. Instead he just shrugs again and makes his way towards the bar.

*

Early the next morning, after a fitful night's sleep, I decide to visit Vince. I need to see him one more time to clear my head. I need to look into his eyes to see if I still believe he killed that girl.

Vince is brought to the visitation room a changed man. His shoulders slump, his eyes are rimmed with red, and his hair has lost its sheen.

'What is it, Detective?' he says by way of greeting.

'I heard you haven't posted bail.'

'I haven't. And what concern is that of yours?'

'I just found it surprising. I can't fathom why you'd want to stay here instead of going back to that beautiful home of yours.'

'Might as well get used to the place,' he says, his voice flat and defeated. He doesn't make eye contact with me. He stares over my shoulder as though he's a million miles away. 'My attorney will either work out a plea arrangement or he won't. Either way, I've decided that I'll be pleading guilty to whatever they charge me with. There won't be a trial. It's over.' He shrugs, his shoulders sagging even further.

I can't believe what I'm hearing. This man who loudly professed his innocence and finally made me begin to believe him, has decided to give up the fight. It doesn't make sense. Even with the evidence we have against him, surely his attorney must have explained there's a chance of acquittal if he goes to trial. That chance is gone if he pleads guilty. Why not take the risk? What does he have to lose?

'Do you want to know what I think, Vince?'

'Not really,' he says distractedly.

'Well, I'm going to tell you anyway. I think you're protecting someone. I just don't know why. That's the only reason you wouldn't take your chances at trial. For one reason or another, you don't want the truth to come out.'

'I don't know what you want from me, Detective. You worked damn hard to put me here, and now you got your wish. Just let it go.'

Vince pushes away from the table and rises to a stand. 'Guard, I'd like to go back to my cell,' he announces. A burly guard strides over to the table and takes Vince abruptly by the arm.

Just before the guard yanks him away from the table, Vince turns to look at me one last time.

'I just have one question, Detective. Please. I need to know the answer.' His eyes are pleading.

'What is it?'

'Was Layla pregnant?'

'No,' I respond, bewildered by his question. There was no

way that Layla Bosch was pregnant. It would have been in the coroner's report.

Vince nods slowly, and I watch as he allows himself to be pushed and pulled, shuffling his feet along the faded floor where so many prisoners have walked before him.

I walk out of the visitation room, still confused as to why Vince would choose to stay in a place like this. I'm so distracted with my thoughts as I walked down the long corridor leading to the exit, that I don't notice Nicole Taylor until I walk right into her.

'I'm so sorry, Mrs Taylor,' I say, suddenly coming back to reality.

Her hands fly instinctively, protectively, to her belly as she regains her balance. 'It's alright, Detective,' she replies as she glides past me.

As I watch her walk away, I finally understand.

The long awaited baby, her subtle tip about the Heatherly Hotel, Vince's sudden change of heart … *Nicole*.

*

Josh is out with his friends tonight, and while I know I should go home and get some much needed rest, I'm feeling far too anxious. And so instead, I'm aimlessly walking the streets of New York City deep in thought. There has to be something I missed on the Bosch case, some stone left unturned that will prove my hunch about Vince Taylor's innocence.

Without realizing where I'd been heading, I find myself standing outside the Heatherly Hotel. The last place Vince was seen before Layla died. I look through the tall front windows, into the stately lobby inside. The bar area seems to be bustling now, unlike the last time I was here. Patrons are sidled up to the cherry-wood bar, long stemmed martini glasses in their hands, and I can see them laughing and smiling through the glass.

A doorman pushes open the entry door, allowing a dapperly dressed gentleman to step out onto the sidewalk. As the door swings opens, the sounds of tinny laughter and lighthearted conversation from the bar floats out into the evening air. I feel drawn to the glittering warmth inside.

I find an empty seat at the end of the bar. The bartender, dressed in a crisply pressed white shirt, topped with a black vest, wipes down the bar in front of me with a worn rag.

'What can I get for you?'

'Gin and tonic, please.'

He pours the drink into a frosty, chilled glass.

I sit and sip my drink, unable to focus on anything other than Vince Taylor and the haunted look on his face as he was led out of the visitation room earlier today.

'Everything alright?' the bartender asks, pulling me from my thoughts.

'Tough day,' I reply.

'Sorry to hear.'

And then a thought occurs to me. We know Vince checked in at the Heatherly the night Layla was killed, but we never interviewed the staff to see if anyone may be able to account for his whereabouts after he checked in. I was so wrapped up in proving that Vince had lied to us that I never considered that his stay at the Heatherly might also be his alibi.

I pull up a photo of Vince on my phone and show it to the bartender.

'Have you ever seen this man in here by any chance?'

'That's Vince Taylor, right? Yeah, he was in here a few weeks ago.'

I feel my stomach drop. 'Do you know what the date was?'

He looks at me quizzically.

I discreetly flash him my gold badge. 'It's really important.'

'Um, I don't know off the top of my head. But I can check for you.' The bartender pulls out his phone while he continues talking. 'He's a real nice guy. I've seen him around here a few times, always friendly to the staff. That night he came down to the bar by himself. Normally I'd go chat for a while if I saw someone sitting alone. I'm just like that, ya know? I like to talk to people. Makes my shifts go by faster. But Vince looked like he was waiting to meet someone, so I left him alone. I remember that he kept checking his watch. It was a Rolex so of course I noticed it. Real nice piece. Anyway, I guess he got stood up, because he was down here for a while and no one ever showed. Oh, here's what I was looking for.' He turns his phone so that the screen is facing me. 'I snuck this photo of him. I know it probably wasn't the most professional thing to do, and the manager here would be real pissed if he knew I was taking photos of a guest, but my girlfriend thinks it's real cool when we get celebrities in here and so I took this to show her. I didn't think Vince would mind anyway. Seems like a real cool guy.'

I take in the photo. Vince Taylor sitting alone on a bar stool, a whiskey glass lifted halfway to his lips. My breath catches in my throat as I see the time stamp. August 24, 2019, 9.47 p.m.. Vince Taylor was here, in this bar, at the time of Layla's death.

'Has anyone else come in here asking about Vince?'

'Nah, not to me anyway. But I was out on vacation last week. Went surfing in Costa Rica. Just got back this morning. Why?'

'I … it's just …' I stammer.

'You alright, ma'am?' The bartender asks, a look of concern spreading across his face. 'You look a bit pale.'

'Yes, yes, I'm okay. I just need to make a call.'

I rush outside sucking in the warm night air in large, gulping breaths. I was wrong about Vince. I was so sure that he was our guy that I saw what I wanted to see. I bent all the evidence to fit my preconceived notion of his guilt, and I failed to see anything that didn't fit with the narrative I created. An innocent man is sitting in jail because of me.

I quickly dial Lanner's number.

'Yo, Barnes! You still in the city? I just left a bar with my buddies, but I could easily be talked into more drinks …'

'No, no, listen. I think we made a mistake.'

I tell him where I am, and about the conversation I just had with the bartender, the photo he showed me. Lanner falls silent.

'This is my fault,' I say, panic rising in my voice. 'I rushed the arrest.'

'There was plenty of evidence that pointed to Taylor. It really looked like he was our guy.'

'I have to call the ADA handling Taylor's case. I need to get the charges against him dropped.'

'You understand that's out of our hands now, right? Our job is to make the arrest and recommend the charges. Which we did. It's up to the District Attorney's office to decide whether they want to prosecute after that.'

'I know, but I have to at least *try*.'

'Well, I'll tell you this much, Chief McFadden isn't going to be happy that you're running around doing the defense's job now.'

I hang up with Lanner and dial the number for the Assistant District Attorney assigned to try Taylor's case. After she's finished grumbling about the unreasonable hour of my call, I tell her about the new witness I've found. About Vince Taylor's alibi.

"This is a disaster,' she says. "This bartender's testimony would kill us at trial. It's only a matter of time before Taylor's legal team tracks him down too. His attorney is good. I've been up against him before. I'm certain that he will be looking to talk to everyone who was working at the Heatherly that night. No one ever thought to interview the hotel staff before Taylor was arrested?'

'No,' I confess. 'I … I dropped the ball.'

'Great. So all we have is circumstantial evidence against Taylor. He might have lied to us about his whereabouts the night of the murder, and even about the extent of his involvement with the victim, but we have no murder weapon, and nothing putting him in Central Park the night she died. I was willing to go to trial with this since the vic's diary claims that Taylor was supposed to meet her the night she was killed, but now that there's a witness that will give Taylor an alibi, that changes everything. This trial would be a joke. The DA isn't going to want to prosecute a high-profile case that is going to end in an acquittal and an embarrassment to this office. It's an election year and he has a conviction rate to maintain. You guys really rushed this arrest.'

'I'm sorry, we were under a lot of pressure too, but I should have figured it out sooner."

'Well, if you don't think Taylor killed this girl, then who did?'

I feel my stomach turning over. I haven't told anyone yet about my suspicions about Nicole, and I know how crazy it's going to sound. 'I think it was the wife. But it's just a hunch. I think he's protecting her.'

'A hunch, huh?' the ADA says, sounding unamused, 'Well, we have even less evidence on the wife than we do on Taylor. If we drop these charges against Vince Taylor, it's very likely they'll both walk, unless you can find something solid, something that definitely puts the wife in the park with the victim that night …'

Chapter 53

Vince

Ten Months Later

I rock my daughter in my arms, her long lashes sweeping her cheek as she sleeps with her tiny fingers curled around mine. I love every inch of her, my daughter, Emily Grace Taylor. She is perfection swaddled in a soft pink blanket. I breathe in the scent of her. I wish I could bottle it up and save it forever, so that I'll never forget the sweet strawberry scent of her hair, the newness of her skin.

I feel a tear slowly slide down my cheek. A combination of immeasurable joy and desperate sadness that I'm not sharing these precious moments with Nicole, the way we once imagined we would.

Although we're still married, in the technical sense of the word, we've been living separate lives since the charges against me were dropped. She's staying at the house in Loch Harbor and I've been living in the apartment overlooking Central Park: the place where Layla, and our marriage, took their last breaths.

Sometimes I still can't believe that the charges against me

were really dropped. Jeff said it was because the bartender at the Heatherly remembered seeing me the night Layla died. Apparently he'd even taken a picture of me sitting at the bar around the time she was killed. I've never been so happy to have my photo snapped in public. But I know that was a lucky break. If that detective hadn't kept digging, I might have spent the rest of my life in prison.

I suspect there are a lot of people who still think that's where I belong. Even though I was never tried for Layla's murder, and Shannon eventually issued a press statement explaining what happened, or I should say didn't happen, between us nearly twenty years ago, it took months for the hate mail to die down. Nearly every day my mailbox would be stuffed with angry letters calling me a rapist and a murderer. At first I shut myself in, refused to face the public, but after a while, I slowly began accepting offers to make talk show appearances, to give interviews to the press. I put my face, my name, back out there into the world and set the record straight. I'm humbled by how accepting people have generally been, the support far outweighing the hate these days. And yet it still frightens me how close my life came to being destroyed, thanks in part to Nicole.

I could have forgiven her if she'd been honest with me up front, if she'd told me what happened to Layla. But I can't forgive that she, even for one second, believed those things Layla had written about me. I can't get past the fact she went to the press and effectively condemned me in the court of public opinion. She might as well have put the cuffs on me herself.

I'm not sure that Nicole and I will ever be able to undo the damage we've caused each other. But I'm trying. We have a long road ahead of us, but I'm doing my best to forgive her. How can I resent her for lying to me, for betraying me, when I'd done the same to her? Besides, she is, after all, the mother of my child. And she's paid a heavy price for her hand in what happened to Layla.

Since she was a little girl, Nicole dreamed of someday being a mother, and after years of heartbreak, that dream was finally going to become a reality. But Nicole didn't get to stand in her nursery, soaking in the golden glow of her pregnancy. She didn't get to smile with unbridled happiness that she was bringing a new life into the world. No, she spent the entirety of her pregnancy, and every day since, worried that she would be taken away in handcuffs. Not knowing if she'd be able to hold her daughter once she finally arrived.

As far as I know the police never found any evidence that Nicole was in Central Park the night Layla died. She was interviewed shortly after my release, and was asked, for the first time, where she was that night. 'At home,' she'd said. 'Alone.' I'm not sure Detective Barnes believed her, but there wasn't much she could do about it. She couldn't prove otherwise, even after a thorough search of our house. There was nothing linking Nicole to Layla, and they couldn't show that Nicole was anywhere near Central Park the night Layla was killed. Evidently Nicole paid cash for the tolls into Manhattan when she went to meet Layla. She later told me that she'd intended to cover her tracks from me should I happen to check our credit card bill, but I suppose it had the added bonus of concealing her whereabouts from the police as well. Barnes may not have caught up with Nicole yet, but we can't be sure that she's finished digging. That's a burden Nicole will have to carry with her; she'll always be looking back over her shoulder, the past never too far behind.

As for me, I've decided to remain a silent investor at KitzTech. Now that the charges have been dropped, I could fight to regain my role as CEO, but I don't want to. Not yet at least. It's time that I finally put my priorities in order. I want to spend this precious time with my little girl. Work can wait, because babies don't keep. Before I know it, she'll be too big to hold in my arms any longer.

I may have gotten things wrong with every other woman in my life, but I'm going to get it right this time; I'm going to give my daughter the world.